IN BLACK & WHITE & COLOR

SHAMROCK MCSHANE

WAYWARD WRITERS PRESS

CONTENTS

	VII
1. Chapter 1	1
2. Chapter 2	13
3. Chapter 3	29
4. Chapter 4	45
5. Chapter 5	59
6. Chapter 6	75
7. Chapter 7	93
8. Chapter 8	97
9. Chapter 9	115
10. Chapter 10	127
11. Chapter 11	145
12. Chapter 12	155
13. Chapter 13	173
14. Chapter 14	185
15. Chapter 15	197
16. Chapter 16	215

17. Chapter 17   231

18. Chapter 18   247

19. Chapter 19   255

20. Chapter 20   263

For Mary June, who believed in miracles

CHAPTER ONE

Jesus stood with arms outspread, facing the rising sun. Beneath the dome, inside Ascension church, with its terrazzo floors, its frescoes alive with Tuscan flair, bright with azurite and ultramarine, its marble statues and saints and stories in pictures, at the baptismal font, someone was pouring water over Danny-Boy's head, and he looked up.

A dome makes it possible for there to be lots of space and light. That's what makes it right for a church. You enter and you're lit up. Your spirit is lifted, it's high and mighty, in a good way, because a church ought to be all about goodness, the path to righteousness, which is pretty much straight up. That was the source of all, its soul, Mother Church. In the Gospel according to Luke, Jesus goes up into the sky and disappears.

Nobody had ever asked Danny-Boy if he wanted to be a Catholic. They baptize you only days after you're born, in their view, to prevent your soul from going to Limbo, the place that was neither Heaven nor Hell, nor Purgatory, but rather the place for the unbaptized babies who died, because, presumably, even God couldn't bring Himself to send a newborn babe to Hell, even though it was already guilty of Original Sin, from which no one is exempt, and from which baptism alone could save you, such that if you were going to die right then and there, you'd go straight to Heaven. The fact remained, no one had consulted him, and he wasn't just baptized, he was baptized Catholic. Maybe you could be born Jewish, but nobody is born Catholic. It was as if you were born Catholic. And you just might spend the rest of your life trying to escape it. The nuns and priests and the school and the Church, all of that was waiting for Danny the moment he emerged from the womb. You started out too little to understand, but there were the robes and garments.

It had been astounding to Danny in the stories of the Bible and then in the even harder to believe stories in history books that a number of people had been killed. Killed, mind you. And the numbers grew, not just in the way of numbers, but in the way of chance and whimsy, Cain killing Abel, ok, but the Walls of Jericho tumbling down, Goliath's head hacked off, John the Baptist's too, the Civil War, Hitler, the Holocaust, Hiroshima, mind numbing shit, and the very first time one of the numbers hit him, it overwhelmed him, because he knew how sad and scared he was when Pop died and he realized suddenly and with absolute certainty that everybody had to die and there was absolutely nothing to be done about that, except everything you could do to not let it happen, not to you and not to anybody you loved or they loved or anybody really, which meant everybody, so that if 50 people were killed, the psychological repercussions would be devastating and permanent, unimaginable, and then to be multiplied by 100, 200, millions.

It was time to watch TV. Now it was always time to watch TV. When he started watching TV, he got up before TV came on. He looked at a test pattern until finally and suddenly the Star-Spangled Banner blared, and the Stars and Stripes flew. The first thing to do in the broadcast day was to remember how we won wars. Remember General Pershing.

It had all happened before. Everything had happened before. That was the point – an endless chain of cause and effect. It was an unfolding. Baptism. God. Bible. But already in the middle of things. Now, Danny-Boy is in it and discovering it.

This is the story of a boy who grew up in the middle of things. In the middle of the twentieth century, in the middle of America, in the middle class, in the middle of his family, the whole world changing, as he grew up, from black and white to color. He could see it vividly but not clearly. Everything was in close-up. Not everything. There's the world and its historical and current events, its politics, its great men and women, artists, and athletes. Then there is Daniel's life, his family, friends, enemies, church, and school. Background and foreground. Long shot and close-up. They are bound together by time and space.

It all seemed to start promisingly enough, moving up from bungalow to house, from Riverside to Oak Park, the specialness of being the baby of the family, and of being the favorite, even after his younger brother came along, because his younger brother was a mistake, was damaged, while Dan was gifted, talented, creative. Such promise, such potential.

It's easy to imagine Dan if you just take everything you know and eliminate about 75% of it, and then shake it up and spill it all out and put it all back together so it fits. In the end, he had a joyful life that he made every effort to fuck up with a capital F. He did it to himself. What did Dan want? Dan wanted a major letter. A great big black F on the chest of his snow-white Fenwick High School letter-sweater.

You try to think it all through, your place in history, which is really just a passage of time, a parade of events and characters, this pageant, and it all seems to be spinning around in a carousel, so fast that it blurs, and at every moment, as you look at it hard enough to see something, some shard of the mirror with the reflection of that sliver of reality in it, and you breathe, and the passing of time seems to separate you from all other living beings – because you are alone, alone with your problems and your thoughts and your self. You have to be confronted, so you seek out confrontation.

There were no cameras then. Before there were cameras. The camera is new in human history, and before it came along there was no way to preserve or record what people really looked like, besides painting and sculpture, which are necessarily subjective, and poetry and prose, which are abstract and which could never really describe someone with factual accuracy enough so that you could see the person, all of that would be practically useless in the future to anybody who wanted to know not just what Grampa looked like or looked like in his younger days, but what you yourself looked like, no way to verify, if just for yourself, that you used to be good-looking or trim. Everybody and everything was more present tense in the past. Because of the camera.

Joseph Kettlestrings and his family arrived in what would become Oak Park, Illinois, from Yorkshire, England, in 1833. Four years later, he bought up the heart of Oak Park for $1.25 an acre. The deed was signed by President Van Buren. The Village would name a street after Van Buren, and one day the Finnegans would live on it.

Frank Lloyd Wright took a hard look at Chicago and saw what he called "an immense gridiron of noisy streets. Heavy traffic crossing both ways at once, managing somehow. Torrential noise. A stupid thing, that gridiron. Crosscurrents of horses, trucks, streetcars grinding on hard rails, mingling with streams of human beings in seeming confusion and clamor. The gray soiled river with its mist of steam and smoke was the only beauty, and it smelled to heaven. This place is the first American city I have encountered. It holds rather more than a million people with bodies and stands on the same sort of soil as Calcutta. Having seen it, I urgently desire never to see it again. It is inhabited by savages. Its water is the water of the Hooghly, and its air is dirt."

The Chicago Fire burned down the whole city, and Oak Park appeared as a refuge, nine miles from the loop, with paved roads, streetlamps, water and sewage, telephones, police and fire department, library, and an opera house. By the end of the 19th century, there were enough churches and Protestants in Oak Park for people to start calling it Saints' Rest. "When you get to where the saloons stop and the steeples start, you'll know you're there."

It was October, Indian Summer, when the fire broke out. It jumped the river. Flames at hurricane speed. The world hadn't seen the destruction of a full-blooded city like this since the Romans laid waste to Jerusalem. The fire left seventy-three miles of streets in rubble and ashes, a hundred thousand people homeless, and eight months later, the city granted three thousand liquor licenses. There was almost nothing left. Well, there was something left. Factories mostly. Meat-packing plants. Railroad lines. Missus O'Leary's cow kicked over a lantern, and the fire started in her hay in her barn, and it practically wiped out the whole city, but O'Leary's own house doesn't even get touched. Explain that. Explain it? Micks. Catholics. Papists. Everybody knows the communists started the fire. That fire was rained down on the City of Sin as a punishment. We've got to rebuild this city! Whore houses over here, saloons over there, dope houses down the street, freak shows, dime museums all along the avenue. A glorious stirring sight!

Meanwhile, in Oak Park, Henry Austin bought out all the saloons and dumped the liquor in the gutter. Then he wrote a resolution into the village charter to outlaw liquor licenses. The Village was so grateful that Austin Boulevard, the border between Chicago and Oak Park, was named after him. The churches were built. Episcopalian, Congregationalist, Methodist, Baptist, Presbyterian.

Frank Lloyd Wright moved from the dirt air of Chicago to Oak Park and discovered what he thought "a place fitted and adapted to be set aside from the distractions of the busy city," a place where he could develop his unique prairie style, flat, everything that sticks up an exaggeration of what's already there. Wright was 22, just married, when he built his home in Oak Park, hugging the earth. He wanted to weave together interior and exterior. He didn't like rooms that were little boxes, so he figured you could "borrow" space from adjoining rooms with doors, the wider the better. Open the doors and you could see from one end to the other, all the way through. Wright designed the Unity Temple. It didn't have steeples, because it wasn't a church. It was a Temple, like Solomon's. The village filled up with ethnicities, white ethnicities, folks from England, Scotland, Germany, Scandinavia. And Ireland.

Irish genius discovered an altogether new way of spiriting a poor people thousands of miles away from the scene of its misery. The exiles, transported to the United States, send home travelling expenses for those left behind. Every troop that emigrates one year draws another after it in the next. Thus, instead of costing Ireland anything, emigration forms one of the most lucrative branches of its export trade. – Marx, Capital

"A kick in the arse is better than no fight at all." – Pop

Pop, it seems, left everything behind in Ireland, mother, father, family he never spoke of, all of it, and he never said anything about sending back traveling expenses for those left behind either.

When James Finnegan's regiment of the British Army was transferred to Canada, he deserted and snuck into the United States, two crimes for the price of one.

James Finnegan, before he was Pop, a poor Irish lad like many and many a poor Irish lad in the late 19th century, in the dim backward and abysm of time, he yearns to leave the old sod, but how? So, he heads downtown in Derry and signs himself up at the recruiting station and joins the British Army.

He does, does he? Does he call the town Londonderry, too? He's going to fight for Great Britain, is he? Britannia rules the waves. Off he goes. His son, his only child, his pride and joy, Connor Finnegan, will be born in 1915, into a world at war. His father is 24 and well shut of the British army. And his father's brothers and sisters? Let's see. They're Irish Catholics. What do you think? He has lots of brothers and sisters, and fare thee well. While James Finnegan is winding his way in and out of the British Army, meanwhile in Germany, Fraulein Barbara Budden is about to embark for America as well. Why? It's the land of opportunity. And Germany isn't. Wilhelm Schmidt will be leaving too.

If James Finnegan had wanted to hook up with an Irish lass over here, he might've picked Gwen Collins. Likewise, if Wilhelm had wanted a hometown girl, he might've hooked up with Barbara. It was the new world that crossed their stars, the Irish lad marries the fraulein, the German lad marries the Irish lassie in a new world and a new century, America drawing them like a magnet. Did they have any idea where they were going and what they were getting into?

When World War I broke out, Pop wasn't in it. He was an illegal immigrant in Buffalo, New York, where he met a poor girl from Germany named Barbara, practically an indentured servant, and married her. Together they made a good team, climbed out of poverty, God knows how, a pair of illegal immigrants.

Connor was clever, handsome, and talented, with an artist's eye, the mind of a mathematician, and the hands of a craftsman. They were still living in Buffalo, not far from the border that James Finnegan sneaked over, nor far from the dock where Barbara Budden landed. Somehow, another somehow, they made their way toward Chicago. It was too terrible to enter. They stopped outside it, at Saints Rest. Connor was born into a black and white world, where cars were new and there was no such thing as

TV, and D.W. Griffin was inventing the movies and poisoning them with racism. Orson Welles was born in 1915, too, and was living in Chicago.

Pop turned down a get-rich scheme to put in with a barnstorming football team called the Decatur Staleys, unless this was just a bit of his blarney, in his fine brogue. The Staleys would become the Chicago Bears. Pop favored drink, and his general counsel was: "A kick in the arse is better than no fight at all."

Edgar Rice Burroughs was churning out Tarzan books, sitting in his stately abode on Linden Avenue, comfortably penning in Oak Park an image of Africa, a place he would never visit, and Black people he could only imagine, that would warp minds all through the century, while casually admitting, "I began to write not for any particular love of writing. It was because I had a wife and two babies, a combination which does not work well without money." Yeah, right, on Linden Avenue no less. When he had what he considered loot enough, he bought a huge ranch outside LA, formed his own company, and hawked Tarzan books, comics, toys, movies, and fan clubs.

Mary Schmidt was an Oak Park girl, born and raised in Oak Park. She went to Ascension and was schooled by the Ursuline nuns. Mother Columbo was her piano teacher. Ascension had only been open a few years. She fell in love when Connor Finnegan scored Fenwick's first touchdown. At least that's what Connor said. Fenwick High School, like Ascension Grammar School, was just getting started, too. Connor was in Fenwick's first graduating class, but there were no jobs. So, he enlisted in the Army, where he rose to Second Lieutenant. Then there was another world war.

Hemingway disputes with Tolstoy about war. He would never dare to step into the ring with Tolstoy as a writer. This wasn't about writing; this was about war. Hemingway can dispute with everybody and anybody when it comes to war, because he's been to war. Tolstoy's been to war too, but Tolstoy's got a blind spot – his hatred for Napoleon. That messes up Tolstoy's otherwise great book, *War and Peace*, in Hemingway's humble estimation, that and Tolstoy's consequent theory that great men are little more than puppets whose strings are pulled by the blind forces of history. What Tolstoy was saying was the same as saying a coach doesn't affect the outcome of a game. Is history a game? Certainly, games are history. Everything is history.

Hemingway takes up a whole chapter of Dan's life. Begin again and concentrate. That was Gertrude Stein's advice to young Hemingway. And he did. He took her advice and learned a lot from her, although he was loath to admit it, she being a lesbian, and he being so sexually insecure. His macho profile was mostly a pose, but he was too much of an artist to escape introspection, and so he had to keep writing, or at least try, no matter how much it cost him – it turned his own hand against him, and, of course, it killed him. It didn't matter. He didn't have a chance. That's what death is – when you run out of chances.

Page after page, character after character, Tolstoy tells us what no one can know, people's innermost feelings, their confused memories, blind spots, how two contradictory feelings, inclinations, desires, apprehensions, exist simultaneously, what everyone was feeling, how it all happened, whatever it was, call it history – except it's not, because there really was no Natasha, nor Bolkonsky, although there was a real Napoleon and an Emperor Alexander.

Maybe someone could write this book to try to figure out how Dan got so fucked up. When you try to figure out what went wrong, you end up doing the same thing Tolstoy did when he wrote *War and Peace*; you have to keep going back and back. At some point, you realize that you could just go on this way forever, so you've got to just pick a point to begin.

There's no other choice. It doesn't mean you can't still go back. But there will necessarily be a point from which the chronology is going forward – the middle of the 20th century. But the story extends as far back as ancient times, biblical times. Suddenly, it's 1950 and J.D. Salinger is holed up in an office of the *New Yorker*, writing *The Catcher in the Rye*. Here and there is a glimpse of our novel's architecture. It's all about Time.

Your life isn't something you can fix the next day. Your life is something that happened, that has already happened. You've been shaped and molded, and it's set. You can break it, but you can't fix it. It's already fixed. For good. Something bad happened. Something bad is happening. And we're just watching it happen. We do something, and we make up the reasons for it afterward.

Connor didn't get to the Philippines till near the end of the war. He was with the Army in Manila when the war ended. Number One Son Ciaran, Dan's big brother, the Golden Boy, was three years old. Connor was 30, Mary was 25. Neither of them had been to college. Fenwick and Trinity were the peaks of their education. And then they had a daughter and named her Norine.

Fenwick provided Connor with an education sufficient to get him invited to MIT fresh out of the Army, and the GI Bill would pay for it, but Com Ed would give him a steady paycheck, plus he could move up. The future was in electricity.

The money, the family income, was coming from Commonwealth Edison, under the direction of its boss, Tom Ayers. Connor was an electrical engineer, and creative-- part-architect, part-inventor-- producer of petty bourgeois wealth, the tangible results appearing in the form of his porcelain dachshund overflowing with silver coin and folded cash in his saddlebags, and the final piece of evidence would be membership at the Riverside Country Club. "Your father turns on the streetlights." That's what Mary told Danny-Boy. It took Danny a while to figure out she was joking.

What Connor actually did for Commonwealth Edison, Danny didn't know, and he was too self-involved to bother to find out. It wasn't his thing. It was math. It was work. Something that required graph paper and calculations and blueprints, all of which came under the general heading of electrical engineering, which reached an apex of achievement in Marina City, the height of modernism, and Connor was illuminating it, blueprints spread out on the drafting table that he had built himself. Connor was successful. He knew Mr. Ayers, and Mr. Ayers knew him.

Connor was the best pool player in the house. They were the same skills he applied to golf and at the drafting table. And he could throw a football with a spiral and snap to it. Maybe he really did score Fenwick's first touchdown. He could ice skate. He would skate with Danny, his sister, and his big brother when Carroll playground was flooded and frozen over. He could swim. He could draw. He was an artist. He read books. Nonfiction. History. He read and subscribed to *Time, Newsweek, US News & World Report, The Tribune*, and *Sun-Times*, and he brought the *Daily News* with him home from work to read on the el. He knew how to fold a newspaper properly to read it on the el, folding it vertically, not horizontally.

Dan's adventures will take him in a widening circle, west to Maple Park, across Harlem Avenue eventually, and out of town that way, into the town of Forest Park, and east beyond the playground and the school to Oak Park Avenue. To the north, where the expressway is in progress, he will venture into the caverns being carved through town to connect Oak Park to the great city of Chicago.

Dan's big sister Norine likes to think of herself as the Little Mother. Mary could use a little help because she's going to have another baby. Dan is five, his big sister, the Little Mother, is 10. His big brother, Ciaran, the Golden Boy, is nearly 15. Dan was the baby. Not anymore.

The baby is still in his crib when the first seizure occurs.

Chapter Two

Age of Reason. When did you start to figure out that this was not the life that you wanted to live? They call that the Age of Reason. As Catholics, you were taught that it starts at age seven. Seven years old. That's when God can hold you accountable for your sins. That's the age at which you should've known better. Up till seven, you're golden, which not coincidentally is also when Freud says all the really bad shit coalesces into a tight little ball in your mind, when you are polymorphous perverse, but you're innocent in God's eyes, He being apparently blind to all the bad shit Freud could see that you are prey to, pun intended, and if God were to take you then, in your innocence, you would go right to Heaven, and what a lucky devil you'd be. But the innocent babe who dies unbaptized must spend eternity in Limbo. Doesn't seem fair. Whether or not you have free will in no way relieves you of the responsibility for your actions, but it counts for something that you are in no way responsible for the situation you find yourself in – to start with – and for quite some time, until finally you're making decisions of your own free will – and by then it's too late. You are no more capable of making a decision of your own free will than a stone is able to choose which way it's going while rolling down a hill. You are free to choose to roll the way you're rolling.

No man is free from sin, not even a child who has lived only one day on earth. – Saint Augustine

The scene opens on Danny's first communion. There's a spiritual leaflet in the pew. It contains prayers and an anecdote about Pope Pius X, who was recently canonized. The religious instruction explains as best it can the mystery of transubstantiation.

Dear Child Jesus, I humbly ask Thee to help me in all my dealings with my parents and teachers so that I may follow faithfully the example given by Thee. I beg Thee to make me always willingly obedient to my dear parents as Thou wert obedient to Thy gentle Mother, our Blessed Lady, so that all I do may bring consolation and happiness to them, and greater honor and glory to Thee, my God and my All.

There was once a little boy who used to take off his shoes on the country road and walk home barefooted, because he wanted to save his shoes so his parents would not have to buy shoes for him. If he was out in the field in the morning and he heard the church bell ring, he knew there was probably a priest going to say Mass. On one occasion, when he did not have his shoes with him, he borrowed another boy's shoes so he could serve the priest's Mass.

He wanted to be a priest, but his parents could not afford to pay for his education. He then studied so hard that he won a scholarship to the seminary.

After he was ordained a priest, he spent all his money on poor children and their parents. He never had anything left. When he was already a Bishop, a certain Monsignor said Mass in his church and he himself prepared breakfast for the Monsignor because he had no servant.

THE BISHOP OF WHOM YOU HAVE JUST READ IS SAINT PIUS X, AND THE MONSIGNOR WHO VISITED HIM WAS FUTURE POPE PIUS XI.

Let Us Pray.

Come, Holy Ghost, and help me to realize whom I receive in Holy Communion. Help me to realize that it is my Jesus, who, though He is God and Man, was always obedient to His Mother and Foster Father until he was a grown-up Man. Jesus, because He loves me and wishes to come to me, hides Himself under the appearance of a little bread.

Danny had just turned seven. It was a stretch to think he could read this, much less that he would. Maybe if he got bored enough. They gave you stuff like this in church, where you couldn't just whip out a comic book. Mean Gene would've snuck a comic book in, a little Superman action in church.

We have a narrative here, a story, purportedly true, about a poor Italian boy. We don't know his name, and we don't know that he's Italian. We'll have to deduce that for ourselves later on when his identity is revealed. For starters, he's just a poor boy walking home a long distance without shoes, by choice, because he wants to save his parents the cost of buying new shoes. He's a sweetheart. He's a saint. Where's he walking home from? He goes to school. So, later on, he's out in the field, where he doesn't wear his shoes either, apparently, maybe this kid never wears shoes, he hears the church bell ring.

They ring it whenever a priest gets it in his head to go and say Mass. Like on a whim, a caprice. A wing and a prayer. The kid somehow knows this, and he also knows that for some arcane reason, the priest needs an altar boy to assist him in saying Mass properly. He could say it by himself, if he were stranded on a desert island, say, and he needed to say a Mass to save his soul, but who knows why a priest would need to save his own soul, being a priest and all, if his soul's not in a state of grace, what business has he administering the sacraments? His sacred duty. See: Graham Greene, *The Power and the Glory*. You are a priest forever. The Whiskey Priest was still God's man on earth.

You are a priest forever, after the order of Melchizedek. – Psalm 110:4

The Mass was a ritual that presented itself as a kind of magic, a miracle, Jesus entering your body, and it could only be performed by this one magical, miraculous man, and only miraculous for that one moment and for that purpose, however, because when the sermons took a liberal turn or ventured into current affairs, the offending cleric would be met with general opprobrium by the conservative parishioners like Dan's dad. The Mass was a re-enactment of the Passion, from which, in the Thomist system, all the graces and sacraments were derived. Only the priest drank the wine, not the laity. Yeah, and the altar boys back in the sacristy.

The priest stood with his back to the laity who were in the pews facing the altar. After the Ecumenical Council, however, the Mass was said in English, and the priest faced the people, who became his audience, and he was like an actor in a play. Danny could identify with the robed man with his back to everyone, but when he turned around, he had the whiskey face of Father Riordan, who looked like the devil. Jesus!

The Ecumenical Council was a party hosted by the jolly pontiff, John XXIII. Everyone loved him except assholes. The altar turned around, and the priest faced the laity, and the words were in English instead of Latin, and you had to turn and greet your neighbor. But the Mass wasn't about other people. It was about taking Jesus into your life. It was between you and him, or you and the trinity, if you could sort that out. Consubstantiality. The Trinity. Father, Son, Holy Ghost – three distinct personalities in one divine substance. What makes it metaphysical is that it makes no literal sense. Most things, when they literally make no sense, are nonsense.

John XXIII died, and the College of Cardinals met in the Sistine Chapel to choose the new Pope. Waiting to elect the new Pope, clouds of smoke would be emitted. Black smoke – not yet. White smoke – new Pope. Saint Thomas Aquinas said that when a man became a priest, he underwent an ontological change – he became something different from everybody else. Aquinas was a wop. His family thought it would be all right for him to become a Benedictine, but the Dominicans got hold of him. They wanted his majestic mind to do battle with heresy. A priest is a mediator between God and the people. But somebody who stands in need of a mediator with God cannot approach God on his own.

Do not address any man on earth as Father, since you have only one Father and He is in Heaven. - Matthew 23.9

A priest can make Jesus appear. Nobody else can. But there was nothing whatsoever in the words and actions of Jesus that indicated any desire or need for priests and nuns to perpetuate his religion. Let us not forget that the only reason Dan might be preoccupied with shit like this was that he had plenty to eat, slept between clean sheets each night, and lacked for nothing. This was no longer a working-class family. Welcome to the petty bourgeoisie.

Monsignor Prince Gerald in his black button-up cassock with its blood-red lining. The Pope wearing a crown that was three crowns stacked on top of each other, a triple-decker crown. The kid runs off barefoot to go serve Mass. He borrows another kid's shoes. And that boy's a saint.

In God's eyes, maybe. We don't know. But our boy goes and serves Mass. He wants to be a priest in the worst way. Is that good? What about the shoes? He ever start wearing shoes? He doesn't want to. His family is poor. They can't afford to send him to priest school. The seminary. It costs money to go to the seminary. An education ain't cheap. You gotta pay to be a priest. You gotta go to the seminary to be a priest. Priests must come from wealthy families. Our boy wins himself a scholarship. They give out scholarships – that's big of them. You take a vow of poverty. Is that a promise to be poor, or just end up poor? God only knows.

Danny told the kids at school that the Pope was coming to his house for lunch.

You cannot take communion if you've committed a mortal sin. You'd have to go to confession first and confess your mortal sin before you could take communion again, and if you do take communion when you've committed a mortal sin and not been forgiven, which the priest wouldn't know about because he can't read minds, just turn bread and wine into body and blood and make Jesus be alive inside you, anyway, if you made the priest give you communion after you had committed a mortal sin and not been forgiven, it would be another mortal sin on your soul, for which you were to be held responsible for all eternity, and it only took one mortal sin to send you to Hell, so you would be doubly fucked, best just never to take communion again, if you could live without Jesus being alive inside of you, but once he was in you, why would you have to take communion again anyway?

The host was kept in a tabernacle in the sacristy, but it could be put into a little to-go box called a pyx if the priest had to take it to somebody who was sick and needed Jesus in their mouth, or the priest could put the host in a monstrance, a contraption like a trophy, and hold it up to people at a benediction. The Mohawks cut a priest's fingers off, so he couldn't celebrate Mass anymore because he didn't have his consecrated fingers to hold the host.

Augustine had preceded Aquinas, and Augustine was Plato's man, and Augustine held that the people, the faithful, were the body of Christ, and the communion bread was a sign of that body, and you ate it, like food, and the people were gathered together for a meal, to share a meal, which is what the followers of Jesus did to remember him, whenever two or more of them gathered together, he was there. He told them so at the Last Supper. Do this in remembrance of him. The logos became flesh in Jesus. And thus, we eat our words. All of it made Dan gag. Well, something made him gag. The host. The wafer. The "little bread". They hadn't practiced that part. They practiced everything else, but there was no practicing that, the actual welcoming of the Lord and Savior under your roof – the roof of your mouth, where He got a little stuck. They had practiced walking in a line in an orderly manner and dipping the fingers of the right hand in the holy water and blessing yourself with the sign of the cross and genuflecting and entering the pew, but there was no practice swallowing sweet Jesus – because that would've been a sacrilege and you'd burn in Hell.

So, presumably, a child would have to wait until the actual mystical experience to know how his untutored and traitorous body would react to the presence of Almighty God in the person of the good and gentle Jesus hiding Himself in a little bread. Don't chew Him! One's teeth must never touch the host.

Father White placed the host upon his tongue and Danny took the Lord Jesus into his mouth, and he was careful not to touch Jesus with his teeth, but nobody had told him that you had to let Jesus melt in your mouth like an M&M before you tried to swallow Him, so, when Danny attempted to draw Jesus down his gullet by means of peristalsis, the circumference of the disc exceeded the aperture, and he started to choke on the thing.

Do not chew the host. If you chew the host, you will go to Hell. Ok, he wouldn't chew it. But a terrible thing was happening. He couldn't swallow it. He couldn't swallow the damn thing. Jesus! Jesus Christ! Sweet Jesus, help me! Mother Imelda was patting him on the back.

"Daniel, are you all right?"

He didn't want to cough Jesus up. He wanted to say I'm ok, but he couldn't because he wasn't. Why wasn't this happening to anyone else? If you choked on the host, it was because you were unworthy, and Dan was choking on the host.

Explaining how the metaphorical is really literal becomes quickly more and more absurd. Jesus as Bread and Wine. Think about it. Now think about it with all the rational thought of western civilization gathered into a wrecking ball to swing at shit and see what you get. Or, you can just accept it, believe it, go thy way, and sin no more. If God and the Church were one and you were commanded to believe in miracles, even though miracles would only prove that God was not God, how could you believe it, how could you rationalize it, how could you reconcile the blatant contradiction? Why was it called the host? Like the host of a party? It's just a wafer. That's the miracle. Looks like a wafer, but it's really the Body of Christ. His body, not his blood. His blood's in the chalice that the priest drinks from. His blood's the wine. The priest gets that. Secretly, the altar boys would sample both, the wafers and the wine. The whole backstage area of the church reeked of red wine, until it would be overpowered on occasion by the pungent smell of incense burning for the dead.

Later that day, while exploring the caverns of the under-construction Congress Expressway, Dan lost his first communion missal, in which he had ignorantly written the names of both pairs of grandparents on the memoriam page, even though none of them was dead yet, he prayed to St. Anthony to help him find it, and St. Anthony didn't do shit.

Danny and his fellow communicants were born shackled to an original sin. That was what started it all, the first sin, the first mistake, and after that, we were all fucked. We were addicted to sinning, couldn't get enough of it, sinners all, generation after generation. It wasn't anything Dan thought up. He didn't invent it. He inherited it. Primitive accumulation. The capital to get it all started had to come from somewhere. It had a starting point.

"Adam bit the apple, and thereupon sin fell on the human race." – Marx

The first thing that Marx wants to get straight in the *Grundrisse* is the notion of the individual and the meaning of freedom – how it's an invention, the result of a historical process, just like everything else. The individual and his rights can't exist without the means for living like that being in place already. Obviously, that's why it's hard to know much about many individuals who lived thousands of years ago. It's like talking about individual ants.

And all that believed were together and had all things common and sold their possessions and parted them to all men, as every man had need. – *Acts 2:45*

Capital's faux-biblical fable is that of the grasshopper and the ant, the capitalist being the ant and the rest of us poor schlubs the grasshoppers. In reality, in history, what we find leading up to Danny's birth is conquest, enslavement, racism, exploitation, theft, brute force, and murder. There was no getting over the bad feeling in looking back at it, even though the sun was shining and the people you cared about seemed happy, and there were good things to eat, enough to gorge yourself, and you did. Overproduction. There was no way to look back on it without feeling guilt. But, come to think of it, he had felt guilt all along. Was it possible to recognize one's immaturity, to be willfully immature, to be fully conscious of it, and still be immature? Is it the process of becoming enlightened? It wasn't called the Enlightenment because they were enlightened; it was called the Enlightenment because they thought they were getting there. And by there it is implied there is a place to get. Where was this all leading? Was it all a story without a plot, without a hero, just a jumble of words and images and sensations and events? What of this notion that he was the only thing in the world that he could control? Could he? Could anybody? Can we possibly control ourselves? We want to control the pain. We want to control the circumstances when the circumstances are beyond our control.

Ascension was a Catholic grammar school taught by Ursuline nuns. The school was nestled right alongside the church that had Jesus atop its dome, looking east toward the rising sun and the city of Chicago.

Ascension had been there since 1912. The priests came first, led by Father McDevitt, the pastor. Four nuns showed up and taught 200 kids. By the 1950s, there were a thousand kids going to school at Ascension. The real church building didn't materialize until 1929. It was the Depression, and both Fenwick and Ascension called for major outlays of capital. How does that happen?

When Danny walked through the door at Ascension Grammar School, the idea that he would be spending the next eight years of his life there never entered his head. He knew it, but he had no notion of its impact. He hadn't even been to kindergarten. Everybody else had. Nine grades in one building. Kids who were six years old and kids who were 14, and all the kids between. It was the fall of 1957, and he would not leave until the spring of 1965.

The kindergartners were in a classroom on ground level alongside the gym. When Dan started in first grade, and his class went to P.E, they came to a halt at the bottom of the stairs. There was a door on the left that went to the kindergarten and a door on the right that went into the gym; all the other kids would remember this or remember that from when they'd been in kindergarten together, and Danny just wanted to get to the gym.

The descent down those stairs was always a good time to try to beat the shit out of somebody. Class changes in general were like that. Danny managed to avoid most of it. He could run, he could play, he was small, but he was tough. He was Dan-Man. He had beaten up a couple guys who pushed things too far on the playground. (No, he hadn't) He could punch, and he could move, and, best of all, he could punch and run away, run the hell away.

Dan got dressed for school in his Ascension uni – the powder blue shirt and clip-on navy-blue tie, the navy-blue trousers, cuffless, that he tried to wear the way Paul Gleason wore his, above the shoe tops so his white socks showed, because Paul Gleason was cool and he wore his pants that way. Paul Gleason was the coolest kid at Ascension. He was handsome and athletic and came from a big family of the best south Oak Park Irish-Catholic stock, his father was a lawyer and one of Fenwick's most honored alums, and there were eight kids in the family. The Gallaghers were pretty cool, too. They had nine kids.

Why was it cool to have all those kids? Because their house was like a playground, like Never Never Land, with kids popping up all over the place all the time. The Gleasons' house was cool because everything was so well organized – there were lists of chores posted, assigning tasks to the various brothers and sisters, and the house was always clean and uncluttered, and the two-car garage was beyond a paved backyard that had been turned into a basketball court and they flooded it in winter and turned it into an ice hockey rink. How cool was that?

The Gallaghers' house was cool because it was so unorganized, a towering three-story castle off Jackson Boulevard, overstuffed with kids and toys and games and sports equipment. They only had one more kid in the family than the Gleasons, but it seemed like a dozen.

And all the kids went to Ascension, one or more to each grade level. Everybody Dan knew went to Ascension, all the Clarence Alley Boys. They all lived in the shadow of the dome atop Ascension. Eight years of nuns. Eight years of these women with their faces in white frames, hair hooded, bodies in billowy black so that all you could see of their skin was their face and hands, the rest of them shapeless beneath their habits. Boys' Lavatory. Girls' Lavatory. Dan needed to go to the lavatory. You have to ask if you can go to the lavatory, if you can use the lavatory, if you can be excused, and you have to say, "Mother, may I", not "Mother, can I", or you'll be in for a disabusing of your ignorance.

A magical event was about to take place, and everyone was saving their pennies for it. Mission Day was coming, when the entire school would turn into a great carnival, no classes, and the gym became a fairground, lined with booths of games, prizes, candy, popcorn, soda, to raise money for the Ursuline nuns to cover the earth with the grace of the Sacred Heart of Jesus. The classrooms were all locked, and the action was in the gym and the Pine Room. It seemed to the little kids remarkable that school could be turned into a fun house full of games and candy and soda, and all you had to do was play. All for a good cause. All those pennies were going to help and feed and care for little black babies in Africa, who could now live and be Catholic and go to Heaven. This was Mission Day. There was a ring toss, a cakewalk. You lost. Shit. Try again.

Danny, the kid's name was Danny. Eventually he would call himself Dan, and he would sign legal documents Daniel, but when he tried to go from Danny to Dan, insisted upon it, because he wanted to be treated like a man, his family and his friends teased him and called him Dan the Man, which was then contracted and made acceptable to him as Dan-Man. He could live with that.

Ciaran was so much older than Danny, he was more like a father than a brother, someone to be hero-worshiped, lionized, the Golden Boy, football star, boarding a train in Union Station downtown, off to college and ROTC and then a tour of Vietnam. The Golden Boy left home for good.

Dan went for a haircut at Leo's Clip Joint on Oak Park Avenue. He was seven years old, and he bounded into the chair.

"What'll it be, partner?" Leo asked.

Dan reached into the pocket of his jeans and pulled out a photo he'd clipped from the *Oak Leaves*.

"What's this?"

"That's my brother Ciaran. Number 30," the kid said. In the photo was Ciaran Finnegan, Fenwick Friar running back, holding his helmet by his side and kneeling alongside phenom Coach John Jardine. "I want my hair cut just like that."

"You mean a crewcut?"

"No. It's gotta look like that."

"You got it, kiddo."

Dan was jealous of the new baby. He would try to scare the baby in his crib, make him cry, try to scare the living shit out of him, and he succeeded beyond his wildest dreams. Dan would sneak up on little Brendan's crib and peek over the edge and make faces at him and make him cry, and then Dan would run away before Mary came to his aid, and one time he went to scare the shit out of Brendan, and Brendan scared the shit out of Dan instead. He was having a seizure, not that Dan had any idea what that was, but Brendan was all seized up, eyes glazed, rocking his head hard against the bars, teeth clenched. Scared the shit out of Dan so bad he screamed, and his mother came running.

Since it seemed that no one was quite sure what epilepsy was, it didn't much matter that Brendan was misdiagnosed with epilepsy; what really messed him up was the treatment – a double daily dose of Dilantin. When Brendan had a seizure, his eyes would glaze over and his limbs would stiffen, and he'd rock against the first impediment he met, and there was nothing to be done about it, just wait it out. Are the drugs doing him any good? Wait and see.

Mary had managed to get her hands on some Lourdes water, and she was anxious to try it out on Brendan to see if it could cure him of epilepsy. She prayed to Saint Jude that it would. It wouldn't. Nothing happened. Mary was sincere. She believed. She loved Easter and Christmas and high Mass on Sunday, and she carried rosary beads with her wherever she went.

It's not easy to say the rosary. It takes time. You have to know all the different prayers to say and the order they go in. And you have to say the prayers aloud, or at least move your lips, or it isn't going to work. Your prayer isn't going to have any efficacy.

From November till March was white. The world was frozen. There was snow. You had to coexist with the snow. But when you were a kid, you couldn't imagine living without it. Not just the fact that you could play in it, but you could catch it in your mouth as it fell, and although you wanted no part of yellow snow, the pure white stuff was perfectly good. Ask an Eskimo. You could make an igloo out of it, well, an Eskimo could. Guys made forts out of snow. After Christmas one year Shock and Jimbo Kidd and Rug Olson dragged a bunch of Christmas trees into Gaffney's yard and built a fort out of them. After a while they got rotten and started to stink.

Big kids *skitched*. You'd sidle up to a car slowly making its way along a frozen snow-packed street, best at night, and just as the car was about to pass by, you would duck down and grab a hold of the rear bumper, and squatting down there, you would be pulled along, sliding over the snow and ice. The driver couldn't see you in the rear-view mirror, but if you wriggled or swayed, he could feel your weight tugging at his bumper as if he'd caught a fish. Sometimes he'd be alarmed and stop the car and get out, and you and your guys would scamper out of sight, sometimes just around the other side of the car, so that when the driver got back inside and started to drive, you'd repeat the whole joke. More and more drivers responded by speeding up. And you'd be off on a thrill ride for as long as you could hold on. It was insanely dangerous, slalom skiing on an icy street where you could just as easily encounter a dry patch of concrete, the driver purposely fishtailing to try and shake you off. There were horror stories of kids whose feet went out from under them, and they were swept under the car's rear wheel and crushed. It was a game. You'd start off fastened to the rear bumper next to a friend or two, and off you'd go, bumping, bouncing, sliding. One by one, you'd be shaken off, knocked over, sent sprawling and tumbling over the snow. And then you'd scramble out of the street before you got run over by the car behind you that was honking at the driver ahead of him to let him know he had skitchers on his rear, and if he didn't understand, it just pissed him off and he'd honk back.

As children, we feel free to believe in our own immortality, which gives us boundless courage to face dangers we will shudder over for the rest of our lives, like skitching, or like skateboarding down the ramp to the el platform at Oak Park Avenue, somehow avoiding a crash landing on the third rail. His gramma Gwennie was taking Danny downtown on the el to Marshall Fields' to see the Christmas displays in the windows and then go inside to escalate from floor to floor, each one a different world of luxuries, rising to the top, and there was Santa Claus.

Imagine paying the tuition for your kid to go to a private high school in 1929? How did a couple of immigrants pay for that? They'd only been in the country for ten years, and Fraulein Barbara didn't even speak English when she got here. And how did Grampa and Gwennie manage to send their daughter to Trinity? The Finnegans had two cars in a two-car garage. A car for Connor and a car for Mary, a boy in high school at Fenwick, a girl at Trinity, a boy in grammar school at Ascension, three different private schools, three different tuitions to pay, and a boy in public school – first at Lincoln and then at Horace Mann, after Mary had shopped around for the best special education classes, whereas the private Catholic schools had none to choose from.

Danny goes to pre-school at Carroll Playground with his chums Gene and Mary Jule, who live with their Nano down the block, and life revolves around the playground. After pre-school comes kindergarten, but Danny-boy doesn't go. There's a gap there in his education. Is it not required? Kindergarten through twelfth grade – isn't each step required? But maybe you could skip it if you wanted to. If your mother wanted to, that is. You don't know enough to make an informed decision. You are completely uneducated. That's the point. Your mother did that to you. Held you back, stunted your intellectual growth. Nah, we just skipped it. Skip that step. The foundation. He stayed home with his mom. He had a little brother now. And that pissed him off.

He didn't want a little brother. Danny-boy already was the little brother. Now they had a baby. But Danny-boy was the baby. Yeah, he was.

Chapter Three

You want to wear those clothes – that's why you want to be an altar boy. You like the costume, admit it. Costumes? Uniforms? Special gear, yeah, so? You have to learn the responses. In Latin.

But there are two altar boys. If the other guy knows his stuff, you just sort of mumble it, just like in the chorus, you just pretend. You pretend. If you don't have the balls to do it, don't do it. Takes balls to be an altar boy. If you don't have the balls to be an altar boy, you're never gonna have the balls to be a priest, and if you can't be a priest, you can forget about being Pope.

It was only on occasions like Thanksgiving or Christmas or Easter that they ate in the dining room. Normally, they ate at the kitchen table. His father was at the head of the table, Dan at the foot, his sister and mother on one side, Gramma and his little brother Brendan on the other. At dinner, before saying grace, they made the sign of the cross, and Brendan, who was lefthanded, would always do it wrong.

"Say grace, Brendan."

"In the name of the Father, and the Son, and the –"

"Other side."

"Holy Ghost. Amen. Bless us, O Lord, for these Thy gifts, which we are about to receive, from thy bounty, through Christ Our Lod. Amen. In the name of the Father, and the Son, and the –"

"Other side."

"Holy Ghost. Amen."

Mary perpetually intervened to prevent him from accidentally swearing allegiance to the devil.

In Ascension church, the communion rail stood between the priest and the communicants. An altar boy has got to hold the paten just under their chin, the skinny gold plate, in case the host should fall when the priest is putting it on somebody's tongue. All of these people lined up, kneeling down, and then one by one, with their eyes closed, sticking out their tongue. There was a fine art to mumbling a bunch of shit that sounded like Latin.

What's the worst thing in the world? That's easy. Having to go to school in the morning. Having to go to work. Having to go to school without having done your homework. Having to go look for work. Being in the Army. Being in Jail. Being sick. Getting beat up. Getting beat up while you're sick. Going to Hell. You should go to confession. Every two weeks. So, things don't get out of hand.

There was only one thing to do if you wanted to get into Heaven. Confess. Bless me, father, for I have sinned. My last confession was two weeks ago. Two weeks ago? You lying sack of shit! Confess your sins.

"Bless me, father, for I have sinned."

And then he would lie about how long it had been since his last confession. You were supposed to go every two weeks. At least once a month. Like getting a haircut.

"Doth not even nature itself teach you, if a man have long hair it is a shame unto him" –

Corinthians

The Seal of Confession. If someone tells a priest in confession that he killed somebody, the priest can't tell anybody. How fucked up is that?

Dan didn't say what it was he was lying about. He was lying about lying. He made up sins to confess to. Normal sins. Petty venial sins. Confess everything, and God will forgive you. Clean slate. You'll feel better. Just the opposite. What makes you think someone is going to feel better because they just said out loud everything they're ashamed of? They're not relieved, they're humiliated. Now for your penance, say ten Our Fathers and ten Hail Marys. And if you skipped out on that, it wouldn't work. You were only going to get into Heaven if you happened to die in a state of grace. Say an Act of Contrition. You were supposed to confess your desires too, your impure thoughts, sinful ideas. Yeah, like he'd be doing that.

Get yourself a cheeseburger – they're great. Can't. It's Friday. Can't eat meat on Friday. Why not? Catholics can't eat meat on Friday. Why? Christ died on a Friday. So? So, Catholics don't eat meat on Fridays. But you can eat fish. The Apostles were fishermen. So, it was good for business.

At Ascension and later at Fenwick, the nuns and priests believed in corporal punishment. Isn't it wrong to beat children? And what about those who beat children? Should they be beaten? Is it wrong to think some men should be beaten, deserve to be beaten? Unless no one deserves to be beaten. The nuns and priests would slap you in the face. Confirmation, a slap in the face. You were confirmed in your faith. Christianity, the belief that one should turn the other cheek. Love one another.

Dan was in second grade when he fell in love with Tina Bartram, who was in second grade. He was also in love with Miss Parelli, who taught second grade and wore silk stockings with a black line that ran from her heel somewhere up the back of her leg. It was not the same as with Tina Bartram. He wanted to marry Tina Bartram. He wanted to do something else with Miss Parelli.

Tina Bartram lived just half a block away across Van Buren Street. She was tiny and petite and looked like a porcelain doll. She had light brown hair that she wore pulled back to accentuate her perfectly round face, and Dan yearned for her in a nearly spiritual way because of her delicate cuteness, and thus he never said a word to her.

Captain Kangaroo and his friend Mr. Greenjeans were Danny-boy's daily companions. They fed carrots to Bunny Rabbit and danced with Dancing Bear, and sometimes a lot of ping-pong balls would suddenly pour from above on their heads. Mighty Mouse and Popeye and Superman and the Lone Ranger, and Sky King, and then Flash Gordon. Sex and violence were part of the game now. Somehow, you had to put the two of them together in your head to come up with Flash Gordon and Superman and even Roy Rodgers – it was all about sex, damsels in distress, not just Dale Arden and Lois Lane, but all those sci-fi princesses in need of rescue in their tight slinky dresses. Puberty had arrived.

From that moment on, Dan would try to do the good thing. Always. Not to slip back into the bad things, no matter how much he might want to – because there was another part of him that did not want to, that knew it would be better not to, even if he were bored, even if everything else felt useless, he would just have to accept its uselessness and do it anyway, do it until doing what was good felt good again – because sometimes it did – but even if that feeling would never come back he would have to do the good thing anyway because it was better than doing the bad thing, which always made him feel bad afterward, the way he felt right now. Because he had committed a sin. Even if there was no God, there was still sin.

Dan goes to Church with his parents, and when they come home, he dons his pretend priestly vestments and celebrates Mass. Layer by layer, the priest got dressed for Mass, saying magic words with each garment, kissing them before putting them on, the pure white nightgown, and finally, the chasuble over the top, a very fancy robe with the sides cut out, no sleeves, embroidered with gold thread and changing colors with the season.

There were all sorts of hats and capes and gloves and do-dads, sashes, all color-coordinated and tricked up with designs and symbols to indicate a hierarchy, ascending to a higher plane.

There was a crying room, a room behind glass, with pews just like the rest of the church, but walled off, where families with crying babies could attend Mass without disturbing the prayerful peace of others. There was a metal clasp on the back of each pew where a gentleman could attach his fedora. There was the *Dome*, the weekly Church newsletter with its announcements of couples betrothed and married, babies baptized, and Masses for the dead. You could make a donation to the Church to have a Mass said for the dead. You had to be dead to have a Mass said for you. Someone else would have to do it for you. Having a Mass said for you after death was meant to impart some indulgence, some lessening of the time your soul spent in purgatory.

The blessed virgin. This is where complications set in. The virgin birth. How could that be possible? It's not. It's a contradiction of the laws of nature, and trying to sort it out in your head as a little boy after he had gone to Mass on a Sunday morning, mimicking the priest, adorning himself with makeshift vestments, or, a few years later, memorizing enough Latin responses to repeat at the appropriate moments as an altar boy, reconciling logic, sex, and reality, with the immaculate conception and the Trinity and the dual nature of Christ and a life for everybody after death, the only question being where, all that could make you crazy. It was incredible, yes, but Dan believed it, that the Bible was the Word of God, that God Himself wrote it, put pen to paper, moved the hand of the scribe, first Moses, then all the speakers of the Old Testament, and then the evangelists of the New. It was true, every single word of it. Jesus Christ, it was the Bible. Dan was past seven. He had reached the age of reason, so he had to know this. People carried the Bible around with them, some of them, and a Bible could stop a bullet, and there were miracles even now, like the appearances of Our Lady of Lourdes and Our Lady of Fatima. The Last Supper was the first Mass, and Jesus was the priest. He made the apostles priests, and when he died, they all became bishops, and Peter was the first pope.

The Old Testament had the best stories. The Old and the New Testaments were two completely different, seemingly irreconcilable books, featuring two different Gods. In the Old, he was a hard ass named Yahweh. In the New, he was God the Father, who had a Son named Jesus, who was also God, and somehow floating about ethereally there was the Holy Ghost (Protestants said Holy Spirit), who was God as well, so there were actually three of them, the Trinity. The Holy Ghost was depicted in scripture and in pictures as a white dove, or once as tongues of flame appearing above the heads of the eleven apostles, Judas already having hung himself out of guilt over betraying Jesus for 30 pieces of silver that he promptly cast away in remorse, none of it, not even the love of the Holy Ghost, could save him from the fires of Hell at that point, so why'd he do it? For the money? And he realized immediately that it wasn't worth it, that he'd been trick-fucked by the devil, who had demonic power, which must have been unequal to God's, He being omnipotent, so this power of the devil's must have been ceded to him by God, from whom all power derived, and here the logic became further entangled in contradictions that Augustine and Aquinas would endeavor to resolve. The Old Testament seemed not to engage in such abstractions. It wasn't that kind of debate in which Samson, say, was about to participate. He dealt with his opponents with the jawbone of an ass. The Bible made everything possible. If you believed the Bible, then, by definition, you believed that miracles could happen, because they did, it was right there in the Bible. You had to believe in miracles – if one was going to happen for you.

If you believed, and Danny Boy believed, then you were more afraid of going to Hell than you were of dying. Makes sense. Like Pascal's bet. You can be as afraid of death as you like, but there's no getting around it. Heaven or Hell, on the other hand, could go either way. When you start to realize how much time has gone before, you see that time used to pass much more quickly then than it does now. The lives of historical people, in fact, all people who are dead, seem to have passed by very quickly.

Danny-boy was in love with the Bible and stories from the Bible all the way back to Moses, even though Moses was not a saint, saintly though he may have seemed to Danny-boy, because it had been determined that there could be no saints until Jesus came along, although even Jesus himself was not a saint, explain that one, he was God's Son, a member of the Holy Trinity, which included God the Father, God the Son, or Jesus, or Jesus Christ, or the Christ, or Jesus of Nazareth, or Galilee, who was born in Bethlehem, all of that before you even get to the poor Holy Ghost, who was also a Person of the Trinity, but, somehow, without actually being a person, but a ghost, but not the ghost of some person, more like a spirit, but called the Holy Ghost, and if you said Holy Spirit, you must not be Catholic.

His mother prayed to Saint Jude, the patron saint of lost causes. Mary, the mother of Jesus, the blessed Mother must have been like Dan's mother Mary, who, when she was angry, never said Goddamnit like his dad, but instead always said Godblessit, and she never raised her voice. And Norine, Danny-boy's sister, the Little Mother, what of her? She loved her mother to the point of imitation.

His father wore a Saint Christopher medal around his neck all his days. He didn't take it off to swim or shower, even. When speaking of Dan's big brother Ciaran, Connor would quote the Bible: "This is my beloved son, in whom I am well pleased." He would also quote Charlie Chan and refer to Ciaran as his Number One Son, and Dan as Number Two Son, and poor Brendon as Number Three Son.

Surprisingly, it was Dan's older brother Ciaran who was the first in Dan's experience to express disdain for organized religion. Ciaran called Mass the Big Show. After his priesthood phase, when he had entered agnosticism, Dan twisted his big brother's put-down into a license, into meaning, since the whole thing was just a show, you could arrive late and leave early. He started going to a different Mass than his parents. They always went to 10 o'clock Mass, so he would go to 11, arrive late, entering through the vestibule, dipping his fingers in the holy water at the entrance to the pews, walk all the way up the side aisle, enter the pews nearest the side door near the baptismal fount, and exit, only to wander around aimlessly, into the courtyard between the church and school, where the kids would play at recess, amble past the kindergarten classroom and peek in at the room his peers had occupied but he had not, past the gym, and following the alley all the way to Van Buren and the expressway, before heading home with the crowd that streamed from church past the castle on Euclid.

Still, Danny loved going to Church. The *Big Show*, Ciaran called it, and Ciaran meant it in the most cynical way. It was just a show and no more. But not to Danny. To Danny, it began as a magnificent, glorious story. It was the Bible come to life, and you couldn't beat the Bible for stories, for characters, for all-out weirdness. The Church depicted it in paintings and sculptures and stained glass and design, and manufactured the words out of Latin.

There was no way his mother and sister were going to miss Midnight Mass on Christmas Eve. Dan would go too, because if you went to Midnight Mass on Christmas Eve, then you didn't have to go to Mass on Christmas Day, like it was some loophole. Midnight Mass. Snow and ice and the cold air that held your breath in a white cloud before letting it go.

Inside the church was packed, there was a choir singing and an organ filling the church with beauteous sound.

When Dan was born, his big sister Norine was five and in kindergarten, and his big brother Ciaran was nine and in the third grade at Ascension, being taught by the Ursuline nuns. His mother Mary had been taught by Mother Columbo to play the piano. She had taken lessons at the convent across the street from the church. Ciaran, Norine, and Danny would each take piano lessons from the nuns as well. Only Ciaran, the Golden Boy, applied himself.

Mary bought sheet music and played the piano throughout the day, whenever the mood struck her. Something magical happened when NBC televised *Peter Pan* with Mary Martin live! A play. Acting, pretending. The boy who refused to grow up. It was filled with music, and the stories came to life through people pretending to be something they were not. It was Mary who loved Mary Martin as Peter Pan, Jimmy Cagney as George M. Cohan, and Judy Garland and Sinatra and Tommy Dorsey and Liberace, and it was Mary who played the piano and collected knick-knacks. The Euclid castle was filled with music, whether Mary was playing the piano herself or listening to the stereo.

One day in the spring, when Dan was getting ready to graduate from Ascension, he got a letter in the mail, an exceedingly rare occurrence. It was a personal note of congratulations and encouragement, written to Dan as a response to a letter Mary had written. What could possibly have inspired this woman, his mother, to write a fan letter to George Wallace, and to tell the world's most famous and dangerous racist about her talented young son who was about to graduate from grammar school? Let's take a wild guess – racism? How could Mary be a racist? Easy. It wasn't like she had to buck a trend. It would have been hard for her not to be a racist. That would've been the hard thing to do, and then how would her marriage work, considering she was married to as racist a man as any in town? Connor didn't like Pollocks or Wops. He didn't like Bohunks either, whoever they were. It was funny. It wasn't funny. It was and was not funny. Casual racism. Intense racism. You can't have it both ways. Sure, you can.

Dear Dan,

Your mother has written me and told me that you were graduating from Grammar School. Education is a most important factor of our lives today. It is important that we strive to get all out of it that we can. Education is like everything else in life – you get out of it what you put in. I know that you are the type of person who aims for the top and tries with all his might to get there. If I may ever be of assistance to you, please let me know. Good luck in your future and with best wishes, I am

Sincerely yours,

George Wallace

Governor

GCW/jbk

He was touched. He responded personally. (Well, he dictated it.) To Dan. Mary was an admirer of George Wallace. Mary, who made Danny's lunch to take to school and put it in a paper sack, and he could smell his peanut butter and jelly sandwich mixed with the aroma of the brown paper and it made him think of his mother making his lunch and he loved her, and she had written a letter to the biggest racist in the land and she must've told George Wallace how much a few words of encouragement would mean to young Daniel.

"That was nice of him, wasn't it, Danny? When someone goes out of their way to do something nice for you, you should appreciate it."

Mary had been afraid when Ciaran played football that he might get hurt. She only went to one of Ciaran's games, and that was in his senior year when the team honored the mothers of the senior players, and the mothers all sat in the stands at Oak Park Stadium together and wore carnations. And then four years later, he was flying a helicopter in the war that she wouldn't watch on TV.

Impressionist paintings are dots. TV is dots. So, if you put all of the blue dots, all the dots of each theme, in one place, then cluster and map each scene, you can then join all the themes together by chronology. *In Black and White and Color* takes place in the middle of the 20th century in the middle of America, in the Chicago suburb of Oak Park, Hemingway's hometown, where the saloons stop and the steeples start, and the paradigms begin to shift. A novel is like a movie is like a painting is like a poem is like music is like a statue or a piece of architecture.

Brendan was not going to follow the same path as his three siblings. He was going to go to public school – because that's where there were special education classes, which he needed, due to what was being diagnosed as epilepsy, manifested by seizures, and the debilitating effects on his brain, his speech, and his coordination caused by the Dilantin he took daily. No nuns for Brendan. It was the public schools that were equipped for the likes of Brendan. The mission of the good Ursuline nuns was the perfection and polishing of minds that could absorb the Latin of the Mass, whereas public schools were for the masses, including the disabled.

In the Catholic schools, with their nuns in grammar school and their priests in prep school, there was clearly something holding it all together, but in the public schools, there was nothing holding it all together, and so it didn't just fall apart, it flew apart.

Cartoons, for a child, are preferable to human beings. Infinitely. The test pattern was on the screen. You had to wait till 6 am before the shows came on, and then it was all documentaries about World War One and World War Two, General Pershing winning the first one, then Ike would come along and win the next one. Finally, the cartoons would come on,

Popeye, Mighty Mouse. They were comforting hero sagas. Here I come to save the day! If you were a little kid, you took that just as seriously as Mighty Mouse did. He was a mouse; you were a mouse. Mighty Mouse flew alongside the Lone Ranger and Tonto. From the Lone Ranger in black and white to the Lone Ranger in color – and it turned out his outfit was powder blue!

Ride along with the Lone Ranger, Hopalong Cassidy, Gene Autry, and Roy Rogers. This was when cowboys settled things. It was time to fall in love with violence, with fistfights and shootouts, and, best of all, war, with tanks and machine guns! Cap pistols. The Fanner-Fifty was a revolver that would allow you to keep firing for 50 rounds, as you fanned it with the side of your hand like the cowboy did on TV. Somehow, it didn't hurt his hand. Had to ride a horse.

Everybody had to ride a horse. So there had to be a whole bunch of horses, and horses didn't start out here. Horses are not native to North America, and yet the Native Americans learned to ride them as well as horses have ever been ridden.

Les Preludes by Liszt was thundering the majesty of Mongo and the heroism of Flash Gordon, as portrayed by Buster Crabbe, and his heroine Dayle Arden and her rival, the evil and voluptuous Princess Zora, daughter of Ming the Merciless. Hitler may have been the evilest man who ever lived, but for scaring the shit out of a kid, you couldn't beat Ming.

For a while, only a few shows on TV were in color. Some shows started out in black and white, and then the next season they were in color. The movies had been in color since *The Wizard of Oz*, but for a while it was divided pretty evenly between black and white movies and movies in color, and it meant one thing for a movie to be in color and another for a movie to be in black and white, but exactly what those things were was hard to say. You couldn't see any show in color unless you had a color TV.

The movies were there too, waiting for Dan, but the line that had preceded him was not so long as the one tracing all the way back from Aquinas to Aristotle. The movies were a new art, a 20th-century art. You could grasp it from the beginning, not just the experience of your first trip to the Lamar theater to see *Old Yeller*, but back to silent movies, Buster Keaton, Charlie Chaplin, Harold Lloyd, unceasing cathartic evidence of what fools we mortals be.

Color was used for musicals and comedies. If you were going for realism, you used black and white. Ingmar Bergman wrote a play called *Woodcut,* and over the summer, he took his ensemble to the country to make a movie of it in black and white called *The Seventh Seal*. Danny was four years old that summer. There he is in the backyard in the wading pool, trying to get Mary Jule to take her swimsuit off while Max Von Sydow as the Knight plays chess on the Swedish seashore against Death.

This was the height of American prosperity, for the prosperous. The whole family would get in the car and go for a drive. No destination. Just drive. Marking the centennial of the Civil War, kids were wearing blue and gray Yankee and Rebel caps that you could buy in a dime store. Everybody in Oak Park wanted a blue one, of course. Why? Blue won.

There was the Davy Crockett coonskin cap. There was the foreign legion cap, which had that extra piece of cloth hanging off it to keep the back of your neck from being fried in the desert, and when his mother wasn't looking, Dan snatched her scissors and snipped it off.

"You ruined your hat – why?"

"It was wearing a dress."

Dan wants to be like Ciaran. He can run fast, too. Really Fast. He challenges the fastest boy on the playground, John Raynard, his friend Roger Raynard's big brother, to a race – and loses. He is shocked. He thought he was the fastest.

"Follow Fenwick's Fighting Friars." Dan's Introduction to alliteration. But what's up with a fighting friar? Fighting for what? And with whom? Who picks a fight with a friar?

Robin Hood versus Friar Tuck. And Friar Tuck won. They fought with big sticks, bow-staffs, as they met on a fallen tree limb that stretched across a stream somewhere in Sherwood Forest. The same trope was played upon by a cartoonist in the sports section of the *Chicago Tribune* before and after the Prep Bowl, Mayor Daley's Prep Bowl, the Chicago city championship of high school football, depicting a Fenwick Friar in his robes being met by a Schurz Bulldog at the midpoint of a limb stretched across a brook. At stake was a ripe apple, labeled *City Title*, which the Friar was reaching for and for which the Bulldog was slavering. That cartoon appeared on Friday, the day before the game. On Sunday, the day after the game, the consequent cartoon appeared, with the Friar's staff sweeping the Bulldog into the waters, while plucking the apple at the same time, and with the swoosh of his staff, the 40-0 score emerged, woosh! It was perhaps the most dominant display of high school football prowess ever.

There was a further irony that escaped the cartoonist in the sports section. Carl Schurz was a German American who fought in the revolution of 1848 against the Prussian army, and then was a Union Army general in the Civil War, and then a US Senator. The Schurz Bulldogs were named after a great abolitionist. The Fenwick Friars were named after a slaver.

Like a dam bursting, the line of scrimmage exploded, and Friar fullback Jim DiLullo shot through, and suddenly he was behind the secondary and streaking for the endzone. Unstoppable. And the defense was suffocating and attacking, daring offenses to throw because nothing could be gained on the ground, and then this wounded duck would appear, a quarterback's last gasp, thrown as he was going down, and the Friar defense gobbled it up.

That Prep Bowl made Fenwick the King of Sport, and, more than that, it could never be taken away and never surpassed. Not only were the Friars undefeated, a perfect 10-0, capped by a city championship, but their dominance was absolute and complete, witnessed by 92,000 fans in Soldier Field.

Danny had watched intently all that fall from the stands in Oak Park Stadium, that wonderful, majestic brick and concrete one-sided stadium with an entrance on Lake Street right in the center of Oak Park, and the visitors seated humbly in bleachers across the field. There was an arrangement then between the two schools, Oak Park High and Fenwick, to share the stadium during football season, which worked out nicely since the Huskies played their games on Saturday, while the Friars were members of the Chicago Catholic League, one of two leagues in the country to play their games on Sunday, the other being the NFL.

The Friars wore high-topped black spikes, with white laces on Sunday, black laces during the week, running their wing-t offense, running it and running it. They probably threw 30 passes all season. That's in ten games. If they threw more than three times a game, that was a lot. They were a machine, they were like the Spartan army, just gutting the defense and plowing through, and, since most everybody was a two-way player, then flipping it over and annihilating the other team's offense, blowing it up, stomping it dead, or causing it to cough up fumbles or panic into interceptions. John Gorman played quarterback and safety. He was a ball hawk. On a sunny Sunday afternoon in October a wounded duck appeared against the blue sky above the field of Oak Park Stadium, and for a moment it looked like it might sail beyond Gorman's grasp, over his head, and it looked for that instant like it just might be that rarest of birds, a completed pass, when Gorman somehow arched his spine and reached back over his head with both hands, and the ball dropped into his grasp behind his head.

Wunderkind coach John Jardine stayed at Fenwick another two years before moving on to the college ranks, first at Purdue as Jack Mollenkopf's offensive line coach, then as head coach at Wisconsin, where he turned the program around. And then it collapsed. Jardine would only live to the age of 54, dying of stomach cancer. He was booed off the field by Wisconsin Badger fans who threw bottles at him and his players after his last humiliating defeat. He was in terrible pain. When the Friars crushed Schurz 40-0 in the Prep Bowl Jardine said: "This is the happiest moment of my life." He was 27 years old, and he was right.

CHAPTER FOUR

*J*esus was taken up and a cloud received him out of their sight. – Acts 1-9

The nuns at Ascension were in charge of the school, but the priests would drop by, and everything would stop.

It is easier for a camel to pass through the eye of a needle than for a rich man to enter the kingdom of God. – Mark 10:25

But it could happen. The Lord could work in mysterious ways. Suddenly, Mr. Bogardus decides to give his property to St. Mary's in *The Bells of St. Mary's*. The Lord could turn the heart of the King of Assyria to aid the Children of Israel. Neither the King nor Mr. Bogardus seemed to get credit for their noble deeds.

In the dark bus on the way back to Ascension from the eighth-grade trip to Crystal Lake, kids were cutting up and couples were making out, and it seemed like they were on their own now and could do as they liked. Convinced that Father White was not on the bus, Johnny-D laughingly called out: "Where the hell's our chaperone?" And out of the dark, Father White's voice thundered: "I'm right here." God's silence. Had been broken. Dead silence followed.

Danny loved Jesus, who had to be the nicest guy who ever lived. Jesus would understand, and even if he didn't, he'd still give you a break. He'd still love you. Same went for the Virgin Mary, and no doubt Joseph was a nice guy too, why else would the Virgin Mary have married him and why else would he put up with not even being allowed to fuck his own wife, so that she could be the Virgin Mary, still, nice a guy as he might be, praying to Joseph probably wouldn't do shit for you, so Danny confined his prayers to Jesus and Mary, and sometimes St. Jude, who was the patron saint of lost causes. Maybe Joseph could intercede for you, but he didn't really carry any weight; he wasn't even a saint. *Saint* Joseph was actually *another* guy. Mary's Joseph was just Joseph *the Carpenter*.

He wasn't a saint? How could he not be a saint? What were the rules for sainthood? One was you had to perform a miracle – through God, of course, like when Moses made water spurt out of a rock so the Israelites could get a drink in the middle of the desert, that was really God's miracle, not Moses', and it couldn't make Moses a saint anyway because saints have to believe in Jesus, or it might be a case like Our Lady of Fatima appearing to some little girl, so the little girl became a saint.

The Virgin Mary and the month of May were celebrated in the court-yard between the church and the school. The Virgin Mary, remember, is still living, because she didn't die; Jesus couldn't bear that, so she was taken up to Heaven bodily, thus the Feast of the Assumption. Quite an assumption. The resurrected flesh and blood of Jesus spent just forty days on earth among the living before his Ascension into Heaven. For Catholics, sainthood is the ultimate trophy. Not just Heaven as a reward for a life well lived, but to be imbued with such holiness and grace that your name would be elevated, like knighthood. What do you have to do to be a saint? The College of Cardinals has to name you one. That's all. It's like the Roman senate making Caesar into a god.

Jesus was a very nice man, a kind and gentle man who was also extreme-ly wise, who taught a gospel of love and peace and justice and virtue, and that was why people loved him and why they killed him. You always hurt the one you love. Most people were perfectly indifferent toward him. He was a common criminal. As are we all.

Jesus could command nature, and if you mixed him with Buddhism and Taoism and Confucianism, you got wisdom and compassion, instead of a preoccupation with sin and sacrifice and redemption – fuck that, it's repressive. Instead, Karma. Jesus could be the answer to free you from your past karmic deeds and restore your original nature. Who you really are, and you are good. You will like you. You'll love you. The concept of sin and human depravity is alien to the universe of karma.

Frank Lloyd Wright had a design for Carroll Playground that he called a kinder symphony, but the Village board turned it down and gave the commission to one of his students, who used the same aesthetic, then the village parks were all named after authors of classic children literature – Lewis Carrol, Robert Louis Stevenson, Hans Christian Anderson, James Barrie.

We watch Danny-boy growing up, starting on Clinton Avenue in south Oak Park, playing at Carroll Playground and in the neighborhood, around the block, with his friends Gene and Mary Jule, walking to Ascension with his sister, from first grade to fourth grade, and then the family moves to Euclid Avenue, a stone's throw from the school and church. He calls himself Dan now. He has two passions – sports, all of them, and pretending. He is only aware of the former.

The Irish famine of 1846 killed more than a million people, but it killed poor devils only. To the wealth of the country, it did not the slightest damage. Ireland is at present only an agricultural district of England, marked off by a wide channel from the country to which it yields corn, wool, cattle, industrial and military recruits. – Marx, Capital

Marx was writing in 1865 about Ireland being England's bitch, its farmland and fodder, and the excess labor was shipped off to America,

Land of the Free. Thus, Ireland was depopulated, and it was just a place to get out of by the time Pop was born, a few decades after Marx saw it for what it was, capitalist addition by subtraction. Joining up with the Brits must've been a common ruse, so it took some guile on Pop's part to convince the Crown of his loyalty.

Existential questions. And what about Grampa, Wilhelm Schmidt, Mary's father, an able-bodied young German mechanic, when there was a war between Germany and the USA? These were the questions uppermost in the mind of God as it extended through Dan into the third millennium CE: Why did the Burkes go to Saint Bernadine's? How did Connor Finnegan get downtown to work before the construction of the expressway that would carry the el to the suburbs?

And then it was summer, and the Finnegans were off to Lake Lawn Lodge for two glorious weeks.

Connor Finnegan must've been taking down a good chunk of change at the Edison Company. Enough to take his family to Lake Lawn, a retreat for the employees of Commonwealth Edison, for a couple of weeks every summer. Enough for two cars, a two-car garage. Enough to have the Clinton house remodeled and send the kids to private schools, and then enough to buy the corner house on Euclid and Van Buren and widen its driveway and outfit it with a two-car garage. But not enough yet to join the Riverside Country Club. He'd have to wait till he cashed in his Edison chips and started his own business for that.

For two weeks every summer the family encamped on the shores of Lake Delevan in Wisconsin in a cottage on the grounds of a resort called Lake Lawn Lodge, two weeks that became the centerpiece of the whole year, to be looked forward to in rapt anticipation, and then to fade into memory regretfully, a moment you had wished to remain in forever, and it was used up, you had consumed it, devoured it, a day at a time, fourteen times.

The lake, the indoor pool in the timber lodge, the wooded trails alongside the lake, everything was alive with aromas, the lake, the woods, the air, the girls. There was a dance hall where bands would play swing music, and couples would dance, and Danny and his summer friends could peek through the windows at them.

There were no baths or showers in the cottages, so everybody trooped over to the shower rooms in their robes, towels, and clogs. There was no refrigerator in the cottage, and a guy would come by and deliver a big chunk of ice. The Iceman cometh to the cottages of Lake Lawn Lodge. The block of ice went into the icebox. The lodge, on the other hand, was a grand sprawling hotel, carpeted, air-conditioned, and with an indoor pool. In the cottages, there was no air-conditioning, but sleeping near the lake in the cool night air of Wisconsin was sublime, pungent, and sweet.

At the Assembly Grounds across the lake, Dan's cousins were staying in a big two-story house just a few hundred yards from the lake. At night, Dan and his cousins would catch lightning bugs in their hands, and they would glow on and off in the dark.

The gift shop in the Lodge at Lake Lawn sold comic books and magazines, and being Delevan, Wisconsin, the sports magazines were full of Packer pix and stories that Dan would pore over while lounging in the cool cottage by the lake. Dan went into the gift shop in the hotel to page through the magazines and comic books until he was forced to settle on a purchase.

The football mag was mostly about the Packers, the greatest team in the world, except for one story about the Bears. It wasn't too long ago that the Bears were the best. They had once been the Monsters of the Midway.

They battered and bloodied Y.A. Tittle to his knees in Wrigley Field to claim the title.

The Bears were training in Rensselaer, Indiana. Willie Gallimore was one of the sweetest running backs anybody had ever seen, swirling and darting and side-stepping trouble with amazing speed. Willie Gallimore had style. Billy Wade was the quarterback. Ronnie Bull and Rick Casares were the halfback and fullback. Dan envisioned them solely based on the power and suggestibility of their names, in Proustian fashion. They were real people, but they were also fictional characters in a narrative Dan alone was reading.

Willie Gallimore could go sideways faster than most players could go straight. And then, *Two Bears Dead*. Running back Willie Gallimore and tight end Bo Farrington killed in a car crash during training camp in Rensselaer.

Death butted into Dan's vacation, and at Lake Lawn, when it was the second week and then only a few days were left, and he was counting them down to the last day, he was sadder each day as the end approached. Knucklehead. *Enjoy* it.

A pretty girl about his age, slim, lithe, with curly brown hair that glistened when she rose out of the water, would tell Dan he kissed like a fish. Because he had never kissed a girl before, and he didn't know where the noses went, and if your nose doesn't go to one side or the other, the two of you meet head on, smooshing noses. Like fish. You have to tilt your head. Blew that too.

That girl at Lake Lawn Lodge said Dan kissed like a fish, and she made fun of him, and the whole vacation disintegrated right there. Two weeks of heaven turned into two weeks of hell – because she was everywhere, with her sleek tan skin and slick black bathing suit so tight on her bottom, laughing at him and glaring at him and getting all her friends to do the same. They shut him out. Why did you always want something you couldn't have? And why must he always be given a taste of it before it is snatched away from him? Why did he have to know what he was missing? They had found each other the first day, and all two weeks lay ahead of them.

One summer, Danny "worked" each day of the vacation at the stables, leading the ponies into their traces, and all the stable hands got to know him, and the next year he came back and none of them remembered who he was at all.

The stables were alongside the playground, just a slide and some swings, and you'd go there in the evenings, just as the sun was going down and it was starting to cool off a little, and you could swing, sit on a swing with a couple other kids, boys and girls, and talk.

They swung up into the twilight of the Wisconsin sky that was purple and black and painted with unnumbered sparks, unlike the orange gray of the Chicago sky, and the talkers were matching each other, going for height, sometimes swinging together and sometimes in syncopation, and then level and swung easy and low, and let their feet touch the ground lightly, just a touch slower until they stopped. It was dark now, and the lightning bugs were glowing and flashing on and off.

Danny found out there was a school called Knox College, and he figured that was where his dad had gone to school. School of Hard Knox. It was like the stone bass. When Danny was little and they were at Lake Lawn for their two weeks of wish fulfillment in the cottages near the golf course, the lake, and the lodge, Connor and Danny would stroll down to the pier in the evening, and Connor would talk to all the folks fishing, and Danny wanted to fish too. So, so one time, Danny brought his little toy fishing pole with him, and Connor tied a stone around the end of the line and told Danny they were fishing for stone bass.

Mary spotted the house on Euclid in the real estate office listings and her heart leapt. It was available. They could buy it. They could live there. Imagine it. It's two blocks from the el, a block from Oak Park Avenue. Gerber's hardware store is right there. The A&P, the bank, Brinkerhoff's drugstore. We could swing it. Up, up, up. From the Riverside bungalow to Clinton Avenue to the Clinton house remodeled to the Euclid castle. Build a two-car garage. Widen the driveway. Screen in the porch. The corner house meant you lived on two streets, Euclid and Van Buren, and it was the biggest house on the block. It was a castle.

You could go down in the basement and play a game of pool, drink a beer. A game of pocket billiards, as perfected by Willie Mosconi. Connor was a Mosconi man all the way, smooth, knew all the angles, how to apply english to make a ball hug the rail. The pool table was magnificent, full length, with firm cushions and pristine green felt stretched over slate, and a ball return, all made of dark wood, with chutes that ran underneath the table and emerged at the foot where they could be gathered and racked. If you were a little boy, you could crawl underneath the table and watch the balls rolling home when Dad or Pop made a shot. And they made a lot. They were good. They could run the table. When an errant shot would ricochet with an unexpectedly fortuitous result, Pop would exult: "A kick in the arse is better than no fight at all."

Connor mounted a backboard and hoop on the side of the garage in the alley. Dan could shoot hoops now whenever he wanted. He could play pinners off the front steps and imaginary football games in the backyard. He was in Heaven. He was in the middle of Oak Park, Illinois.

When they went to swim at Ridgeland-Commons, Johnny-D kept two fingers across his left wrist where he wore his watch, so his skin wouldn't tan there, and that way he could show everybody how tan he was. Plus, he wanted to make sure people didn't think he really was that color. He was sly and he looked like Maury Wills and could steal bases like him too, and hit both ways, righty and lefty.

What would you grow up to be from watching "The Honeymooners", "I Love Lucy", and "Amos and Andy"? "Leave it to Beaver" was a parody of Danny's own family's existence. Beaver and his big brother Wally, like Dan and Ciaran. "Father Knows Best" exhibited what it was like to have a sister. Dobbie Gillis just wanted to make out, but he was going to follow the rules. His buddy Maynard G. Krebs just wanted to avoid work. "The Honeymooners" was a parody of their existence, too. The husband with wild schemes, a big heart, and a bad temper, and the pretty, empathetic wife who loves him and really rules the roost. The Mystic Knights of the Sea had a double meaning, and Dan merged the two. The Mystic Knights of the Sea was the lodge where Amos, Andy, and Kingfish were members. The K of C were the Knights of Columbus, and so Dan wondered how in the world his dad could be a member of the same lodge as Amos and Andy.

Going My Way played the Lamar when WW2 was going full tilt, with Bing Crosby as a young Catholic priest and Barry Fitzgerald as an old one as Irish as you can get. There in black and white was the Catholic school with its nuns and priests, in the city, all concrete and gray. This must be the way it was in Chicago. It was a kind of fantasy template for Ascension, nuns, priests, moving from black and white to color, from city to suburb.

Then came the sequel, *The Bells of St. Mary's,* a movie on TV that the Finnegan family could watch together in the living room, Mom and Dad in their separate recliners, Norine on the couch,

Danny-Boy lying on the living room carpet with his head resting on their collie Pokey's back, Ciaran in college, Brendan, Dilantin-ed-out, upstairs asleep. Dan's mythology required no audience but himself. Henry Darger must have felt the same way. The purity of Henry Darger, the great

Chicago primitive artist, lies in the hopelessness of his ever finding an audience. He was his own audience. And he was right there in Chicago. Dan must've walked right by him once or twice downtown, going in opposite directions on Wabash Avenue underneath the el.

It's the same as Danny making up a basketball league in the basement, as playing pinners off the front steps, as playing a football game against himself in the backyard while announcing the play by play. The purity of Henry Darger was to accept fully that his world was imaginary. There, he was able to confront his demons and defeat them or be defeated by them, but to persist, nonetheless. His secret world of art, his Dead Sea scrolls hidden in a cave. Dan was pretending to be an athlete, the same way he was pretending to solve a math problem or play the piano or get girls.

Henry Darger was living on the west side. Dan walked past him on the street. They walked past each other. His life intersected with Dan's. So did the riots at the Democratic convention, the war on Vietnam, the race riots, and Martin Luther King being murdered.

So, there we were, fellow Americans, with the Checkers Speech in black and white with Howdy Doody and Two-Ton Baker and Kubla, Fran, and Ollie, and the playground and Gene and Mary Jule, dissolved into the 60s, where Black people would appear.

Gene and Mary Jule Morrisey were red-haired, freckle-faced twins who lived with their Nano down the block on Clinton Avenue. They moved away in third grade to live with their mother on the south side of Chicago. The south side was a vast expanse of territory, unlike the north side. The Ascension kids replaced the Clinton Avenue friends, Gene and Mary Jule, and the Burkes.

Mean Gene liked to read comic books, *Superman, Batman*, and the like. Danny's sister Norine liked to read *Betty & Veronica*, and Danny studied them, absorbed by the notion that first he would prefer blond Betty, and in the next moment, raven-haired Veronica, never once considering why it had to be one or the other, they were both so delicious, yet the blond aura of Betty was distinct from that of Veronica, and they, though they were only ink drawings on a page, must have tasted and felt and smelled subtly different.

Why were Gene and Mary Jule living with Nano in the first place? Gene and Mary Jule were the products of a broken home. There was no dad. The Burkes had a dad. They were a real Catholic family, and they lived right across the street on Clinton Avenue. They weren't a big Catholic family; they only had five or six kids. And they went to church at Saint Bernadine's, which was just as far away from Clinton as Ascension, but it was across Harlem Avenue in Forest Park. Nano was Gene and Mary Jule's Grandmother. Their mother lived on the south side of Chicago. Their parents were divorced. Catholics weren't supposed to get divorced. The Pope said so, and the Pope was infallible on matters of faith and morals, except when it came to the Nazis.

Gene would one day enter the seminary. Mean Gene would one day become a priest. Father Mean Gene. Maybe he would harass the bishops the way he did the seven patrol boys. Maybe he would abuse boys, too, but probably not. Probably that would just piss him off. The Legend of the Seven Patrol Boys. Gene went to kindergarten and Danny-boy didn't, so, it was hearsay as well perhaps as hyperbole, but according to both Gene and Mary Jule, Gene got into an altercation that turned physical with an eighth grade patrol boy, who called to his partner for aid, and then another patrol boy and another patrol boy joined in, until there were seven of them, all to quell one skinny little kindergartner, which might be hard to fathom, but not if you were a would-be kindergartner yourself, albeit sheltered from the experience.

Gene and Mary Jule moved away, but not before the hot summer ended, and the three of them were playing in the kiddie pool in Dan's backyard,
and Dan talked Mary Jule into removing her bathing suit. Gene didn't give
a shit. He was Mean Gene with everybody else but Dan. With the rest of
the universe, he had a terrible tendency to explode into tantrums, fights,
and wreckage, on the playground, or at Ascension, where he got into it
with one and all, kids, nuns, priests, it didn't matter. But Gene never got
mad at Dan, and Dan never got mad at Gene. There was nothing to get
mad about. All they did together was play and have fun, all up and down
the block.

Dan's circle of friends began with Gene and Mary Jule. Then came
the Burkes across the street. Then came independence. Dan would ride
his bike to make deliveries for Paul's Drugstore, on the other side of the
bridge over the Congress Expressway. Working for Paul's was where he
would discover Benson and Hedges cigarettes in a box, which was very
intriguing. So, Dan was tooling around town on the cruiser, Ciaran's old
bike, delivering prescriptions. He got paid by the delivery. He kept his
money in a cigar box. He and the Burkes would hang out in their tree house
and count their money.

Houses, side by side, block by block. Catholics, Protestants. There
were Jews, but who knew? Muslims? Who had ever heard of such a thing?
Religious questions devolved into such mysteries as: Why do the Burkes
go to school and church in Forest Park at Saint Bernadine's instead of
Ascension? Why does the Protestant church on Harvard Street have a
bowling alley in the basement?

The 50s happened on Clinton Avenue; life happened at Carroll Playground. One time, they put on a circus. There were bleachers set up, and
there were concessions being sold, and it was at night with all the lights
on, and kids were in it as clowns. And Danny was the little clown at the

end. He had his hobo make-up on and a bowler hat. And then he wasn't. Roger Reynolds got the part instead. Who cares about the circus? Roger Reynolds ended up playing the little hobo instead, and not only was the skit a hit, winning loud laughter and applause, but as the clowns ran out of the ring, the little hobo was last, and his pants fell down, and the crowd erupted in laughter that rose to a cheer. Everyone would remember that moment. Well, Danny would remember it.

At Ascension, Dan hung out with the guys: Roger Raynard, David Gallagher, Paul Gleason, Len Larawitz, known as Shocker or Shock, Rug Olson, and Larry Sullivan. Then there were the Clarence Alley Boys: Gump and Johnny-D and Jack Lepper, who didn't like Dan for some reason. Guys called him Jack Strap like Jockstrap, and so did Dan, and he didn't like it, so maybe that was it.

At first, it was about winning. He was good, he was lucky, he was talented. He could do no wrong. And then it went away. It seemed to be all about losing, and maybe it was, but it wasn't really about Danny after all. It was about becoming. It was about the whole world changing from black and white to color to black and white again, and if focusing on the experience and inner life of one little loser paints a picture less than hopeful – that's the point. It explodes into color again.

Moby Dick was on the summer reading list, and Dan read it at Lake Lawn Lodge and loved it. All that minutia about whales washed over him, and he didn't care how long it was taking to get to the point; he was at sea, without having to go to sea, which he would have hated, would have scared the shit out of him.

Dan never wanted to leave the playground. Peter Pan never wanted to grow up. By pretending, by trying to slip away, by quitting, by lying, by doing everything he could think of to avoid responsibility, to grow up.

Talking about Dan or America? The USA? No, Dan. The USA would never grow up.

Danny somehow knew that it was in sports that you found out what you were really all about, so, with each of these sports, it was becoming clear that many of the world's greatest athletes were Black. So, what did that mean? Only that those athletes were setting the standards of excellence, and that their accomplishments were something to aspire to, but none of that earned you any points among the racists.

Tuesday, at ten thirty in the morning, air raid sirens go off, every Tuesday. It would be a hell of a time for the Ruskies to attack, everyone would think it was just a drill, which might be good timing really, because everyone would routinely take shelter.

The whole world was being made over. It would take just three years for twenty-four new countries to come into existence. They had been European colonies. The 50s slowly turned into the 60s, but it didn't take long for the 60s to catch fire. The difference was as graphic as the contrast between Eisenhower and Kennedy.

To get to Kennedy, you had to get past Nixon. Everybody at Ascension was for Kennedy. A kid wearing a Nixon button, like Charley Clover did, would be pummeled by his classmates and his banner torn. Dan just watched. Charley Clover was a jerk, and he picked his nose. He had been caught picking his nose. He picked Nixon, and he picked his nose; he was doomed.

CHAPTER FIVE

A nd this kid named Nathan Degrorio said it was all bullshit. Nathan Degrorio could punch holes in anybody's argument and make fun of it mercilessly. If you jerked off, you would go to Hell.

Nathan laughed: "That's a bit much, don't you think?"

Reading the Old Testament, it appeared that God was a giant asshole, and this seemed to be the mission of the Bible, to turn the Asshole of Part One into the Nice Guy of Part Two. He didn't undergo character development; however, he was just replaced by somebody else, like the new James Bond. There was a different Jesus in every gospel, too. Bond, James Bond. Christ, Jesus Christ.

At the end of *Goldfinger* came the announcement that James Bond would return. The same thing with Jesus. He was going to return. Those first Christians thought it would be any day now, but after a century or two, they had to develop a long view, that Christ wasn't coming back any time soon, or maybe he wasn't actually coming back at all – it was all a metaphor. After a year or two, Bond aficionados would figure it out too, but they wouldn't call it a metaphor – they would call it bullshit, which is what Nathan DeGrorio did on seeing *Thunderball*. Bullshit, right from the start when they made Sean Connery look dorky wearing an old-timey football helmet without a facemask, strapping on a jetpack, and farting up into the sky.

Dr. No was a turn-on. Honey was her name. In one scene, she was rendered unconscious and slung over a villain's shoulder. Bond would have to rescue her, among other things. Dan anxiously looked forward to this scene in the movie, but it failed to be translated from the page to the screen. In *From Russia with Love*, the SMERSH assassin Grant drugs the beautiful spy Tania's drink and then attempts to garotte Bond as they grapple beside her unconscious body. Bond wins. In *Goldfinger*, a nude woman becomes lifeless, limp, and gold, and we have finally arrived at the complete objectification of a woman – we've turned her into gold, into money. Ages 12, 13, and 14. On the heels of eight years of nuns, the weird sisters.

How could you believe *Dr. No*? The difference between what a 13-year-old believed and what a 17-year-old believed was wide. The difference between what philistines believed and what Nathan Degrorio believed was light years.

James Bond, *National Review* called him The Conservative Agent. He was fighting as a soldier of capitalism in the Cold War, which apparently had just been waiting in the wings for World War II to end, an undeclared hostility between Communism and the so-called Free World.

The USA and the USSR had been allies in World War II, but then again, the Soviets and the Nazis had been allies at the beginning of World War II. Things change. The British Invasion, James Bond, and the Beatles. The Rolling Stones. *Time* magazine, *April 8, 1966: Is God Dead?* Hadn't Nietzsche settled this a hundred years before?

The bells were ringing the Angelus at Ascension, Injun Summer outside, as depicted in a color cartoon in the *Tribune*. Color funnies. The *funnies*. In color on Sunday. Dick Tracy, Prince Valiant. Gil Thorpe. There went that crippled lady, her name was Maureen, dragging her wretched body with the aid of her walker past the Euclid castle every single day, no matter the weather, to go to Mass. "Morning, Maureen." She only smiled back, and it took all the effort of a saint; she was in such pain, all she could do was smile, and she couldn't speak. Presumably. Presumptuously.

Dan had a set of golf clubs and a bag to carry over his shoulder so he could ride his bike with the guys, Johnny-D, Denny Doody, and this kid named Chester, to Columbus Park on the other side of Austin Boulevard in the great city of Chicago. He had three woods, a five iron, a seven, a nine, and a putter that was gold (it looked like gold anyway), and he polished it with chrome cleaner. He also had a TAD tennis racket, strung with catgut, in his equipment room. He had a hockey stick with a curved blade that he wrapped with black adhesive tape. He had two hockey pucks that he kept in the freezer in the basement.

Dan switched the light on at the top of the stairs and went down to the basement to get his clubs. They were in the storeroom alongside his dad's workbench. His dad's clubs were in there too, and they were in a bag on wheels, and there were a lot of them, really nice and new and well-maintained, and all the accessories, towels, tees, golf glove, brand new Titlist golf balls, and a bucket of old balls he was planning to take to the driving range,

This kid named Chester was short and skinny, and he had one leg totally crippled or lame or something, so that he couldn't bend it, and he could barely run, but he'd try. It was kind of pitiful, really. Guys felt sorry for him, plus he was rich and guys mooched off him, and here he was tagging along on the golf trip, riding their bikes to Columbus Park with their golf bags slung over their shoulders, Chester lagging behind.

Golf was one of those games, like tennis or pocket-billiards, that unless you're Gump, you're going to need some serious instruction to master the fundamentals. Whatever it was, Dan didn't quite have it. He hooked it, he sliced it, he duffed it. Meanwhile, Chester couldn't hit the ball very far, but he hit each shot dead-on straight as a ruler. By the seventh hole, he was five strokes ahead of everybody else.

The basement was Dan's indoor stadium. The Derrymen played their home games there, the Derrymen being the imaginary team from Derry, Ireland that Dan invented. The fans were jamming the place. You could feel the excitement. And then – an electric hum, loud and growing, and it was not the legendary Tony Lawless, the Rockne-like football coach turned athletic director, setting the needle on the phonograph record and cranking up John Phillip Sousa as the Fenwick Friars emerged onto the court, no, it was the Beatles!

"Baby's good to me/ You know she's happy as can be/ You know she said so/ I'm in love with her/And I feel fine!"

Danny put on his black Chuck Taylor Converse All-Stars with the white laces. Not white low-cuts like practically everyone else. The Boston Celtics wore the black Chucks, and so did the Fenwick Friars. He kept his gear in the storeroom in the basement. In the bowels of the stadium.

Going from season to season. Spring, the ice is melting. Time for basketball in the alley. Spring on Clinton Avenue, learning to ride a bike. Learning. Learning to swim. Learning to ice skate, roller skate, grip a baseball, a tennis racket, a pool cue, a golf club, overlapping grip, choke up on the bat, how to putt, how to chip, how to drive, how to pull the ball, how to bunt, how to punt, shoot a slap shot, lift the puck, throw a forkball, a spiral, make a lay-up, a jump shot, a free throw, a hook shot, a bounce pass, chest pass, behind the back.

They all happened over time, gradually, turning into habit, techniques employed without thinking and honed to perfection, well, as good as you were going to get, and mostly all thanks to Connor and Ciaran. Over time meant that while Dan was learning how to ride a bike, Lenny Bruce was making jokes that would get him thrown in jail, crafting monologues that morphed into dialogues and could travel in time back to Calvary and hear what Jesus said to the two thieves being crucified alongside him, while Danny-Boy pedaled unsteadily down the alley with both Ciaran and Connor running alongside him.

Now for Christmas, Dan received among his many gifts a bottle of English Leather. He did not have sideburns yet, to his regret, but he did have some acne going, which made him feel as though he was getting somewhere, might as well smell like English Leather so the broads would go for him. He used Vitalis. And Clearasil.

In his dad's dresser drawer: White collared shirts, fresh from the laundry, wrapped in cellophane, the collars starched. Silk ties, subdued colors, stripes. An electric shaver. Dad shaved every day, sometimes twice. He never once in his life grew a beard. Once in a while, on vacation, he might have a few days' stubble.

They say things are perfectly calm in the eye of a tornado. Just two blocks away from the house on Clinton Avenue was the playground that took up the whole block, Carroll Playground, named after Lewis Carroll, presumably because playgrounds are for children, and Lewis Carroll, whose real name was Charles Dodgson, by profession a mathematician, also an amateur photographer, especially liked little girls.

At the heart of the playground was the shelter house – so called because it was where everyone went to warm up when the playground turned into an ice rink in the winter. The whole vast field would be flooded when the freezing temps arrived, and dozens of people would come to skate.

You can't play hockey on figure skates. Why not? Because it gives you an unfair advantage.

How? Because you don't even have to skate, you can just stand on your toes and run around. What's wrong with that? Nobody else can do that.

They've got hockey skates on. That's the point. Seems like they're the ones wearing the wrong skates.

The Blackhawks' Bobby Hull, the Golden Jet, could fire off a hockey puck with his slap shot at 120 miles per hour. There were six teams in the National Hockey League: Blackhawks, Rangers, Bruins, Redwings, Maple Leafs, and Canadians. They beat the hell out of each other. The Blackhawks had never won Lord Stanley's Cup. Gump Brecca's favorite player was Gump Worsley, goalie for the Red Wings. Of course. Gump had named himself after Gump Worsley. And everyone respected it. His real name was Jim, but nobody ever called him that, not even his parents. His father was a doctor, and Gump was a straight-A student, and Dr. Brecca called his son Gump – out of respect. He was the most skilled player at every game, with one caveat: he was not fast at all.

Gump lived on Scoville Avenue, a street named after James Scoville, President of the Prairie State Loan & Trust Bank, who at least did one good thing after he bought up all the land from Oak Park Avenue east to the Chicago city limits; he gave Oak Park a library. The Scoville Institute, better known as the Oak Park Public Library. Ernie Hemingway would walk into the world of books there.

In the shelter house at Carroll playground, there were legendary games of steal-the-bacon, and that was where Dan first got the notion that he could be the greatest athlete in the world – because he was a shade quicker than a dozen other six-year-olds sitting in a line on opposite sides of the floor, cross-legged. Steal-the-bacon required guile, speed, quickness. Red Rover: brute force and intimidation. Dan was more adept by far at the former than the latter.

The sports world, like everything else, was well underway before Danny ever came along.

Before sports hit him, there was the unorganized play of Chase. Adventuring came before sports – tree climbing, all-purpose climbing, scaling buildings, getting up on roofs, and traveling anywhere on your bike, and by the time you got to your teens, you'd be ready for a drink, you'd cop a smoke, if you had the nerve, and Danny had plenty of nerve, and not much common sense, in fact, practically none.

There was a ledge about ten inches wide 10-feet off the ground all around the Presbyterian church on the next block, across the street from the playground, and you could climb up onto it and you could try to make your way, either face to the wall or back to the wall, all the way around the church on the ledge. Why? To see if you could.

Kennedy against Nixon. It was a tough choice for conservative Catholics – to vote for the liberal Democrat, Kennedy – but he was a Catholic, and he played touch football. So why shouldn't he take over from the aged king? The prince becomes king, revitalizing the kingdom of Camelot. President Kennedy said we could get to the moon by the end of the decade. What a dream world. And then *bang*. It all ended. Everything seemed to be going along just fine until Kennedy got shot. Eisenhower had been like the country's Grampa. Then we got Young Dad to replace him, and our new Dad was handsome and Irish and Catholic, and he played touch football with his brothers.

Tackle football without pads. There were a couple of kids at the playground who just wanted to mess Dan up. They were lying in wait for him. The villains: Brian Cunningham, Jimbo Wilkinson. There was a whole life there on Clinton Avenue; there were four seasons revolving around Carroll playground again and again and again. And then they moved a mile away to the Euclid castle, and they lived there, three blocks from Ascension, and Dan was home from school for lunch and watching Bozo the Clown on WGN when the President was shot. Kennedy was murdered, having completed little more than half his first term, and it was a pretty sure bet he would've been re-elected, especially in light of the way LBJ would crush Goldwater. But then Johnson would go on to serve only one term before the War in Vietnam made him say: Enough of this shit! By then, it was *that* year, one of the most tempestuous in history, when childhood would vanish forever into Dan's past. Anything was possible now. Everybody knew that after the President had been shot.

Lenny Bruce would take you through a whole movie in your mind, when out of his diatribe would emerge a dialogue, and suddenly he's playing two guys talking to one another, or a man and his wife, or himself and his auntie, or Jesus on the cross and the guys being crucified next to him. He imagines these scenes, the thoughts of these characters – the Texas cop aghast as Oswald gets shot by Jack Ruby – "Oh Shit-uh!"

Johnny-D, the sardonic wit, standing at Kennedy's gravesite in Arlington National Cemetery along with the other patrol boys, quipped: "Let's blow out the eternal flame."

Chase was the ultimate running game. The first thing was to set the boundaries: You couldn't cross Jackson Boulevard on the north, Van Buren on the south, Euclid on the west, and Wesley on the east, the whole block inside those limits – the church, people's yards, the alley – all of it was in play.

Jimbo Kidd was the good Jimbo. Jimbo Wilkinson was the bad. They were both tough, but Jimbo Kidd would joke with you, while Jimbo Wilkinson would shoulder you as you tried to walk past him in the hall. If you were tough, you were going to box in the Silver Gloves. They fought it out for the heavyweight championship of Ascension. Jimbo Wilkinson kicked Jimbo Kidd's ass.

Dan would close the door to the bedroom he shared with his little brother, whom he barred from entrance most of the time, and set up a table alongside his record player and stack of 45s, and he became a deejay playing the week's top ten.

Johnny-D took the gag a step further. He went public with it, acting as if he were broadcasting wherever he went, catching sight of an imaginary Frank Sinatra crossing the street and calling out to him loudly, "Frank! Frank Sinatra! Yo, Frank!"

Johnny-D would pretend to be Steve Allen doing his man on the street interviews, and he generally conducted himself in public as if he were hosting a talk show, and he would broadcast wherever he went. If you walked around with him, you became his second banana.

It pours forth, Dan's life, in the middle of the century, where Truman is followed by Eisenhower, Kennedy, Johnson, and Nixon, five presidents in all, Rocky Marciano retires, Ezzard Charles and Jersey Joe Walcott take turns at the title, Ingemar Johansson winds up with it, knocking out Floyd Patterson, and then Patterson wins it back, only to be humiliated twice by Sonny Liston, who in turn is humbled twice, most mysteriously, by Cassius Clay, who turns into Muhammad Ali, whose license is suspended when he refuses to be drafted into the Army in the middle of the Vietnam War.

Dan walked down the hallway between classes. This was when things happened. In class, it was predictable. But between classes, the unexpected happened. Barry Lugan, a big jerk, shouldered him.

"What the hell?"

"What's your brother doing again?" he asked – because Danny had been spreading the word around.

"He's flying a helicopter in Vietnam."

"Yeah? Bet he gets killed. The gooks are always shooting helicopters down."

And that was it. Dan threw a punch that only bounced off Lugan's head, and Lugan came back at Dan with a punch of his own that landed flush on his mouth and drove his tooth, one of the canines, into his lip, and when Dan touched it with his tongue he was amazed at how perfectly like his tooth the hole was shaped, and then it welled up with blood that he had to swallow to pretend like nothing happened.

And in the beginning, there was George Mikan, who was schooled at DePaul by Coach Ray Meyer, who lived in Oak Park. Mikan was tearing up the NBA, clearing guys out with his forearm and hooking with either hand, winning five titles and then retiring, like Rocky Marciano, the two white champs, short and tall, champions of the black and white era, and then color arrived, Elgin Baylor making moves that were hard to believe, and then Wilt the Stilt, who made it even harder to believe what you were seeing, and then Bill Russell and the Cooz and the Celtics to more than match them, and during that span, the Celtics won eleven titles!

The Cubs, Jesus, the Cubs.

There was nothing in the sports world that could ever bring peace because its essence was turbulence, volcanic energy. Emotions would have to come into play. Bullies would win, the strong would survive, and even if you managed to make it to the top, it would only be to discover that it was all an illusion, and you would have your license taken away like Ali, or you would die in a plane crash like Rocky. Sports ended in reality.

What was it about boxing? There doesn't have to be anything about boxing – it just *is*. It is the primitive social interaction, as natural as running, and so it fell naturally into Dan's purview of the sports he played and loved: running and jumping, track and field, baseball and softball, football, basketball, ice hockey. The Clarence Alley Boys played everything.

Connor mounted a hoop on the back of the garage in the alley of the Euclid house – you'd bang into the wall of the garage every time you drove for a lay-up. There were hoops mounted on the sides of garages in the alleys all across town, and Dan would take his ball and head out and go from one to the next, shoot a few, and move on, or wait till he finally heard another ball bouncing and someone else showed up to play. "You wanna play? "

This was the sports world, the true world, where you could put a stopwatch on somebody and the result would be true; there could be no bullshit about it. That was how fast you were. That was how high you could jump. That was how many points you scored. These were the trophies you won. There were the guys you beat and the guys you couldn't beat, and then there was everybody else that you'd have to find out about.

The fighters had been fighting their way through the 20th century, from John L. Sullivan and Gentleman Jim all the way back from the Marquis of Queensbury and then blasting forward to the great Jack Johnson beating a white man. Rocky Marciano thought the greatest fighter who ever lived was Jack Dempsey. But who could dispute what Joe Louis did?

Bum of the month! Only they weren't bums. Louis took out a top contender every month or so for a decade. Then he retired – and should've stayed retired, but he didn't, and others fought for the crown he had, like Lear, given away. Jersey Joe Walcott surprised Ezzard Charles to take the heavyweight crown. He promised to give Charles a rematch the following summer, which left Rocky Marciano to fight the great Joe Louis to be next in line.

Neither Marciano nor Louis wanted the fight. It didn't matter. The fight was planned for the Polo Grounds, but Bobby Thompson messed that up by sending the New York Giants into the World Series there, so it was on for Madison Square Garden. Dan was five weeks old. Sonny Liston was in jail and wouldn't get out until Danny was nearly seven. Louis was 6-2, 212. Marciano was 5-10, 187. The Brown Bomber's legs quit on him and his punch was gone, and in the 8th round Rocky knocked him down, then knocked him down again, and not just down, but, humiliatingly for them both, Rocky pummeled Louis while he was hung up on the ropes, and then knocked him clear out of the ring, except for one leg that trailed after him as he fell and rested on the bottom rope as he was counted out.

In Oak Park, nobody considered Italians to be white people till Rocky Marciano won the heavyweight title. Then they were white because he was white, and he was white because he beat the black guy.

Rocky Marciano was going to defend his belt for the sixth time. Big deal. When you get to about two dozen, let us know. Because that's what the Brown Bomber did. Still, Rocky was going to quit on top, undefeated, 49-0. Rocky Marciano was the Heavyweight Champion of the World, the only undefeated heavyweight champion ever. Marciano, a white guy, not even six feet tall and short-armed, but he had beaten an over-the-hill Joe Louis, who had been as good as there ever was, to claim the title, and he had beaten Jersey Joe Walcott and all the top contenders, everybody who stepped into the ring with him, and then he got the hell out of the ring before Sonny Liston could come along and decapitate him.

He still had more fights left in him. Why couldn't he fight Patterson? You don't think people would pay to see Rocky Marciano fight Floyd Patterson for the title? Rocky said he was going to stay retired. He could've retired, and he could've just not *told* anybody he was retired. After a period of time, though, he would be compelled to face a challenger. This goes back to Beowulf.

The boxing world was corrupt and crooked, that was a fact, but that wasn't because it was integrated, the first sport to be integrated, it was because the Mafia was behind it, and the same forces that swung secret deals with managers and robbed the gate and paid fighters to take a dive fixed most of Rocky's run, not in the outcome, but in the profits, were backing Sonny Liston now.

Floyd Patterson versus Sonny Liston, the fight that would send Dan to Hell. Floyd Patterson was a nice guy. Anybody could see that. And because Floyd Patterson was a good man, and Sonny Liston was a bad man, it made all the sense in the world if you were about 11 years old, like Danny. There was no appreciation of the sweet science anywhere else in the house, in the neighborhood, in Oak Park, because the heavyweight championship of the world was a contest between two Black men. No one was the least bit shy about using the n-word. They might not go around shouting it in public, that was low class, but it might certainly pop up in a normal private conversation, or, more directly, as in: The so-and-sos are selling their house to n-words. That was when the thing had to be confronted, had to be stopped. An all-white neighborhood was one thing, an all-white school was another, an all-white church, all-white churches, so, ok, all-white town, so who's going to object to the private use of the n-word, when the entire environment had been erected to exclude Blacks?

Ruth, the Finnegans' colored maid, visited once a week to clean, until Mary caught her stealing and had to let her go. Bullshit. What if she did? Danny stole all the time. Danny was a thief, a petty thief, stealing the loose change his father left next to his wallet and keys, Danny even stole candy bars from a store once, and he was consumed with shame and guilt, and so was Floyd Patterson, slinking away from the fight in disguise, humiliated, knocked out by Sonny Liston in the first round. Patterson had packed a disguise in his bag before the fight – a fake beard and mustache – in preparation for the eventuality that he might lose. He thought ahead.

Norman Mailer and William F. Buckley were going to debate each other in Chicago at the Medinah Temple on the eve of the Patterson-Liston fight. The *Tribune* reported: "In what was billed as a political debate between a conservative and a hipster, William F. Buckley Jr. and Norman Mailer met before a crowd of 3,600 at Medinah Temple last night to discuss (but only when they felt like it) the subject: 'What Is the Real Nature of the Right Wing in America?'" The transcript of the debate was published in *Playboy*.

It was getting harder and harder to fight Communism, since the Reds' propaganda machine could whip up worldwide outrage at the blatant racism in America, so racists like little Danny here took the assimilationist mode of thinking and cheered for Floyd Patterson to beat Sonny Liston, while the segregationists like his mom and dad turned a blind eye and a deaf ear to the whole sordid affair, even as it unfolded a few miles away on the south side of Chicago in Comiskey Park.

Danny had taken on a general cast of guilt about his little brother's predicament, a guilt as heavy as the one the nuns and priests laid on everybody, that of Original Sin, and so it was God's will and Danny's sin intertwining when he laid his head on his pillow that night and there was his transistor radio underneath.

The fight lasted a little more than two minutes. It began briskly. Patterson may have been outsized, but he could really pack a punch. He had a left hook that he threw from out of his crouch, and it landed like a bomb when it connected with a jaw, as it did Johansson's. Ingemar Johansson? No joke. A *Swede*? He was no joke. Well, Rocky *Graziano* thought the whole heavyweight division was a joke after Rocky *Marciano* retired. *Wops. Dagos.*

Danny could picture it, listening to the blow-by-blow account through his pillow. What's the big deal with the kid listening to the fight on the radio, with the radio under the pillow, nobody can even hear it, who's it going to bother? It comes on too late, that's all. Danny cannot take that radio to bed with him; he'll be awake all night. Danny *was* awake all night.

Patterson had been given a pep talk by no less than President Kennedy. All right-minded, red-blooded Americans were counting on him to beat Sonny Liston. President Kennedy also wanted James Bond to pitch-hit for us in the Cuban Missile Crisis. President Kennedy had put his hand on

Floyd's shoulder and whispered to him that America was counting on him to beat Liston. The pressure was on.

Eddie Machon wasn't the fighter Patterson was, and he had stayed with Liston, but Machon was elusive, a slick boxer who made a point of avoiding being knocked out. On the other hand, Patterson was going for a knockout himself, despite having packed a fake beard in with his gear to wear as a disguise in case he should lose. Who does that? Who prepares a disguise to escape in disgrace after defeat? He knew he was going to lose.

Patterson came out ducking and throwing that hook. He wasn't going to run and hide. Liston kept coming forward, too. They were going to move in and throw punches. They were going to *fight*.

Patterson was doing just fine, ducking and weaving, looking for an angle to launch that lethal hook that took Johansson out, until he mistimed his duck and ducked right into Liston's uppercut, adding his own momentum to the force of the blow. It rocked him. It stood him up. He tried to grab hold and clinch. He'd been able to do that just a moment earlier when he found himself within Liston's long reach in the center of the ring. It was simple then, but somehow now, even though the fight had just begun, it seemed to require more energy than he could muster. How much time was left in the round? Maybe he could weather it. He tried to cover up, and he got hit again, and this one he hardly saw coming, just caught it out of the corner of his eye, something black.

Once Liston stood Patterson up with that uppercut, it was easy pickings. He nailed Patterson good with a left hook, and it was lights out. Sonny Liston was the Heavyweight Champion of the World. It was a school night, and the fight came on too late. There was no moral dilemma. Danny felt just as shameful and guilty as Patterson, with the important exception that Danny could just put that persona aside, the one that identified with Floyd Patterson, and he could identify with a completely different hero, but he would never be able to shake the feeling that he had caused Floyd Patterson to lose that fight in Comiskey Park by disobeying his mother, who had told him not to listen to that fight on his transistor radio, and this was God's punishment, to live in an evil world where Sonny Liston was Heavyweight Champion. This was a dark time. It was a dark time for Sonny Liston, too – he had his own demons and lethal enemies, and he was not long for this world and was due in a short time to meet a violent end, while Patterson had only begun his humiliation. First, Liston beat the living daylights out of him *again*, and then he would make the mistake of incurring the wrath of the Greatest of All Time.

Danny was convinced he was the cause of his little brother's condition, and from there it would not be a long jump to thinking that he was responsible for Floyd Patterson losing the heavyweight championship to Sonny Liston. It had not been due to Danny that Patterson had *won* the title, of course. That was the fault of Ingemar Johannsen.

CHAPTER SIX

T he 60s flashed from black and white to color. As soon as Johnson became President, with that hangdog look and Jackie standing next to him in her pink blood-stained dress, the USA and its meaning were given a good shake in the kaleidoscope of sentiment and empathic response of patriotism at odds with reason, and it all added up to: it felt bad. Johnson was President, the nation was at war, spies and assassins were loose in the world, and there was no need for Catholics to be Democrats anymore – unless you were in Chicago. As always, Oak Park, Saints Rest, prided itself on being *not* Chicago.

Camelot was long dead. Even before Kennedy was shot, all sorts of sneaky shit was going on with the CIA and the FBI. J. Edgar Hoover had practically invented the FBI, and so the FBI did pretty much whatever he wanted, investigated anybody he wanted to investigate, investigated the hell out of them. But nobody was looking when DeMare swung that election for Kennedy by turning out the vote of Chicago's dead.

In *Armies of the Night*, Norman Mailer made a distinction between the Civil Rights march on Washington and the Vietnam War protests. The Black Panthers, and other Black militants, and Black protesters were out for justice, not peace, so they weren't joining up with the *peace* movement; no, they were joining the *anti-war* movement. Their fight just wasn't with the Viet Cong.

It was Ike's half-ass idea to split Vietnam in two and let Ho Chi Minh, who'd been elected by the whole country, govern just the north, while the new country of South Vietnam would be ruled by one of the few Catholics to be found, a fellow named Diem, who was then overthrown and killed the same year as Martin Luther King's I Have a Dream speech, same year Kennedy would be shot, and Dan was in the sixth grade. His sister was *not* home for lunch. She was at Trinity. Ciaran was in college in Minnesota. Connor was at work. There was his mom, Gramma, and his little brother, and Bozo's Circus playing on WGN, which was interrupted. The President has been shot. The President is dead.

Dan went back to school after lunch. We had seen our President shot to death. Then we saw Jack Ruby shoot Oswald on live TV. Jesus Christ, is this real? Is this really happening? We watched Kennedy's funeral on TV. Everybody. The whole family. And everybody else in America. The President's funeral. There was a horse in the street, a riderless horse, in Washington, DC. A little boy saluting. Jesus.

Dan stood on the corner on the school side of the East Avenue bridge over the expressway. It was a blessing that the Euclid castle was west of East Avenue to aid his lame sense of direction. Which way was east? Toward East Avenue. The Church with Jesus atop its dome was on East Avenue, so the sun rose in the east over Jesus every morning. It was a crisp November day, and Dan was just hanging out, no school because of the President's funeral, and all the kids were wondering the same thing. Did that just happen? Things happen because other things happened, not because we wish them to happen. Sometimes they do.

Stan Roe had a brace on his leg that kept it straight. It ran all the way down his leg from his hip to his heel. Stan Roe was a crossing guard, too. He and Dan and Nathan DeGrorio had all been assigned to the corner of East Avenue and Van Buren, in front of the church, in the dead of winter, hard-packed snow and ice on the streets and sidewalks. One good thing about being a crossing guard, besides being able to tell other kids what to do, was that you got to go to class late, because you had to wait at the corner for every last kid to come to school, and then, of course, you would lollygag on your way as much as you could. Once the bell rang and there were no more kids coming, the three of them turned finally to go, it was cold, and that was when Stan Roe's legs went out from under him and he jack-knifed onto the sidewalk.

Dan stopped, but Nathan kept on walking for a few paces. Then he stopped and called over his shoulder, "You all right, Stan?" He never looked back, just kept on walking. Dan hustled to catch up with him, and Nathan was laughing like it was the funniest thing he had ever seen in his life, and maybe it was. Dan sniggered and Nathan stopped dead, looked him in the eye, and said:

"You all right, Stan?" And doubled up again.

Dan told his mom, "We're going to do a skit. "

"You and Nathan DeGrorio?"

"And Paulie and Kenny and Charlie McCallister. Yeah."

"What's it about?"

It was called The Uncle Freddie Show. Oddly enough, it was just like a routine on the latest comedy album by Bob Newhart. But not really odd at all – Nathan DeGrorio just cribbed the whole act, plagiarized it. He was a joke stealer. The biggest joke of all was that he got away with it. The skit was approved, and on with the show! A bunch of fifth graders in a Catholic school acting out Bob Newhart's cynical nightclub act with Nathan playing Uncle Freddie, a grown-up, hosting a kids' show with obnoxious kids that he plays for laughs.

Bob Newhart. You know he's from Oak Park, right? No shit. Bob Newhart projected the image of an Oak Parker, a St. Giles grad, trying tactfully not to fuck things up, no matter what things they were or how ridiculously fucked up they were already. Nathan DeGrorio's record collection included not only Lenny Bruce, Bob Newhart, and Bill Cosby comedy sets, but also Frank Sinatra, Dave Brubeck, and Oscar Petersen. Nathan sat in his bedroom by himself and played a Bob Newhart comedy album, and then he stole a long bit that Newhart did and presented it as a skit, recruited a cast, and began rehearsing it to be performed on stage in the Pine Room for Mission Day. Everything except the cynical tone of it was entirely out of character for Nathan DeGrorio, who was going to be the star of the play, Uncle Freddie, in a satire of children's television called "The Uncle Freddie Show".

They met at Charlie McCallister's house, in the rec room in the basement, where there was plenty of room to rehearse, and Mrs. McCallister was always so nice and made snacks for everyone: Nathan, Charlie, Kenny Allerton, Paulie Fossner, and Dan. She was the nicest lady, Charlie's mom, and she used to joke with them when they'd eaten every snack they could beg, "Are you sufficiently suffullsified?" she'd chirp.

They rehearsed for a couple of weeks, more than they needed to, because the snacks were so good. And then, at the very last moment, in the wings, just before they were to step on stage, Nathan put a hand on Charlie's shoulder and said, "Charlie, we're not gonna use you." The look on Charlie McCallister's face was one of disbelief, dumb shock, and on Dan's one not quite of bewilderment, but of wonder, and he wondered whether maybe that moment was what Nathan had been aiming for all along. Why was another question, but Dan had to admit it was just like Nathan; he was back in character. And so, on with the show, without Charlie McCallister, who just stood in the wings like a moron. Charlie's mom was so nice. Nathan must've had it in his mind from the beginning. That must've been why he cast Charlie – for his mom.

Danny and Nathan would watch "The Man from UNCLE" together at Nathan's house. "Come on over if you want to," he said. So, Danny would head on over there in the early evening, walking east, alongside the expressway, past the church, and once beyond the immediate neighborhood, the setting changed from middle class to lower middle class and the melding of urban and suburban. Nathan lived one block from Austin Boulevard, the border between Oak Park and Chicago.

Napoleon Solo was being pursued by two agents of THRUSH through the streets of NYC, and he led them a merry chase, but finally they caught him, two henchmen, and they tossed him into the back seat of a car. The funny thing was, Solo simply squirmed across the seat and hopped out the door on the other side of the car. Brilliant! That was something to remember if ever you were captured and thrown into the back seat of a car.

Dan and Nathan were watching "The Man from UNCLE" in Nathan's room, and his mom came to the door with a plate of cookies. Before she could cross the threshold, Nathan met her, took the cookies, and slammed the door in her face. Nathan's mom knocked on the door again, and Nathan started singing: "I hear you knockin', but you can't come in."

Dan was going with Nathan to see a movie called *From Russia with Love*. Then Dan was reading the book. Then *From Russia with Love* was playing on a double bill with *Dr. No*. Ads proclaimed: James Bond is back-to-back! Then *Goldfinger* came out. Dan and Nathan rode the el downtown to the Woods theater to see a morning showing. Then he was reading the book. The paperback featured a wrap-around screenshot from the movie of the nude girl who gets painted gold curving around the spine of the book, with the title and author's name frustratingly blocking the view of her bare butt. Dan used his imagination.

Goldfinger. It sounds ridiculous because it is ridiculous. But nothing is ridiculous if you take it seriously. There is nothing people take more seriously than gold, which is ridiculous. Then Dan went with Nathan downtown to see *Thunderball*, and Dan was disappointed, while Nathan flat-out hated it.

Nathan had already been a grown-up when he was hosting the Uncle Freddie Show. So, by the time he and Dan hit high school, Nathan had moved beyond "The Man from UNCLE" and "I Spy". Even James Bond had failed to please after *Goldfinger*, and not just the movies, but the books. *You Only Live Twice* was the end. Nathan shrugged. Atlas shrugged.

Nathan DeGrorio was not happy, but he didn't care about that either, and this lent him a brave cast of stoicism, because he just soldiered on alone. He wore rubbers. Not condoms, rubbers – that you wore over your shoes in the snow. Only old people wore rubbers. Nathan was an odd duck. There was no other kid like him. There were kids who were odd, but they weren't smart. There were kids who were odd and smart, but they weren't funny. There were kids who were odd, smart, and funny – but they weren't mean, and they weren't smarter than everybody, including all the nuns and priests.

For Dan, it was the summer of reading books in trees, reading *For Your Eyes Only* and *The Spy Who Love Me,* up one tree in Fox Park and another in South Park. Nathan opened the world of culture for Dan – movies, tv, and music. They had all been in his life before, but now James Bond was intriguing Dan to turn the pages of a novel. It changed everything. While at the same time, all the passions he had from the start continued. He naturally becomes an altar boy, an athlete, a liar, and a thief.

Jill Malloy was a classmate in sixth grade, medium height, slender yet curvy, with curly dark hair, dimples, vivacious and popular, and out of Dan's league, and he yearned for her in a straight-out lustful manner. He was not enamored only of her pretty face, but of her legs and butt and the way, when she sat in the desk ahead of him, in her knee-stockings, and she would dangle her shoes off her feet and expose her bare heels and high arches, and sometimes her penny loafers would slip off entirely and there would be her stockinged toes and all, and Dan loved her from head to toe, but would never say a word to her. He told Nathan he had the hots for her, and Nathan said Dan wouldn't even know what to do with her if he had the chance.

"Are you in love with Jill Malloy? "

"Look, nobody's in love with anybody, ok? You *like* somebody. "

"You like her? "

"Shit yeah."

Jill Malloy was of the same general type as Annette Funicello. Brunette. Raven-haired. Veronica, as in Betty & Veronica.

Nathan cut into the reverie: "You wouldn't even know what to do with her." Nathan said the same thing about the *Playboy* models they ogled in the basement of Nathan's house along the expressway. It seemed like you could do sports, or you could do girls. You could do sports, or you could read books. You could read books, or you could watch movies.

"Do you even know anybody who's got a girlfriend? "

"How about Gump?"

"Don't think Gump *wants* a girlfriend."

"Why? Is he queer?"

"I don't think he even thinks about it."

"How's he do that?"

None of them had girlfriends, not Johnny-D, nor Jack Strap, nor the Deering twins. None of the girls had boyfriends. The kids were all bachelors and bachelorettes, happy, content in their independence. The Three Stooges formed the Woman Haters Club, but there were Girls in the gang with the Clarence Alley Boys: Laurel O'Connor, blonde, and her like, they were Betty Types. Brenda Sloane, busty brunette, a Veronica type.

Then there were the redheads, of whom freckled Lucy Lapperstack was their representative, and she *was* stacked. Bobbie Cosner was a blond pixie, like Tinker Bell. Charise Neville was another dark-haired beauty, and she had a beauty mark on her cheek, near her pouty lips.

And then Dan was going with Brenda Sloan. Johnny-D was going with Bobbie Cosner. Gump was going with Lucy Lapperstack. Everybody was going with somebody. If you were going to be around girls, you didn't want to be all sweaty and gross; you'd want to be all clean and sharp and wearing your madras shirt.

Brenda and Dan were walking past the apartment buildings. There were apartment buildings along the street that looked onto the Congress Expressway, and they included secluded hallways from the front of the building to the alley, straight through, with a lightbulb glowing at either end, where a kid could duck in to take a shortcut or hide or smoke a cigarette or make out with his girlfriend. By eighth grade, Dan would take Brenda Sloan by the hand, and they would slip into the hallway and make out for a record time. Later that year, he would duck in all by himself and extract an English Oval from its flat box and smoke it.

"I've got to get home."

"There's a way through here."

"Where?"

"That door. This hallway just goes through to the alley."

"Really? What for?"

"Come on."

Was he good-looking? Not really, he was short, just average, maybe a notch above. She didn't need to go with him. He had said: "I love you." And in a moment of weakness, she said: "I love you too." What possessed him to possess her hand, to touch her hand and let his fingers slip around it and take hold of it, somehow trusting that her fingers would curl in response? He gave it an instant's thought, and as if on its own, it happened. He didn't have to say, he didn't have to sing, he just had to think: I wanna hold your hand. And they were holding hands, walking along East Avenue, and anyone looking their way could see it.

So here was Danny. We do not have to say it was fate, just as we do not have to say that anything that happened in the past was fate – because it clearly was fate – because it happened and nothing else did. Brenda Sloan was stacked, which made her quite a catch. She was quite intelligent, too. At least as smart as Dan. He couldn't tell what she was thinking. She surprised him with her lust. She was willing to make out for great long stretches. Brenda was the girl Dan went steady with in eighth grade. She had big boobs and walked pigeon-toed, which Dan found fetching.

"Who's got a girlfriend?"

"A *girlfriend*?"

"You know, to make out with."

That was all Dan wanted to do. That was all he'd ever want to do. It would go on forever. They were swimming at the Ridgeland-Commons pool, Dan and a bunch of kids, along with a couple hundred or so other people, and he and Kathleen Hanson were standing in the 4-foot deep section with the other kids, and Kathleen, tan and hot in her sleek white one-piece, leaned back against him and reached back for his hands and took and placed them together on her tummy, and instantly he recognized it as a moment he would not mind abiding in forever.

The Ecumenical Council was churning away alongside Dan's narrative. Genuflect. Dip your fingers in the holy water and bless yourself. Ursuline nuns at Ascension to be followed by Dominican friars at Fenwick.

At the movies now the crowd was waiting beyond the ropes for the next showing. You looked at their faces to see the impression made by what they had just seen, what they had experienced.

Would that be you in two hours? You used to just go to the movies. It didn't matter what time. You'd walk into the middle of it. That was half the fun. Gotta figure out what happened before you got there. What must've happened. Yeah, right, maybe, maybe not. And then stay put, wait for the movie to start over. You get cartoons and coming attractions first.

Then *Psycho* happened. They wouldn't even let you in after the movie started. Before that, the audience, the individual viewers, were in charge. They decided when they would enter the experience, the world of the film. Now the film would demand the same respect as the stage play and the concert. But why? It's disconcerting to the actors onstage to have audience members trooping in and finding a seat after the curtain has gone up, but the actors onscreen don't miss a beat. The other audience members may be put out when someone arriving late has to step over them to get to an empty seat, maybe a whole family or a group. But the same thing happens every time someone leaves their seat to go use the restroom or get some popcorn – both verboten in the high and mighty theatre. The movie theater was wonderfully different, wonderfully anonymous, wonderfully *empty*. People were home watching TV. At the movies, there were *continuous* showings. But now the movie theater owners were going to start extracting the ticket price for each viewing. They couldn't let you buy one ticket and then watch their movie three times. They were going to clear the theater after every showing. They were going to keep the next audience out of the theater until the movie ended. Going to the movies would have to change.

It was the Rome Olympics, when Dan was nine, that made a stir in Dan's sporting heart. It would all make sense in Tokyo, so that by the time the Mexico City Olympics came around he had a thorough schooling in Olympic history, track and field in particular. Tom O'Hara was an anomaly, a great middle-distance runner, breathing the dirt air of Chicago.

Billy Mills scored a great upset win in the 5000 in Tokyo, hanging with the leaders and then unleashing a kick that shocked the world. On the screened-in porch in the Euclid castle, Dan was watching.

Track and field. The village put together teams from each playground and held a track meet at Oak Park Stadium. Dan competed in every event, in the long jump, high jump, shot put, and in every race and relay. They travelled to the stadium in a flatbed truck. Dan rode in the bed of the truck along Oak Park Avenue to Lake Street and the grand brick Stadium, remembering a long sidewalk stretching the length of the playground, and on one side was the playground, and on the other was Lincoln School. The sidewalk was where Dan would race John Raynard, who everybody said was the fastest kid on the playground, but Dan didn't believe it. Dan thought he could beat John Raynard in a race, even though John Raynard was a year older than he was. John Raynard was Roger Raynard's big brother.

"You really think you can beat my brother in a race? "

"Why not? I beat everybody else. "

"Never lost? "

"Not yet."

Then this would be the first time. Dan was fast. John Raynard was faster. He really was. Dan was shocked.

Growing up was all about sports (no, it wasn't), and sports meant hero worship. Sports were about finding that one thing that you were better at than everybody else. Maybe running wasn't it. Maybe running *was* it. Dan could still beat everybody else. He had good speed, better than average speed, not great speed. Maybe he just hadn't found the right event yet.

What about pole vaulting? Pole vaulting? What are you, nuts? Imagine a couple of ten-year-olds trying to teach themselves how to pole vault. Trying to pole vault what? Into what? Into sand?

That's not sand, that's dirt, that's just *dirt*. To pole vault or high jump, you'd have to have a pit, and it'd have to be filled with foam rubber, or you'd immediately break your bones.

Dan was still all for pole vaulting. It required good speed, not great speed. If a pole vaulter had great speed, he wouldn't be a pole vaulter; he'd be a sprinter, unless maybe he was a decathlete, like Jim Thorpe, All-American, as portrayed on the silver screen by Burt Lancaster. No less an authority than the King of Sweden said to Jim Thorpe, "You, sir, are the greatest athlete in the world." Dan wanted to be the greatest athlete in the world. Or the Pope.

Maybe pole vaulting wasn't the answer, although Dan still harbored dreams of Olympic gold and he still thought he matched up pretty well with the skills required – good but not great speed, coordination, balance, athleticism, yes, fine, he was an ace at steal-the-bacon, strength – well, maybe he wasn't all that strong, but he wasn't weak, and he could get stronger, if only he had some weight-lifting equipment. But, no, in the end, after studying carefully pole-vaulters and their technique on TV and live at the Oak Park high school field-house, there would quickly come a point in which you could not just push off the pole, but instead, real vaulters would grip the pole near its end, sprint with the pole tilted slightly up and then dip it down to plant it, and then finally, with the fiberglass pole bending like a bow, they would lift off the ground, and that was where Dan and the world's great pole vaulters parted company, because he just could not stomach the idea of hanging upside down in the air like that, which was what came next if you were going to pole vault over a bar higher than four or five feet off the ground into the sand pit at Carroll Playground, so, finally, pole vaulting was out.

But the sprints were still on. He would try his hand at the 100 and 200-yard dash. He would spend a year of his young life aiming at a mark in the 440. He fancied himself a miler for a time, and when he broke five minutes, he thought he was on his way, but it took all he had to get from 5:02 to 4:58, and, finally, 4:56. He was maxed out.

Finally, Dan would settle on the half mile and set his sights on the world record. Jim Ryun had set a new world record in the half mile practically by accident. Jim Ryun had arrived in the pantheon of heroes with Jim Thorpe, All-American, as played by Burt Lancaster. The mile was too long, the quarter mile too short, so Dan settled on the 880, setting a goal of getting under 2:10, and he got to 2:09. Now, if he could get under two minutes, he would be elite. But he couldn't. He couldn't get any faster than 2:09. Ever. That was it.

He wanted to run a two-mile under 11 minutes, but could get no closer than 11:18, and that was on the cross-country course. Then the distance for cross-country was raised to 2.7 miles, and that was clearly outside his range.

He'd swing from one sport to the next, from one to the other, to basketball when he was discouraged with running, it was more fun to play, until the competition showed him that he was a better runner than a basketball player, and he'd return to running, knowing that when he broke five minutes in the mile that Jim Ryun would have lapped him. Dan thought of his teammate Benny McGill as a superstar because he was about to break 10 minutes in the two-mile, while Steve Prefontaine was blowing up the high school record with an 8:41!

Somehow your fate got tied to your heroes. If Jim Ryun could not outkick Kip Keino down the homestretch in Mexico City, then all was lost. Dan himself must be doomed. How could Dan ever hope to lead his harriers to victory if Ryun couldn't outkick Keino? One thing had nothing whatsoever to do with the other, but in Dan's mind, it did. There was no point in having a hero if you couldn't identify with him.

Ryun didn't have a prayer of beating Keino. There was no way an African runner who trained all his life at high altitude was going to get beat by a boy from Kansas in *Mexico City*. Kip Keino was going to kick Ryun's ass. Keino's coach was absolutely sure of it. He knew there was no way Ryun could adapt to the altitude of Mexico City and that a fast pace from the start would take the wind out of him, and consequently, he'd have no kick left at the end. Enlisting an accomplice, a Kenyan teammate, who might have medaled himself had he not sacrificed his chance with his suicidal pace over the first half mile and more, acting as a rabbit, Keino cruised along in contact with the leader while Ryun labored all the way back in last place, out of contact, beyond reach of a surge, before belatedly making his move with a lap to go.

Ryun knew before almost anyone else that he was going to lose. But Keino's coach had known it first. Then Ben Jipcho, the rabbit, knew, but as the bell sounded for the last lap, everyone in the world knew it. Ryun wouldn't outkick Keino this time. He was cooked. Ryun probably knew he was going to lose before the race ever started. What had begun as a fear over a year before, when his training was interrupted by a bout of mononucleosis, became conjecture for the public that conducting the Olympics at high altitude was going to alter the character of the entire enterprise. The Olympics were going to get high.

Ryun was going to try his best. But his best wasn't going to be his best – because he couldn't train in the heavy fashion he was used to, and he was late in even attempting to acclimate to the altitude, something Keino had done at birth. Given all that, Jim thought he had done the best he could and should be proud of himself for winning a silver medal – but that was all he was going to get, one lousy silver medal for someone America, and Dan, had hoped would be the greatest middle-distance runner of all time. Ryun was a tragic hero, which was to say, he was a goat, a loser. He wouldn't even make it to the finals of the next Olympics four years later in Munich, because he would fall down in the semifinal, like a klutz, and not even qualify for the final.

Not long after that, Ryun became known for stepping off the track. Dan couldn't believe what he was seeing. Ryun was quitting. Like falling out of love. As soon as he stopped loving running, running stopped loving him.

"I'm proud of the race I ran," Ryun would say – for the rest of his life, and no doubt he was, but who could be proud of a silver medal, when you finished 20 yards behind the winner, more thoroughly beaten than any other silver medal winner in the history of the event, when you were supposed to be the greatest miler of all time?

Sure, Dan was proud of what he did, too – except for the parts he wasn't proud of. Ryun at least had an excuse for all his failings. Not Dan. And yet, Dan would have been a fool to trade his fate with Ryun's. Who would want that legacy? Who would want Hemingway's? Or Buckley's? If for one minute he could be Jim Ryun, and experience the pressure, indeed the trauma, the pain of his existence, which Ryun endured with Protestant faith, where there would be no place for the least transgression, Dan would have leapt back into his gnostic skin, preferred solecism.

What's the frame? What makes it go forward and backward. Story-telling. Who is telling this story? Tolstoy? Hemingway? *Citizen Kane*'s frame is the March of Time newsreel. What sort of storyteller can range freely back to Aristotle and Plato, forward to Aquinas, to the Civil War, to a young boy's mind in the mid-50s and 60s? A storyteller who doesn't tell us who he is, who somehow stands outside it, above and beyond it, and can still see into the heart of it, writing in the middle of things, writing in the middle of the night.

Because the Greeks needed a navy to fight off the Persians, Athens put one together. When the war was over, they used it for commercial purposes, and in seeing the belief systems of other people, the Greeks were among the first rational beings to see such beliefs as bullshit – because they were able to compare and contrast, because they knew more, from having sailed to foreign lands.

A sportswriter, journalist, historian, and author. It's just a book about a time and a place. So, it may be straightforward, if not exactly chronological, roughly chronological, peppered with flashbacks and flash-forwards, with a plot moving forward, and a subplot moving backward. Break it all apart and reassemble it, chronologically, going forward and backward all the way to John L. Sullivan and forward from Floyd Patterson to Sonny Liston to Cassius Clay to Muhammad Ali, from black and white to color. And Danny becomes a boxer.

It's a history book that turns into a novel, or the other way around, the novel as history, that's what Mailer called it when he tried it. History comes first. *Studs Lonigan* is a history book. This book, *In Black & White & Color*, proceeds chronologically, season by season, year after year, for twenty years. Dan moves from sports to something vaguely like the arts, but more like imminent disaster. He's a schmuck. It doesn't matter. He's grown into a particular kind of schmuck due to the forces that shaped him, and those forces are the real interest here. The real people and historical events. Dan's consciousness expands, and the world keeps getting more and more fucked-up. We're on the eve of destruction. I can't get no satisfaction. What exactly was his problem? Why couldn't he get no satisfaction? Because of the culture, man, the consumer culture.

Danny? Danny was a sweet kid; in all his hero worship, it was all heart, all love. It was a way to love someone. If he loved you, he wanted to be like you. More than that, he wanted to *be* you. He wanted for there to be *two* of you. He wanted something that was impossible, not to speak of superfluous. Dan had to lie to himself and tell himself that he was good and honest when he knew he wasn't, but if he could pretend to be something, then he might eventually become it.

CHAPTER SEVEN

Dan and Gene were digging in the backyard. Not in a sandbox. In the dirt. There wasn't much grass. It was mostly gray dirt. They were building a highway, an expressway like the one steamrolling from Chicago out into the plains. Nano didn't seem to mind. She was cheerful and happy and kind as always.

A few blocks away, the Congress Expressway was under construction, but here, there were just sticks and rocks to be cleared away to make way for toy trucks. The Eisenhower interstate highway system was a linear graph of mostly straight lines crisscrossing the country with four and six-lane roads, the goal being efficient and easy travel. You swept by the west side projects, gray, brown, broken and crumbling, but swarming with life, windows still being smashed, rat-infested, from a distance it could be seen safely as a prison, except that there were no wardens or guards. They weren't buildings; they were *projects*.

Ike got the idea for the interstate highway that would wreak modernism upon Chicago, and all those Studs Lonigan neighborhoods would die, and the interstate would barrel through all the way across America, crisscross it up and down, and all those small towns would start to die, and the modern cities would rise in all their grandeur and ugliness and squalor, skyscraping, and filling in the gaps with ghettos and housing projects.

Somebody had to build the highway first. The construction would intersect Oak Park Avenue as it headed west, past Harlem Avenue, connecting eventually Chicago, all the way to and from the Loop to the cornfields of Dekalb, but first, all that land had to be leveled, which was not too great a task on the Great Plains, and cleared and paved.

The Congress Expressway was coming through, and Danny didn't know what had been there before. It was gone now, whatever it was. People's homes. Streets where people had lived and worked and shopped. It was gone now, knocked down, bulldozed away, leveled, graded. Traffic all across America had been building up and up and up as cars began to cover the earth, and when Ike had the idea of untying all the knots with an interstate highway system, to cut all that downtown traffic loose, down a chute, and spew it out into the suburbs, it seemed like as good a solution as any to everybody except the poor schmucks who were in the way.

Everything along Congress Street was annihilated, the buildings, homes, businesses, churches, schools, neighborhoods, life in the city for thousands of lives, removed, if it could move, and at first nothing would be left, just a gash, a lengthening crater, spreading west.

It didn't work. If it was meant to eliminate traffic, it didn't eliminate shit. The traffic was worse, and the traffic kept getting worse; a trip into or out of Chicago by car ranged from pain in the ass to nightmare.

The Expressway wiped out neighborhoods, real communities of shared life, daily experience, of families of Jews and Italians and Poles and Irish, and what grew out of the rubble along the crater that stretched to the west? Something to flash by as you sped out of town. Something to travel past. Something that made you avert your eyes. The neighborhoods were replaced with projects and ghettos in which to house poor Blacks arriving from the South. Thus, expressways crisscrossing and shooting streams of traffic in every direction but east, where Lake Michigan stood in the way –

the Dan Ryan, Stevenson, Kennedy, and Congress expressways. The Dan Ryan Expressway was *wide*, 12 lanes across, and it just steamrolled straight through the south side. That's where Martin Luther King got hit on the head with a brick. The Expressway cut through town, and filled it with a clogged river of traffic, with the el tracks running alongside, cars coming, going, streaming, or stalled, in both directions. The Congress Expressway went through the worst of it, where the riots and the fires would be fiercest.

Oak Park was different. There was nothing else like it the whole length of the Expressway. The two exits in Oak Park, at Austin Boulevard and Harlem Avenue, were unique, both in the *middle* of the Expressway. Every other exit, the length of the Expressway would be to the right. Oak Park stood astride history and said stop: My way *is* the highway.

Suddenly, for Danny and kids, there was an expressway where there had been a bulldozed plain and only trucks and workmen allowed – until they all went home at the end of the day and the kids came out to play, like fairies appearing in the woods, and the kids would climb the sandhills and mount the machinery and excavate or pretend to and crawl through cement tubes and tightrope-walk across beams in the twilight.

CHAPTER EIGHT

I t was spring and Dan was playing pinners against the stairs. He had learned it from the Burkes, a typical Irish Catholic family from the south side of Oak Park. There were a lot of Burkes. The ones near Dan's age were Paul and his brother Jerome, known as Rome or Romer, and his twin sister Rose, who went by Ro-Ro. They were all athletes who would play anything, Ro-Ro too, she was fast as hell, like Dan, and she had a couple of older brothers who played on real teams – football, baseball, basketball.

You could play pinners all by yourself against the front stairs for hours. All you needed was a rubber ball and a glove. Didn't even really need the glove since it was a rubber ball, but if you wanted to get better with the glove, you used a glove. You were the pitcher, and then you were everybody else. Your imaginary mound was only about twelve or fifteen feet away from the steps, right in front, so your reactions were going to have to be quick. You could go into a windup, or you could pitch from the stretch. Fastball, knuckleball, palm-ball, slider, split-finger, overhand, sidearm, underhand – the old submarine ball. Nobody really knew how to throw a curve. Except for Gump.

And Dan let fly. The ball pitched into the stairs wherever it might. If it struck between steps, the ball would come straight back at you like a line drive, but if the pitch drove the rubber ball into the edge of the stair, then it would do just about anything but come straight back at you. It might take off like a shot over your head, soaring across the street, and if it landed on the other side of the street, it was a homerun.

A high fly ball into the street, you might be able to shag for an out, or it might drop in for a hit or even extra bases, and you had to make the throw off the stairs to hold the runner. If the ball struck the edge of the step at a downward angle, it would ricochet back at you as a hot grounder, and you'd have to pluck it off the ground or snare it on the short hop, or stretch for it, or reach across your body to glove it before it got by you. Pinners was the best training in the world for fielding, especially for infielders.

"You fancy yourself a shortstop, do you?"

"Natural position. Feel comfortable there. "

"Like nothing can get by you? What about the throw?"

The beauty of pinners was that you could play it by yourself. You could be both teams and all the players. A whole major league season could be played on the front steps. Johnny-D taught Dan the fine points of pinners. He was slick. Johnny-D knew everybody's moves better than they did themselves. He wasn't that strong, but he was smooth and would come up with moves you never saw before.

Johnny-D could bat both ways, righty and lefty, like Maury Wills, the Dodgers' great shortstop, and he would surprise everybody and lay down a bunt to get on base, and then he'd distract the pitcher. He could play all the sports, with specific sneaky moves for each. Of course, all of the guys could play all the sports because that's what they did together – play all the sports. Every day you wanted to play something, so whatever was in season was what you played. Basketball, baseball, ice hockey, football, tennis, golf, bowling, swimming, racing on bikes and on foot, roller skating.

Johnny-D would trick you, pull the hidden ball trick on you, and catch you off base. He'd pretend to throw the ball back to the pitcher, but he'd keep the ball in his mitt and then swipe you with it. It was the oldest trick in the book, but he was so slick with it he'd still pull it off, and then he'd laugh at you, and he could get all the other guys to laugh at you too. Johnny-D was the first guy Dan knew to be adept at psychological warfare.

Willie Mays made The Catch, the most spectacular defensive play ever made in the World Series, when Danny was three. Mays was racing toward the centerfield wall, with the tying run on base, his back to the batter, who hit a towering fly ball that looked like it would either bang off the wall or drop onto the warning path for extra bases, and Mays caught it over his shoulder, whirled and threw a strike to the cut-off man to hold the runner on base. Gump was three years old as well, but Gump was going to master that catch, and throw, and the Willie Mays basket catch to boot, before he was 12, casually holding his glove open at waist level for flyballs to plummet into as safely as into a net.

Follow the story of baseball. It goes back to the 19th century. It's working itself out in a capitalist manner, the same way those seafarers did in Shakespeare's time, the East India Company and the New York Giants, both professional clubs.

Athletes were human beings at the peak of their physical powers, and it seemed to Danny that, having attained such a state of grace, they had entered a timeless moment of perfection, and they hovered there. It had come from somewhere in the legendary past and the time of heroes and the time of Babe Ruth, so that when Danny came upon this world of baseball and there was Willie Mays and baseball cards and gloves and bats and balls and base-paths to run and bases to *steal*, and Nellie Fox always had a plug of tobacco puffing up his cheek and it was fixing to kill him one day. Danny had no idea where it had all come from. He had no idea that the Giants and Dodgers had deserted New York and left it to the Yankees, the white supremacists of baseball, proving their superiority, until the Black guys started showing up. The last major league teams to integrate were the Tigers, Red Sox, and the Yankees, of course.

The Negro League had a team in Indianapolis called the Clowns. Once Jackie Robinson broke the color line, the Negro League was through, all its players greedily gobbled up by big league clubs. The National League had Black players, and the American League didn't. The Yankees and the Red Sox ended up being the holdouts, and as long as the Yankees could dominate the World Series with white players, helped along by nationwide discrimination that kept limiting Black opportunities, the difference between the two leagues could persist, but *all* the other American League teams were going to suffer for it, because sooner or later there's always some truth to sports, and in a fair fight, the better man wins. The Cubs were the fourth team to break the color line, after Brooklyn, Cleveland, and the Giants.

The Cubs won the pennant in 1945, six years before Danny was born, and then they had losing seasons every year since. Jackie Robinson signed with the Brooklyn Dodgers in 1946. The Cubs weren't half-bad that year, finishing in the first division. It'd be the last time for a long, long time. Jackie Robinson had to travel from Los Angeles to Daytona Beach to get to spring training, by car, by bus, by train, harassed and called the n-word all the way, and he wanted to quit before he even got there. He sat by himself at a table in the dining room of the Chase Hotel in St. Louis, and nobody would wait on him. The waiters ignored him. It pissed him off. But when he got to *Chicago*, Wrigley Field was packed. And in the bleachers above the ivy-covered outfield walls, dressed like they were going to church, every Black person in the city of Chicago had come to see Jackie Robinson play.

Bobby Bragan, the Dodgers catcher, betrayed his teammate and went full racist and signed a letter to Branch Rickey, the Dodgers' owner, to inform him that Bragan and the other signees were not going to step on the same field with that n-word Jackie Robinson. Bragan would come to regret it. He would *truly* regret it.

When Danny-Boy was born, Maury Wills was just a teenager, but he was already playing minor league ball. Then he got trapped in it and was still a minor leaguer eight years later. He'd never make it to Ebbets Field. The Dodgers would move to Los Angeles before he ever got a shot at the major leagues. It didn't look like he would ever make it. He couldn't hit. He was afraid of a curveball. He flinched when he saw it coming.

Well, it was coming right at him.

Bobby Bragan saved Maury Wills. That Bobby Bragan. The one who signed the letter against Jackie Robinson. He was sorry. He wanted to do something to make up for it, if there was ever a way. And all these years later, maybe he could still do something.

He saw what was happening, and he knew how to fix it. It came to him when he saw Maury in the batting cage just fooling around, hitting left-handed. He was a righty, of course, and he was only swinging left-handed because he didn't much give a shit anymore. He'd lost his drive and purpose after eight years of trying to bust out of the minors. He was pretty sure now he'd never make it. He couldn't hit a curveball, and he knew it, and everybody else knew it, too, but Bobby Bragan knew why.

"You know what? You're not half bad at that."

"Right."

"I'm serious."

"I'm just messing around."

"You ought to think about it."

"Why?"

"If you hit left-handed against righties, and right-handed against lefties, that curveball wouldn't scare you so much."

"Fuck you."

"Think about it".

"What're you saying?"

"Why do you flinch?"

"Fuck you."

"You telling me you don't?"

"What difference does it make? I'm going home."

"It's natural. Ball's coming right at you. Only natural to shy away."

"Guys hit the curve, and they go up. I've been down here for eight years, and I can't hit it. Eight years."

"Think about it. It wouldn't be coming at you the same way, like out of nowhere, if you looked at it from the other side. You could watch it all the way in. I'm just saying. You should at least try it. Before you go home."

"I appreciate it."

"Of course, you'd have to work at it, to at least be decent, but it looks like you got a good stroke."

Wills thought about it. It was possible. Not at all likely, but possible. He would have to bust his ass to have any chance at all.

Maybe Danny's memories start then, with Maury Wills finally breaking into the majors, but they would be memories of summer, not really memories of baseball until Danny could bounce a rubber ball off the front steps.

The great thing about baseball before interleague play was that you had to imagine what teams and players would do against each other. There was a distinctly different tone, feel, and color to each League. Especially color.

Ernie Banks had a buddy, Gene Baker, the second baseman, who was really a shortstop but was being moved over to make room for Banks. They'd be baseball's first Black double play combo, and they thought they'd take in a movie on an off day in St. Louis, and as they walked up to the ticket booth, the ticket seller just waved them away, and Gene just turned to Ernie and said: "How'd you like the movie?"

Ernie Banks was a good shortstop, but not a great one. He had trouble with throws from deep in the hole. That was Danny's problem, too. Maybe Danny could play second base like Nellie Fox of the White Sox with a chaw in his cheek. Danny could only imagine Ernie Banks at shortstop because all he ever saw was Ernie Banks playing first base. The image you have of a shortstop is totally different from that of a first baseman. Ernie Banks had great wrists for batting, but he didn't have a great arm.

The Dodgers and the Giants both left New York and headed for the West Coast, the highways were spreading, and the suburbs were draining energy from the cities, and the American League was holding out against integration, the racism as stark as black and white, Willie Mays and Micky Mantle.

The Say Hey Kid became famous for the basket catch, as much as for *The Catch*, which was maybe the greatest catch of all time, but Mays was just as famous for the Basket Catch, catching routine fly balls as they dropped into his open glove, held at waist level. Little Leaguers were cautioned not to catch routine fly balls this way, because they would inevitably drop one, but Gump caught fly balls this way all the time and never dropped one. Anything Gump saw a player do on TV, he could mimic. He could bat like Stan the Man Musial or Ernie Banks, he could switch-hit, but he never played on any organized team in school or Little League, never played any kind of organized sport, just with the bunch of kids at the park. Gump could throw a curveball, a knuckleball, and a split-finger fastball -- he had perfected them all with a whiffle ball, and he could pitch overhand, sidearm, or underhand, ala Ted Abernathy. Gump could ice skate beautifully, powerfully, and he was by far the best hockey player on the ice, the best stick-handler, had the best slap-shot, and was the

best goalie too, like his man Gump Worsley. Gump was the best golfer, the
best bowler, just about the best everything, without being very fast or very
strong, or looking at all like an athlete. In fact, he was a little pudgy. Gump's
father, Dr. Brecca, was strict. He made education Gump's top priority.
Gump was his only child. All those superb athletic skills of Gump's were
only allowed to flourish and bloom at Fox Park in grade school, and then
just disappear like smoke, but Gump had been magnificent.

A whole series of contrasts emanated from the world of sports, the way
it felt to root for the Sox as opposed to the Cubs, the way the American
League *felt* as opposed to the National League. The East in the NBA
and the West, and the NFL felt completely different than the AFL. The
contrasts couldn't be sharper.

There were no names on the backs of the players' jerseys. Why would
you even think about putting your name on the back of the jersey? That's
what numbers and scorecards were for.

Mean Gene said he got lost at Comiskey Park, and that much was true,
because Mary Jule confirmed it and she always told the truth, but then
Gene said the Andy Frain ushers took him into a room where he met Little
Louis Aparicio and chaw chewing Nellie Fox, and then he hung out with
them for a while. That never happened. Gene was lying. Other people told
lies, too.

The White Sox played in a bad neighborhood on the South Side in
a ballpark called Comiskey Park, which didn't look anything at all like
Wrigley Field. It looked more like Kiddieland, the amusement park on
North Avenue where you could ride roller coasters and rides that didn't
scare the shit out of you, meant for little kids, a place where Nano had
taken Dan and Gene and Mary Jule, and it was there that Dan would take
Patti Mangione in their sophomore year and make out with her between
rides after having been lustily tossed against her in the tilt-a-whirl.

If you were playing in the field while Sandy Koufax was pitching, it didn't matter whether you were in the infield or the outfield; after a while, you would fade into oblivion. You would disappear and Koufax would be out there by himself, like a concert pianist, and you weren't even there -- because you didn't need to be there, what was the reason for your existence, except to watch him work? He just struck everybody out.

To score runs, the Dodgers would all have to work together, Maury Wills would get on base, and then they would move him around. They only had a few guys with any power. Then they would go out on the field, and Koufax would single-handedly dispatch the other team. The Go-Go Sox ran into Koufax, but that was when Sandy was just starting to get warmed up. Koufax was blowing his arm out, pitch by pitch. Maury Wills was ripping his legs apart, stealing bases. Then came a game in the World Series, and Koufax wouldn't pitch because he was a Jew.

"He's a Jew, Sandy Koufax?"

"You didn't know?"

"I never thought about it."

"I shit you not."

"Hey, Samson was a Jew."

Another thing you could do is collect baseball cards. You didn't want to buy one pack of baseball cards, you wanted to buy two or three and open them right away, and stuff all three sticks of pink bubblegum in your mouth and wad it up in your cheek like Nellie Fox, whose chaw would only kill him one day.

You had to figure out what position you were going to play, so you knew which mitt to get. If there was a track and field meet, you had to figure out which events to enter. You had to know where to line up on the football field, what spot you had in the batting order, and your position on a basketball team. You had to know that, or you didn't even know what you were.

You played pinners and then you could go over to Lincoln, the public school, and rectangles for the strike zone had been painted on the walls, and two or three guys could play, with one guy at bat and one guy pitching and the other guy in the field, which was a pair of asphalt basketball courts side by side, so that sometimes guys would be trying to play basketball while the baseball players were rocketing line drives at them.

Dan went over to Lincoln to play basketball, and two kids were playing baseball against the wall with a rubber ball. They asked Dan if he wanted to play in the outfield, and he said sure. The kid who was up to bat said Dan could use his glove. It was long and flapped over. First baseman's glove. Dan couldn't play first base, and he couldn't much play the outfield, and he sure as shit couldn't play the outfield with a first baseman's glove. This was going to be embarrassing. The guy hit a fly ball. Dan lost it in the sun. When he turned around, it was bouncing over the fence.

Basketball and baseball were both games you could play by yourself – shooting hoops or playing pinners. With pinners though, whenever he popped one up, the rubber ball would slam into the aluminum at the bottom of the front door and make a bang like a gunshot that sounded through the whole neighborhood. He was as good as banned from playing pinners. He could still play, but he had to play cautiously, and the first bang ended the game – like a rain-out. If four and a half innings were completed, it would count, and the stats would be official. That was when Dan was in the habit of keeping stats – for a fictional baseball league.

Danny was 10 years old, on a Little League team full of 12-year-olds. He had been in the Tee-Ball league the year before, while Roger Maris was hitting 61 homers, Danny was batting the ball off a tee. The Yankees were back in business after the Go-Go White Sox had their fling. Fenwick football was at its height. Floyd Patterson and Sonny Liston were enacting their boxing drama. Mayor Daley – DeMare – made Kennedy President. Hemingway killed himself.

The top contenders for the Oak Park Little League crown were Village Savings in the lower middle-class South and Fair Oaks Pharmacy in the upper middle-class North. Billy Novolio of Village Savings had pitched a no-hitter in the first game of the season and hit two home runs. Ernie Banks was playing shortstop for the Cubs now, emerging from the Negro League and taking Chicago by storm. The Cubs were still awful, but Ernie Banks was great. Back-to-back MVPs. He was the best player in all of baseball, and he was a Chicago Cub with a smiling bear cub emblazoned on his white uni sleeve.

That summer, Danny's little league team won the Village Championship. To call it Danny's team is somewhat misleading. It was the Little League team that Danny was on. Danny was just 10 years old when, out of the blue, he was called up to the League to play for the Village Savings team, even though the season was nearly half-over, because the Village Savings' star pitcher, Billy Novolio, who had already pitched two no-hitters, was discovered to have turned 13 years old and was ineligible.

"You got called up?"

"Yeah."

"*You* got called up?"

He didn't even know the *rules*. He sort of knew the rules. He knew three strikes and you're out, but that was about it. The first time he ever went to the plate to face live pitching, he figured he'd just wait out four pitches and take a walk. According to his primitive understanding of the rules, a strike was when you swung at a pitch and missed. Isn't that what happened when mighty Casey struck out?

"Why didn't you swing?"

"What?"

"Why didn't you swing?"

"I was going to take a walk."

"You struck out on three pitches."

"But I didn't even swing."

"You don't have to swing. "

"I know. I didn't."

Danny was an idiot. It was pure luck that carried Danny to that baseball trophy, but it was *his* luck. Danny had good luck. Danny's team won the Village Championship, even though Danny had almost nothing to do with it; his only value to the team was filling out the roster. What did that matter – it was a trophy, wasn't it?

The reason Dan was on the team was that somebody found out Billy Novolio was too old and was ineligible, and Danny was the only player the coach could find to fill the roster spot. Why'd he replace a kid who had just pitched a no-hitter with a kid who couldn't play? Dan could play a little. He couldn't hit. Lots of guys can't hit. Billy Novolio was the best pitcher in the League. And he hit two homers. *Homers*. Dan couldn't even hit the ball, much less a homer. He couldn't even hit a *foul ball*. Well, maybe he could hit a foul ball. Maybe he could *scratch out a hit*.

Dan was ten years old, and everybody else was 12. He was out of his league. If you were a red-blooded American boy in the middle of the 20th century, you loved baseball – even if the baseball itself scared you, even if you couldn't hit worth a lick and you didn't have much of an arm and couldn't make that throw from deep in the hole at short. Neither could Ernie Banks. The Cubs moved Banks to first, where he would hardly have to make any throws.

Even if you couldn't hit, throw, or field, you could still run the bases. That's all Dan really wanted to do. At practice, the coach would have a guy run the bases, and the fielders would practice different situations with a runner or two on base, and that was Dan's favorite thing to do. He wanted to steal a base.

"Idiot, you can't steal bases in Little League. It's against the rules."

The Village Championship was decided in a three-game series held at Ridgeland-Commons field, on the dividing line, Lake Street, between north and south Oak Park. Village Savings, the champions of the South, versus Fair Oaks Pharmacy, the champs of the North. It was an economic division too, the north being significantly more affluent, more like River Forest, while south Oak Park was more like Berwyn.

Village Savings won the first game and was comfortably ahead in the second and on its way to the championship, when Danny Finnegan finally got a chance to play. He took the field at second base and watched a strikeout and a flyball caught in the outfield bring his team within an out of the championship, when a hot grounder came his way. This was where playing pinners was going to pay off. Danny's reflexes were catlike. He pounced, and with a sweep of his glove gobbled up the grounder, pivoted, and then did something so dumb no one could believe it.

"Nicest pick-up I've ever seen," the coach said. Then he started shaking his head.

Inexplicably, Danny's next move was to race over and touch second base – before uncorking a wild throw toward his stupefied first baseman.

"What were you thinking, Danny?"

"I don't know."

"The kid makes the nicest pick-up I've ever seen, and then for some unknown reason, he races over, and he touches second base. There's nobody on first base! There was nobody on first base, Danny."

"I know."

"Now you know. Did you know then? Because it looked like you thought you were going to force the runner on first going to second – but there was no runner on first, you get it?"

"Yeah."

"We were about to win the game."

"I know."

He still had him. He still had the guy, the batter, Danny still had time to throw the guy out, even after touching second like an idiot when there was no one on first, Dan was quick from all those games of pinners. Everybody's yelling at him to throw it to first, and he sails it into the dugout.

The rest of the game was a blur. They didn't get out of the inning till Fair Oaks won the game and tied the series. Village Savings would win the deciding game and the Village Championship the next day, while Dan watched safely from the same dugout that he sailed the ball into the game before. Dan won a trophy. A gold trophy. You had to be good to win a trophy, right? You had to be on the winning team. You had to be good to be on the winning team, right? No.

But you were probably good. The last guy on the bench for the Celtics had a championship ring. Maybe he was a sorry player compared to Bill Russell, but he was on the team for a reason, and probably the reason was that he was pretty good.

Dan was a champion and a goat. There would be no more organized baseball for him. But there would still be pinners, and he could still maintain the stats of his fictional major leagues – which mirrored the actual major leagues. Dan played out the pinners baseball season from the point of view of the White Sox. The Cubs played baseball in real life, but the Sox of the imagined American League played in Pinners Park.

Dan was in the eighth grade now, and he had about had it with school. It was almost summer, and school was just going on and on like it would never end. It was boring, the same old thing every day, day after day.

It was Nathan DeGrorio's idea. He said it would be easy. They started school every day by going to gym class, and the coach, old Chrome Dome, took roll by reading everybody's name, and you had to say here when your name was called. But Chrome Dome never even looked up from his roll book while taking roll. Anybody could call out here; he'd never know the difference. Paulie turned out to be too chicken to skip school. So he would call out here when Chrome Dome said their names.

The bell was ringing back at Ascension as Nathan and Dan picked out a bunch of candy at

Mollie's Candy Shop to take with them to Wrigley Field. Then they crossed halfway over the East Avenue bridge atop the Congress Expressway, paid their fifty-five cents, and went through the turnstiles and down the long ramp and got on the train to go to the Cubs game, heading downtown, thrilling to the rumble of the subway, when the train plunged underground, and it got very dark.

"We're under the river right now," Nathan said in the dark in the rumbling train.

The train stopped, and they wove through the crowd of businessmen and shoppers. They had to transfer from one train to another, and had to go down two flights of stairs, down a long tunnel, and onto another platform, which they did. Nathan knew where he was going. He'd gone to plenty of Cubs games with his dad.

Finally, the train rose out of the subway, and they were on the elevated tracks that circle downtown Chicago. The big, twisted circle the elevated trains run on is called the Loop, and the trains are called 'el's .

They got off the el at Wrigley Field on the north side of Chicago. There was a giant marquee that said: Ball Game Today, Chicago Cubs versus San Francisco Giants. It was only three dollars to get into the grandstands, and Nathan said those were better seats than the bleachers.

They ran down the aisle to the Cubs' dugout. There were all the players they'd seen on TV. Ernie Banks – Mister Cub. Sweet-swinging Billy Williams. Ron Santo. Willie Mays was playing for the Giants. When he went to bat, he looked so fired up you would've thought he'd scare the ball if he didn't hit it. There was the green grass in the middle of the city in early summer, and the ivy on the walls in the outfield, the crackling action, the players larger than life. But, still, a big league game takes a long time. Nine innings. And then the game went into extra innings. Dan looked at the clock in center field and was surprised and then scared to see that it was already past four o'clock. He would be late getting home. He would be really late getting home.

"What'll I tell my mom, Nathan?"

"Just tell her you stopped off at the library on the way home."

That sounded good. Dan decided to explore the ballpark a little on his own and walked all the way around till he got to a gate that led to the bleachers in center field. He decided to check out the view from the bleachers. It was neat. He walked all the way down the aisle to the ivy-covered wall, and the right fielder was about close enough to touch. But when Dan tried to cross back into the grandstands, he couldn't find his ticket stub, and an usher told him he couldn't go into the grandstands. The game finally ended, and the Cubs lost as usual. But Dan could not find his friend Nathan anywhere in the crowd. Dan was alone and lost in the city of Chicago.

He walked all the way around Wrigley Field. Twice. It was starting to get dark. Businessmen and shoppers were swarming toward the el platform. He thought about asking a cop how to get home, but that might lead to more trouble than it was worth. He decided to just get on the el and try to figure it out for himself. How hard could it be?

Getting on the first el was no problem. It circled toward the Loop and plunged underground. When it came to where he would have to transfer from one train to another, that was the tricky part. He paid and went through a turnstile and then through the long hallway, up one flight of stairs, and then another. But somehow, he ended up on the wrong side of a turnstile where he would have to pay again to get on the train he was sure would take him home.

Maybe they should have bought two-dollar tickets to the bleachers instead of sitting in the grandstands or bought less candy at Mollie's. It didn't matter. He had no money to get through that turnstile. There was only one thing to do. He vaulted over it and ran. Dan kept on running. He saw the 'el up ahead and the doors were closing.

Chapter Nine

A new world opened up to every Black person in America, a world that had in it not only bathrooms and water fountains, but restaurants and movie theaters and hotels, a world they had seen, but never lived in, during all their lives, some of which were long and all of which they were used to, if not comfortable with, at least set in their ways, hesitant to change, unsure, *afraid*, so that Black people still lived in fear.

The Civil Rights Act was passed. What could that mean to Dan? All he knew was that he had all the rights there were, and if Ruth, the colored lady who cleaned their house once a week, had a few rights now too, then good for her. It still didn't stop the Finnegans from letting her go. "She stole a pair of Mom's earrings," Norine said. Bullshit.

Ruth came once a week, from Chicago, and she'd mop and wax the kitchen and dining room floors, vacuum the wall-to-wall carpeting, and dust and polish the furniture. She would do a *professional* job. The house was *professionally cleaned*. Hell, Dan stole all the loose change he could lay his hands on, and if there was a stack of ones, who's going to miss a couple ones?

Civil Rights might have been the law, but it's not until somebody breaks the law and gets punished for it that it's *really* a law. So those civil rights workers in Mississippi had to be murdered first, and that was a clear violation of their civil rights. The Voting Rights Act and the Civil Rights Act came out of Lyndon Johnson. Not Kennedy. Not Nixon.

Nixon was coming. To racists the Civil Rights Act was a declaration of war, not the same Civil War as before, not north against south, industrial versus agricultural, this wasn't even Black against white, because Black people, having won their rights, would just as soon be done with it all and *enjoy* their rights, and everyone could live in peace, rather, it was whites against freedom, whites against equality, whites against truth, and Dan was white.

Dad and Mom were Republicans. Oak Park was Republican. There were Democrats in Chicago. Buckley was running for Mayor of New York City. It began as something of a joke. He was running for mayor *sarcastically*. He knew he wasn't going to win, just like he had known Goldwater wasn't going to win. It wasn't about winning. How could it be about anything else? It was about *ideas*.

Dan was graduating from Ascension and Ciaran was flying helicopters in Vietnam. War was something that happened on TV. And in the movies, but that was just Hollywood. Real war happened on TV. The fact was that the war was happening half a world away, and most of the dead people were yellow, and we only saw it on a TV screen, so that it seemed confined to that box, crammed in there with the Beverly Hillbillies and Judy Carne in her mini-skirt, manageable, soft core, a hint of sex and lots of violence and mostly for laughs, all in an effort to sell something. And we bought it. The Vietnamese might turn Communist. So what? The domino theory. We've got to stop the spread. The Communist Control Act made it illegal to be a member of the Communist Party.

Black people were making music that moved you and thrilled you and you could listen to on your transistor radio, which you could put under your pillow and only you could hear it. There were, *mirabile dictu*, even greater advancements to come, like an earpiece, but at that time, it was sufficient to put your transistor radio in your pocket. The transistor radio, snug in its faux-leather jacket, you could take it with you almost anywhere. The transistor radio was the grandest device, because now you could be in the freezing cold, with all your gear on, the big mitts, layers of clothes, boots, in the snow, and be able to listen to Chubby Checker. What was particularly wonderful about having the transistor radio under the pillow at night was that it was not allowed, but how was anyone to know, unless Mom came into the room and caught you? "Hand over that radio, Daniel." But why would she do that? Come barging into a kid's bedroom like that? That was the problem: living with all these people, trying to get some privacy. What do you need privacy for? Good question. What did Dan need privacy for? The life of his mind begins to take shape. It starts with God, then his family, then the place where he lives. It all goes together to produce how he thinks.

Black and white and color were adjectives applied to movies and TV, the 20th century's art, and the debasement of art, both of them powered by capital. That was what brought technology and artists together. Call it capitalism, call it history, or just fuse politics into the whole picture. It came together in the middle of the 20th century, and at first, it was an all-out war between movies and TV. Competition, the 'lifeblood of capitalism', making everything better, because it has to get better or go out of business, and die. If you can call it better. Progress. All an illusion. All of it flying through the projector at 24 frames a second, and then by means of dots like Seurat, beamed electronically into a tube, Davey Crockett and the Mouseketeers and James West in the early *Wild Wild West* and Napoleon and Ilya in the early *Man from UNCLE*, ducking into the tailor shop. The pre-credit sequence came into being in the 60s. The action begins before it's even been announced, before the players have been named, even the title has been withheld.

From Russia with Love Dan could take seriously. So could JFK. The Cold War was serious. But *Goldfinger*? This was where Dan fell in love with James Bond, but the silliness that was essential to a fat villain named Goldfinger was disorienting. Goldfinger was fat, but he was *going* to be sucked out the tiny window of that plane. Just as Dan was growing up – in his mind – his meditation became sophomoric. It didn't occur to him that he *was* a sophomore. Why didn't he have sideburns?

Upstairs, in the bedroom he shared with his benighted little brother, Dan was reading the James Bond book of the movie. Danny could see what diversions the screenwriter had made from the novel. More than that, he was taken simply by the different experiences of film and novel. When he looked up, he had read 60 pages, when before a few paragraphs of any text would suffice, just what it took to sum up a sports story.

Ian Fleming had written the whole Bond oeuvre, and died, thanks to his Bondian habits with tobacco and alcohol, practically before Dan caught up with him, but really the timing was perfect. At the end of Ian Fleming's creative journey, Danny Boy arrived at adolescence, and that was what the world of James Bond was all about. And so, Danny became Dan and entered into the world of literature via James Bond. He discovered that *Dr. No*, *From Russia with Love*, and *Goldfinger* were much more than movies. They were *books*. They were *novels*. He read *The Man with the Golden Gun* and *You Only Live Twice*. They were not like the movies at all. They were infinitely better. *The Spy Who Loved Me* was narrated by a *girl*, probably a decade older than Dan, a damsel in distress. It was hot. In fact, to a reader at age 14 it was really hot.

After James Bond, Nathan introduced Dan to Orson Welles in his bald cap as old Charles Foster Kane crashing the shelves and trashing a room of his mansion and bursting into a hall of mirrors, the cinematography dizzying and searing into memory. Welles was 25, but Kane was decrepit. Ingmar Bergman and Orson Welles were opposites in a universe of opposites, objects and beings completely different from one another, making no sense, not to Dan anyway, except the sense that was inherited or misunderstood or ignored. He was not failing and he was not succeeding, he was just getting older, you might say growing up, but technically and more to the point in Dan's case, since the skull is pretty much the biggest, most grown part of you at birth, he was actually growing down, mired in the mid-20thth century middle class midwestern blues, no longer upwardly mobile, but still looking to take the path of least resistance at every turn.

And how did that jibe with distance running, or going way back, to the days when he wanted to be a priest because he liked the costumes? Tonsure. He wanted one of those. Like Francis of Assisi. Bergman's conflict was between the Church and the theatre. In the theatre, all is simulation and dissimulation. What Bergman was doing was different than what Orson Welles had in mind. With Bergman, you confronted moral and philosophical questions, whereas with Welles, the concerns were more strictly aesthetic.

The post-war renaissance of films reached its height in black and white. *Dr. Strangelove. Breathless. Shoot the Piano Player.* Bergman in black and white. *Citizen Kane. Lolita. Psycho.* NBC started broadcasting all its shows in color. William F. Buckley didn't like the Beatles. He said they were godawful. That was how fucked up he was. James Bond didn't like them either, said you needed to listen to them with earmuffs on.

It was loud before *A Hard Day's Night* started, and the Lamar was packed, there had been a line to buy tickets, lots of talking, laughing, chattering, then the movie started and it got almost quiet but there was a nervous chatter underneath it, anticipation, and then here they came, the

Beatles, running toward the camera and away from a pack of girls who were chasing after them, and the theater exploded in high-pitched screams that barely wavered for the next hour and a half. Black and white.

There was James Brown and the downbeat. There had been Frank Sinatra and Eddy Duchin and Tommy Dorsey and Satchmo and Ella Fitzgerald and Billie Holiday, but now on Danny's tinny transistor, there was Diana Ross and the Supremes. Dan and everybody listened to the Beatles, Dylan, the Supremes, the Animals, the Stones, and the Beach Boys. This could be the last time, maybe the last time, I don't know. Don't you play with me, or you're playing with fire.

Back on Clinton Avenue, with Carroll Playground around the block alongside Lincoln school to the east, on the corner was a two-flat, and Tim Gaffney lived on the bottom floor. He was cool, one of the cool guys. Gaffney was a little taller than Dan. Most everyone was. Gaffney could shoot a basketball. He was tall and skinny and fair-skinned and freckled, and he had a slingshot kind of jumper that he would launch from over his shoulder with both hands. Gaffney could shoot from *outside*. He could *swish* it. He missed more than he made, but anybody who could heave it up there from outside was impressive to Dan.

He wasn't thinking about God or Plato or Augustine. He wasn't thinking about any of that metaphysical shit. He knew that Hemingway was a rich kid from north Oak Park who went to Oak Park High, and he was a Protestant and wrote dirty books. Dan just wanted to read a dirty book. Why? To satisfy his prurient interest. Nathan DeGrorio said that everyone was selfish and that nobody really cared about anyone else, that love was bullshit, and there was no God. What if that were true?

"The bird fights its way out of the egg. The egg is the world. Who would be born must first destroy the world." – Herman Hesse

Nietzsche was a teenager wanting to know what evil was and where it came from, like Goethe's Faust: "Half childish trifles, half God in your heart." What can be gained from this? What can be learned? From Dan's life? Precious little. But not nothing. No, not nothing. Something. Of worth, of value to us all. As a Catholic schoolboy, trained in repression by nuns and priests, expected to attend Mass weekly, to go to confession every other week, when it came to experiencing a healthy sexual appetite and development, he was fucked.

Dan deigned not to dance with his raven-haired date at the Trinity sophomore prom; he would not dance at a dance, but a year later he had become a dancing machine. He had been too shy then, and now as if he were someone else, he was suddenly proud of his moves. Proud of his moods, too. There was no one like him – popular yet aloof, cool guy yet artistic, sensitive.

"Who invited you?" They were in the basement of Jack Strap's house at Jack Strap's party, and all Dan's friends were there, and they had all been invited, but not Dan. Jack Strap didn't like him for some reason. Maybe because he called him Jack Strap, like jockstrap, but his real name was Jack Lepper, equally as ignominious, if you ever read the Bible.

It was simple, what he wanted to do any day was to wake up at whatever time his eyes came open, and if it were early he would have breakfast, and if it were late he wouldn't, and instead of cereal and the sports section, he would just head straight to Fox park to play softball or basketball or touch football – all day, interrupted by a trip to Madison Street to buy some chips and candy and soda and wander past the new car showrooms, maybe be bold enough to enter and check out the new models until the salesmen chased them out. So much of life consisted of going places where you could stay until you got chased out. They would just go back to the park and play some more. When Dan got home, and, remember, he would be doing

what he wanted to do, he would set up his TV table in front of the TV
and watch *Wild Wild West* while eating an Italian Beef from Carm's or
a Vienna hot dog from King's, Roosevelt Road's finest cuisine, in a grease
stained brown paper sack, along with about a pound of fries. That would
be *all right*. That was all he wanted, to play and eat junk and watch TV
and eat some more junk and then go out and play some more, play until the
street lights came on, and then come home, but maybe Mom would let him
stay outside and play chase with the kids on the block, till everybody had
to go home, so home he'd go and lie on the carpet in front of the TV till he
went to bed, preceded by the obligatory bedtime snack – buttered popcorn
popped over the electric stove in a wire popper. Sweet dreams. There was
really no God involved, nor any real need for girlfriends, until there was,
although in the night you might need God – because you were afraid, but
He didn't actually do anything for you, and then it started and whenever
Danny didn't want it, the thought of girls bypassed his head entirely and
went directly for his groin. There was only one thing missing in this perfect
existence: a girlfriend, and lacking that ruined the whole thing.

Patti Mangione was from Melrose Park, also known as Pizza Park for
its population of wops. Patti Mangione was impossibly pretty. Impossible,
that is, for Dan to ever have a chance with her, and now he was going
steady with her. It was cold, and Dan and Patti Mangione were standing
in line to get tickets to see *Doctor Zhivago* at the Lamar, and once they
got inside and settled, she rested her head on Dan's shoulder and they
went to Russia together, to the ice and snow and revolution, and Betty
and Veronica reappeared. Doctor Zhivago, played by Omar Sharif, had
to choose between the dark and the light, the brunette or the blonde,
Geraldine Chaplin or Julie Christie, and Dr. Zhivago chose light, and Dan
chose dark.

Dan would get all his cultural clues from Nathan DeGrorio now, which earned him Nathan's complete disdain. But so what? Schweez wasn't going to lead him there. The nuns and priests weren't. His big brother wouldn't. He was going to be on his own no matter what. There was no one like him, and he was like millions of other people; there was no one like him, and there was nothing special about him.

To watch Joseph Cotton as Jed Leland, Charles Foster Kane's best friend, was like looking in a mirror and a crystal ball. Leland and Kane were both at heart cynics, but Kane's cynicism was on an entirely different plane than Jedediah's, and that was the way it was with Nathan and Dan. Dan was just tagging along.

It was from Nathan that Dan learned the term "dilettante" and, coincidentally, learned that he himself was one, crippled with growing awareness of sex and culture; Nathan's influence was as a teacher. Finally, one must reject the teacher. Time has in it the spinning earth, jumbling history in a kaleidoscope of black and white and color.

"You're going to the movies with Nathan DeGrorio? What are you going to see?"

"*Hour of the Wolf.* It's an Ingmar Bergman movie. Whatever that means."

According to the Legion of Decency, that would mean C, for Condemned, so if you see it, you go to Hell because that's where they show movies like this. Next stop, the Clark Theater for the Ingmar Bergman Festival. You could step on the el and be downtown in 21 minutes, and you would have effectively disappeared. You were no one, walking amid thousands of other no ones. You could do anything you wanted, alone, in Chicago, go places, the Public Library, the Art Institute and sit in front of a Van Gogh, or go to Kroch's & Brentano's bookstore, or a comic book store, the whole city could be yours in complete privacy – because nobody gave a shit about you.

Johnny Lattner's Steakhouse was dark and cool inside and smelled of wood and leather and steak and cigar smoke. In a glass case lit with a mysterious glow was the Heisman Trophy, a crouching bronze running back, wearing an old-timey helmet with no facemask, clutching the pigskin to his chest and thrusting out a stiff-arm. Can't just look at it all day; they'll kick you out.

And what of Nathan DeGrorio? Is he the hero of this story or the villain? This is not a buddy-pic. That would imply equality. Nathan De-Grorio had no equal. Nathan stood apart. There was no father in Nathan's picture. Life without a father, with no siblings, only a mother whom he despised.

"Why do you hate your mom, Nathan?"

Dan never asked. What would have happened if he did? Nathan would probably have pointedly ignored him. He would give you to understand that you would elevate yourself in his eyes if you would refrain not just from asking but from wanting to know, reducing it to the level of obnoxious triviality, and forget about it, as if he had to be reminded that he had a mother. He wasn't going to bring it up while he and Nathan were looking at *Playboy* in the basement of Nathan's house.

"What're you looking at her toes for, Dan?"

"I dunno."

"It's a naked broad, Jesus."

"I know."

"Look at her tits, Dan."

"I am."

"You're looking at her feet."

"They're pretty.

"Boy, have you got a lot to learn."

What the Hell did Nathan know? He'd never been with a girl. But he had seen a lot of foreign movies, and he read *The Story of O* and the novels of de Sade and books that'd been translated from Japanese; he had read everything, so that was how he knew. Nathan tittered at the priest's admonishment to the boys gathered in the Pine Room, separate from the eighth-grade girls, to learn the Church's views on sexual matters. "Feeling girls' breasts," Father White cautioned, flexing his fingers in demonstration, "is no good."

"Don't knock it till you've tried it," Nathan whispered. But Nathan hadn't tried it. How'd Nathan get hold of those *Playboy*s anyway? He kept them in the basement. His mother didn't know about them. His mother never found out about him skipping school that day either. He probably waltzed into the drugstore and bought the *Playboy*s, just because he had the balls to do it. He read the articles too. He read the *New Yorker, National Review,* and *Playboy.*

Nathan was the gatekeeper who didn't give a damn and thus provided an entrance for Dan into the secular world, where you could see Jane Fonda's tits directed by Roger Vadim and condemned by the Legion of Decency. It wasn't as if he felt some sort of judgment descended upon him the moment Jane Fonda's bare breast appeared on the screen, but it was clear to Danny at that moment that there were good people on earth who were virtuous by nature, and there were those who were bad, who were flawed – and Danny was with them. He liked Jane Fonda's tits, and he very much liked her ass, and he didn't know enough yet to even think about whether he might like her pussy, which did *not* appear on screen; he was stuck on her ass, and her tits, and her toes.

Chapter Ten

It was August and Pop was old and sick, and he lay on the couch in the tiny living room of the small house on South Kenilworth, a block from Berwyn, with the Cubs losing on TV. Dan used to walk or ride his bike over and watch the Cubs game with Pop. Gramma would give Danny a cup of soda and some cookies, and he would open several packs of baseball cards that he'd purchased with change he'd stolen from his father's ceramic saddlebag-wearing dachshund. His dad would hang his watch over the pooch's tail, his keys over his nose, and he'd put his wallet in one bag and his change in the other, and if there were seemingly uncountable coins there, a slew of quarters and dimes and nickels, Dan would pinch just enough so that nobody, so thought Dan, would notice. Gluttony had already set in, as well as thievery. He devoured the cookies and slugged the soda as he rifled through the packs filled with cards that he already had, then stuffed all the pink strips of bubblegum into his mouth at once so that his cheek bulged with his chaw like Nellie Fox, the White Sox second baseman.

Dan had been a kid then. Now he was, what, cool? He didn't go to Pop's house and watch the Cubs anymore; he hung out with the Shocker, Rug Olson, and Gaffney. They jetted around town on their bikes.

Great things could happen on your bike. Just a day or two before, Dan was riding his bike home from the pool, with Kathy Winston on his handlebars, Dan was giving her a ride home, and she kept leaning back and resting her head on his chest and pretending it was an accident, woops, slumping against him, falling practically in his lap, and he could have kept peddling all the way to downtown, Chicago, if she had asked him to.

But what about leaving town? For one thing, they weren't in a town. Oak Park was the largest *village* in the world, connected to the big city of Chicago to the east and to the north and south, the big city wrapping around it on three sides, like an ocean with a curving shore.

Everybody rode bikes everywhere. All the guys had bikes. Dan's was the beat-up old tank of a Schwinn that had been handed down by Ciaran. Looked like something out of World War II.

On a hot day in August, Shocker, Rug Olsen, Dog Ryan, and a bunch of the guys rode their bikes to Lake Street to go into Sears and run up and down the escalators the wrong way, run through the aisles. Till they got kicked out, of course. Then what?

Shocker announced: "Guys wanna go to Brookfield Zoo?" It wasn't really a question.

"You know how *far* that is?"

"We go Jackson Boulevard out to Harlem Avenue, cross over into Forest Park. Ride over the Circle Avenue Bridge."

The Circle Avenue Bridge came into view, straight up and straight down, steep, and at the bottom, they would try to make a right-hand turn, at a ninety-degree angle, to head further west, to get to Brookfield Zoo. They could ride their bikes to the Forest Park Pool, just past St. Bernadine's, but they didn't have their swimming suits, and besides, they were on a mission to ride to Brookfield Zoo.

Dan's bike, the 26-inch tank handed down from his big brother, didn't negotiate the turn, and went out from under him, slid into Rug Olson's bike and his took out Gaffney's and they all went down in the street, but

Shock, at the lead, was unscathed and wasn't even pissed off, when they looked up to see the smoking ruins of the Ferrara Candy Company.

"Holy shit!"

"This can't be real. "

Shock was in shock. He dropped his bike on its side. "Jesus Christ!" Who could blame him? The Ferrara Candy Company had burned down, and everywhere, in the grass, on the sidewalk, spilling into the street, were mounds and mounds and rivers of Red Hots and Fireballs. Hot damn! It was the marriage of Heaven and Hell.

They stuffed them in their pockets, crammed them in their mouths, stained their hands and faces cherry red, all the Fireballs and Red Hots they would want for the rest of their lives. Then they jumped on their bikes and peddled fast to the west in the hot August sun, with their mouths on fire and screaming in raucous good humor because they had just scored. It had really happened. It would be on the news. The Ferrara Candy Company burned down. Their tongues and their lips and their cheeks and their hands proved it.

Shocker was a liar, a thief, a cheater, and a bully, and that was what made him a leader. What did it take to win his admiration? They rode single file alongside heavy traffic, then cut through the cemetery. Beyond the cemetery was the entrance to Miller Meadow, and on the other side of that lay Brookfield Zoo. There was a long green corridor that led to the front gates. It had taken half the day to get there. When would they get home?

Shock said, "Who cares?"

To say they rampaged through the zoo would be putting it mildly. They did nothing at a walk, and they did nothing without noise, but then a zoo is meant to be noisy. The monkey house was a scream. In the snake house, they used their voices to try to get a rise out of the snakes. On the grounds outside, chipmunks were overrunning the place. They were practically underfoot, scrambling around all the outdoor exhibits, all up and down the paths, all about the greenway that Brookfield Zoo prided itself on, showing that the zoo wasn't just a bunch of concrete buildings with animals inside, in cages. So, the chipmunks had the run of the place.

Shock instructed Dog Ryan and Rug Olson to climb out on the limb of a tree that overhung the giraffe habitat, and two full-grown giraffes ambled over and ate the leaves off branches that Dog and Rug broke off and held out to them right out of their hands like pets.

It was Shock who started firing stones at the chipmunks, and whatever Shock did, everybody did – if they could. Stones rained down on the unlucky chipmunks.

"Damn, Shock, you hit it! Shocker! You hit it right in the fucking eye! Jesus!"

Dan would never get that image out of his head, ever, the dying chipmunk clutching at the wound Shocker had inflicted in fun. In *fun*.

"Hit it again."

A zoo isn't open at night. When the sun goes down, it's time for everybody to clear out. The guys left the murdered chipmunk in the bloody dirt near the habitat of the friendly giraffes and beat a hasty retreat through the turnstiles to the bike racks and then raced along the green corridor to Miller Meadow, and the sun went from gold to crimson over the trees.

"Getting dark."

"No shit. "

"Getting late. "

It was dark by the time the guys split off in their different directions on their bikes, and they finally got back to Oak Park after their day at the zoo. The house was quiet. It seemed nobody was home.

He didn't know about Pop. That was where everyone had gone – to Pop and Gramma's house on Kenilworth Avenue. Gramma said she was in the kitchen, and he was lying on the couch watching the Cubs game, and she heard him talking, and she thought he was talking to her, but he wasn't, and he said, "Blessed Lady, take my hand," and Pop, James Finnegan, was dead.

Death – terrible and comforting simultaneously, because the Blessed Lady may well have taken Pop's hand, as he had asked with his last words, and led him into paradise, or it might have been that shrieking banshee from *Darby O'Gill and the Little People*.

Next would be Grampa, kindly, jovial Wilhelm Schmidt, retired bus mechanic, popper of popcorn, and dancer while it popped. Gramps smoked a pipe, and the tobacco smelled sweet, not harsh like cigarettes. Dead. Both grandfathers. With whom would he watch the Cubs games now? Nathan? At Grampa and Gwennie's house, there was a wood stove in the basement and a wire popcorn popper, and as Grampa shook it over the burner and the kernels started popping, Grampa would dance a little jig and tell Danny Boy, "It's all in the dance." So it was that Danny attributed popcorn popping properly to the dance accompanying it, more so than to natural causes.

When Pop died, Gramma moved in. The Euclid castle was plenty big enough to accommodate her. Connor fashioned the upstairs so that she not only had her own bedroom but also a sitting room that overlooked the yard. Then Grampa died and Gwennie moved in too, and there was a brief time when both grandmothers lived in the Euclid castle, but Gwennie was frail, and the end was near.

Gramma, however, Barbara Budden, the former indentured servant from Germany, was strong as a mule. She did all the housework, the dishes, the laundry, and mowed the grass with the electric mower trailing its extension cord around the corner of Euclid and Van Buren.

Both grandfathers being gone, then Gwennie gone, served to turn the Euclid castle into the last stronghold of the Finnegans, once the grandparents' houses on Jackson Boulevard and south Kenilworth were sold. Dan took over the room on the first floor that had been his big brother's. Dan was the man now, and he could stay up all night. When he got to high school, he could come home drunk and crawl into bed, and the walls would swirl around him so dizzyingly he could not shut his eyes.

Schweez went to Ascension too and lived in a white stucco two-story house around the corner on Wesley Avenue, across the street from the Flaherty family and the Monacos. He had a sister a couple of years younger, and he had an older brother, starting forward for the Friar basketball team, whom he idolized, just as Dan did Ciaran. He knew what it was like to be in the middle.

The siblings were all spaced far enough apart that they didn't hang out with one another. So, when Dan went to Schweez's house or vice versa, they could go down in the basement and be undisturbed.

One day, Dan and Schweez were roaming the halls of the Oak Park Arms hotel, and they happened upon the radio station on the top floor, WOPA. There was a disc jockey in the studio behind the glass, and he motioned for the two boys to come in.

"Have a seat, boys."

"What the heck?"

"You boys ever been on the radio before?"

"Yeah, right."

"Now, when that red light comes on, I want you to read this. You can read, can't you?"

"Yes, sir."

It was a good thing he was asking Dan, because Schweez couldn't read worth shit. The disc jockey asked: "Why are you reading it so fast?"

"You asked if I could read."

"That's right. I didn't ask you how fast you could read."

"I wanted to show you."

"That's not the idea."

"What's the idea?"

"You've got to put some feeling into it."

And the guy read some stuff like he really meant it, and you could see he didn't mean it, so they left, and they wandered the halls of the Oak Park Arms.

Schweez loved to lift weights. He was convinced that lifting weights was the key to success, and even though he was skinny and never seemed to get any bigger, just taller, he was almost six feet tall in grade school, he kept curling, benching, and squatting. He would get to six-three, almost as tall as his big brother, who had filled their trophy case playing forward for the Fighting Friars. When Schweez was just starting out, he and Dan would do their weight-training together, which meant they would see how many times they could curl or press a ten-pound dumbbell, and somehow Schweez got it into his head that the source of all your power lay in your forearms – like Popeye.

Schweez was a great sports guy, and he lived right around the corner on Wesley Avenue, across the street from Terry Flaherty. There was a trophy case in the Schweez's living room that displayed the trophies that the Schweez brothers had won, and mostly they belonged to his big brother, who played on the Fenwick basketball team, an honor nearly equal to playing on the Friar football team. Schweez and Dan were boxing fans, which meant that they were, among other things, anti-segregationists, as well as fighters themselves, in training, two things that were unique in their respective households.

Cassius Clay won the Olympic gold medal in Rome as a Light Heavyweight, and then he threw the medal into the Mississippi River. Cassius Clay was re-inventing boxing. He had a new style all his own. Floyd Patterson depended on ducking blows. Not a bad strategy, considering there is no hitting below the belt, so you could just duck in and out of your peekaboo sanctuary, and keep moving, always a threat to pop up with a hook packed with all the momentum and power of your legs, and wham! Trouble was the whole thing had to be timed just so, or you would duck right into an uppercut, which is what happened to Patterson twice.

Clay had an entirely different method altogether, one which met with the complete contempt of the boxing establishment. Instead of the traditional, time-tested attack of the duck and weave, Clay used his height, reach, quickness, and speed to back away from punches, pulling his head out of harm's way. Clay would lean back out of reach from even the longest jab, and with dancer-like footwork, he effortlessly side-stepped hooks, while uppercuts were entirely eliminated from the opponent's arsenal as pointless – you were swinging at air.

Cassius Clay. His name was Cassius Clay. Danny was taken with the name. Cassius Clay. There was a name for you. In Shakespeare, Julius Caesar tells us, "Yon Cassius has a lean and hungry look." And Cassius Clay did have a lean and hungry look. He was a light heavyweight. The assumption was that as you moved up in the weight classes, there might be an increase in power, but there was likely to be a diminishment of speed and agility, yet Clay defied all of that.

What could make Danny care again about boxing after Liston had destroyed Patterson twice? The second time, after the exact same thing happened, Patterson became a joke. You could go from hero to joke in about 2 minutes and 11 seconds.

Mom was right. Danny was awake all night. After the fight ended, two minutes and ten seconds into the first round, Danny switched off the transistor radio under his pillow and lay in the darkness with his thoughts. Why had he not imagined this? Why was he shocked? Because he thought that since Eddie Machon had gone the distance with Liston, and Machon was nowhere near the fighter that Patterson was, that it was going to be a *fight*.

At Ascension, there was a boxing tournament called the Silver Gloves.

"You gonna sign up for boxing? "

"Hell yeah."

"Gonna get your ass kicked. "

You wore headgear, padding all around your head, and the 16-ounce gloves were full of padding, and it took a straight shot to the nose to really hurt you, although you could get whammed upside your head pretty good too. Mostly guys just squared off and started slugging, giving as good as they got. In the gym at Ascension, late afternoon sunlight was angling through the high windows in shafts, just mats on the gym floor, and the ring wouldn't get set up till the night of the fights.

You wouldn't find out who you were fighting until after the try-outs and all the practices. In practice, you would fight different guys. Some guys weren't good enough to fight on Fight Night. Not everybody got to fight on Fight Night.

Then the list of bouts for Fight Night was posted. At the bottom of the list, the last names, the lightweights, Tom Deering versus Danny Finnegan, one of the Deering twins. It didn't matter, Tom or Gerry. Danny knew he could beat them both.

You could stand flat-footed and trade punches, which required no special skill, just power and durability, or you could move, circle away from your opponent, out of reach, attack with straight jabs and crosses, dancing, back-pedaling.

Danny didn't fight like Cassius Clay, but he did fight like a boxer, not a slugger. He felt and understood the sport of it, that it was movement and dance and art, not mere brute force and animosity. It was the same as Steal the Bacon, speed, quickness, guile, scoring points, landing punches, it didn't matter how hard, just how many.

Three rounds, three minutes each, with a minute rest between. The sparring sessions gave everyone a notion of the energy expended in fighting someone for that period of time, but somehow, in the practice of it, the passage of time was not a concern. For one thing, there was no bell, just a voice, saying: "time", and there might be stoppages, interruptions for advice or admonishment, and there were no ropes – just the edges of the mats as boundaries, and it was in the afternoon, with shafts of sunlight pouring into the gym through the high windows, and only some kids and Coach Crowley watching. But on Fight Night, with the entire focus of the gym resting on the raised ring that you had to mount stairs to get to and then step between the ropes to enter it, suddenly time began to matter because this was the moment, the instant, the bell, when time became real.

You thought you were fighting the other guy, and the other guy thought he was fighting you, but when the bell rang you both realized you were fighting time, and you were fighting all by yourself, and while you were absorbed in fighting time, the other guy attacked, like a diversion, a sideshow you had to fend off to concentrate on the real opponent, time, who was kicking the shit out of you.

The first round ended, and Danny had never been so tired in all his life. It was funny, Danny was cool and in control against Tom Deering, even though it was his first fight. With Tom Deering, it was all about boxing, scoring points, but the next year against Larry Sullivan, it was about who was tougher, who would win in a street fight; it was about slugging it out. With Tom Deering, in all the confidence Danny had from the start that he was going to win, he kept moving, kept jabbing, and, the same way they say you can't hit a homerun by trying to hit a homerun, so they said, Danny never having actually hit a homerun in all his life, but he believed that was how homeruns were hit, by simply meeting the ball, and he supposed what happened next was something like that. They were boxing each other well; they were *both* boxers, not sluggers, and that was what it took to win the Best Boxer trophy, one skilled boxer surpassing another skilled boxer by the slightest of margins. Danny wasn't thinking about that either. If he had he might have pulled that punch that met so perfectly with the slightest hesitation, the one fraction of a second when Tom might have kept circling but instead made the fatal decision to change directions just then, and, pop, down he went, onto one knee, and then popped right back up, but it was too late. It had happened. It was a knockdown, and the great Tony Zale, who was the celebrity referee, the former middleweight champion of the world and devout Catholic and personal friend to Monsignor Prince Gerald, gave Tom Deering the standing eight count.

A year later, it was Danny Finnegan versus Larry Sullivan. It was a step up in weight class. Danny was no longer one of the littlest guys; he was somewhere near the middle. The Larry Sullivan fight was just two kids standing there whaling away, pummeling each other, a slugfest, and Danny was getting the worst of it, getting hit with the harder shots, getting hit with more shots. He was never close to going down, but neither was he ever close to winning – except for the first round.

The first round went exactly according to plan. When the bell rang and Danny came out of his corner, his plan immediately kicked in, and he started circling and jabbing and boxing, scoring points, *winning*, but all of a sudden, he stopped, he surrendered to his instincts and allowed the fight to degenerate into a slugfest, which he knew he was bound to lose, but at least it would look like he tried. If you swarmed each other and flailed away, both of you would land blows and one of you would get the better of it, but neither of you would be able to wind up or swing with enough space or leverage to do much harm. It was just ugly to watch, the kind of fight that someone would just break up and tell you to go home – and Larry Sullivan clearly won, so, instead of going home that night with two gold trophies – one for winning the fight, and the other for winning the fight the only way he could have won the fight, by being the Best Boxer – Danny was going home with a ribbon, emblematic of *losing*.

Cassius Clay was shaking Liberace's hand on the Jack Paar Show, and he made a face and started to go down on his knees at the supposed force of Liberace's grip. Sonny Liston watched Clay and was convinced he had no punch, no power. "He's a fag, and I'm a man." But it was more than that.

Clay said: "If a man thinks you're crazy, he'll think twice before he acts, because he figures you're liable to do *anything*." Hamlet's logic. Sonny Liston was going to kill that kid. You see what he did to Patterson? Liston's left hook was lethal, he had the stiffest jab in the world, and he had the reach on Clay.

As Liston was getting ready to fight Clay, Rocky Marciano stopped by the gym where Liston was training. "Hey, Rocky," Sonny said, "What do you think you would've done with me?"

Rocky didn't say anything. "I know what I would've done with you," Sonny said. Rocky wanted to fight him right there and then.

Liston at 218, a big heavyweight. Clay at 210, bulked up from his Olympic gold at light heavyweight. Clay was faster than Liston could have imagined and immediately sliced his face open and closed one eye with jabs he recognized only afterward, bewildered, disconcerted, sitting on his stool before the seventh round and complaining that his shoulder was fucked up too, and so, Cassius Clay became the heavyweight champion of the world. Clay said the next day, "I don't have to be what you want me to be, I'm free to be who I want." Cassius Clay turned into Muhammad Ali.

Nobody ever asked to be a slave. Nobody ever asked to be snatched out of their home and strapped down and shipped to another continent. Neither did anybody ever want to be born into slavery. All it proved was that it didn't matter what you asked for. All that free labor, the source of primitive accumulation.

Ali preached in the Chicago Coliseum on Wabash Avenue, not long after Danny saw the Celtics with Bill Russell beat the Chicago Zephyrs there, and when the Celtics walked off the court at halftime, they passed directly under the stands where Dan and his classmates were seated to watch Schweez and the Ascension basketball team play an exhibition game against St. Bernadine during the break. The greatest basketball team in the history of the world was passing beneath him, and Bob Cousy, the Cooz walked through, and his hair was *steaming*.

Muhammad Ali was not the least bit afraid of Sonny Liston. Cassius Clay had been afraid of Sonny Liston. Ali did not fear any man, except Elijah Muhammad, who was the Messenger of Allah. It was comical. Ali flicked a little right-hand semi-bolo punch under Liston's arm, and Liston jumped onto the floor. Jersey Joe Walcott, who was the referee, wandered around the ring when it happened like he didn't know what he was doing either. He didn't count Liston out. Somebody else counted Liston out, and they had to tell Jersey Joe to start counting, because he was letting the fight begin again.

The Ali-Liston rematch was so rigged it was funny. Sonny Liston took a dive so obviously, so awkwardly, he plainly had no idea how it was even supposed to be done, like a bad actor in a B-movie: "Oh shit, I gotta fall down, right?" And then he got up and realized he got up too soon, so he plopped down again, and when he was counted out, he stood right up, not sweating, not even breathing hard. It was bullshit, and he knew it was bullshit, and he knew that everyone could see that it was bullshit.

On the second anniversary of Kennedy's assassination, not even five months after beating Liston for the second time, Ali beat Patterson in Vegas. The three of them had gone around and around with one another and now Ali was on top, the king, the rightful ruler, like King Arthur or King David. Ali defended his crown five times in one year. And then Ali would *not* step forward and be drafted.

Mr. Bobbitt's class at Fenwick High School was called Americanism versus Communism. The first edition of *Capital* came out in 1867. The Civil War was over, and Lincoln was dead. The European nation states were squabbling over the colonies they'd laid claim to throughout the world. Labor-saving devices, machines, and technology made it possible for human beings to live while not actually knowing how to do shit. That was why universal education became necessary, because human beings would otherwise be in danger of becoming too stupid to live. They were smart enough to invent machines to keep up with capital's expansion, to keep up with growing profits, but when they arrived at the point where all they had to do was push a button and let the machines do everything, they couldn't think of anything else to do – because they could no longer think. You had to teach them to read, to add and subtract, otherwise, chaos. You didn't have to teach serfs or slaves or peasants, who didn't need to know any more than was necessary to do the task assigned to them. Now people needed to know more than how to do their job; they needed to know how to be a consumer. What is the proper education for the consumer class?

There's always the danger with education that if the student gets too smart, he, or more likely she, will see through all the bullshit. The guilds had a code. The different trades were called mysteries. A journeyman had to swear to love his brethren with brotherly love, to support their respective trades, not willfully betray the secrets of the trade, and besides, in the interests of all, not to recommend his own wares by calling the attention of the buyers to defects in the articles made by others. Only then could you become a master. Can you spot the mystery?

At the Berlin Conference, the European nations got together and carved up Africa and divided it into portions for each. It was theirs. Whether or not God had given it to them, they were civilized, and Africans were not, and the whole world needed to be civilized, and the civilizers had a duty to civilize the whole world, and they could turn a nifty profit at the same time.

This was Ed Fenwick's view of things, too. He didn't know he was creating Fenwick High School, like God, *ex nihilio,* out of nothing. He believed in God. To Ed Fenwick, God was as real as, say, the Pope. Ed Fenwick cashed in his slaves in 1800. He didn't set them free; he sold them. Some of them he kept for a while to work for him, to slave for him. It was slaves who built his first priory.

The Dominicans cast about for a name to call the order's new school in Oak Park. Saint Dominic might have come to mind. The Church was being championed by the Dominicans in its fight against racism in the suburbs – not racism against Blacks, mind you, racism against *Catholics.* So, they were going to set up shop in Oak Park, bastion of WASPs, to prove their worth, intellectually, athletically, and above all, morally.

And the children of Israel gave out of their inheritance at the command-ment of the Lord, these cities and their suburbs. Joshua 20-3

Right there in the Bible, the priests shall take up in the *suburbs*. In America, where once had been outposts and then settlements and even-tually towns and villages, there would be cities and their suburbs joined by intersecting lines of superhighways, with all the land where the highways did not steamroll their way through to remain country, creating three classes of people to be further subdivided: city dwellers, country folk, and suburbanites.

And I have given thee land for which thou didst not labor, and cities which ye built not, and ye dwell in them. Joshua 24-13

There was no racism at Fenwick, nor had there been any at Ascension. In fact, there wasn't any racism in Oak Park, because there was only one race there. Twelve years of Catholic education, plenty long enough to fuck anybody up to where anybody saying it didn't fuck them up, it probably fucked them up worse, so bad they don't even know. All education is in-doctrination. Buckley made this point in *Up from Liberalism*. At Fenwick, in Theology class, a point was being made that while man is naturally religious, he is not by nature Christian. Why is that? Father Farrell wanted to know. "Because it is not natural to turn the other cheek."

How would Fenwick High School ever come around to admitting girls without admitting the whole boys-only idea was a terrible mistake? That would take some slick spiritual rationalization.

"Times have changed. Girls are now human beings." And besides, enrollment is down, and lots of girls' parents can swing the tuition with ease.

In the spiritual world, in the world of the mind, of Aquinas and Aristotle, the world of ideas, there could plainly be no abortion, no birth control pills, because nothing could be more sinful. But to be against both birth control *and* abortion in the real world was absurd. So, what does the Church do but take it up a notch and make homosexuality a mortal sin, deserving eternal damnation in the fires of Hell.

The Church would fuck you up either way – either you would accept all its dictums and never fuck, never even beat off, and maybe never have sex with anybody except your wife, and then strictly for the purpose of having children, *or* you could try to carry on a natural normal life, fight your repression, and come to enjoy sex *because* it was bad and dirty.

Be perfect as your Heavenly Father is perfect. – Matthew 5:48

If the goal is to be perfect, you're not going to make it, and when you don't make it, you're going to feel guilty.

"It was only in the hands of the priest, that true artist in guilt feelings, that guilt achieved its form – oh what a form! 'Sin' – for this is the priestly name for the animal's 'bad conscience' (cruelty directed backward) – has been the greatest event so far in the history of the sick soul: we possess in it the most dangerous and fateful artifice of religious interpretation. Man, suffering from himself in some way or other but in any case, physiologically like an animal shut up in a cage, uncertain why or wherefor, thirsting for reasons – reasons relieve – thirsting too for remedies, narcotics, at last takes counsel with one who knows hidden things too – and behold! He receives a hint, he receives from his sorcerer, the ascetic priest, the first hint as to the 'cause' of his suffering: he must seek it in himself, in some guilt, in a piece of the past, he must understand his suffering as a punishment." – Nietzsche

There had been something weird and creepy about priests almost from the beginning. Priests and nuns. How many kids were abused? Whom would you tell if it happened to you? Nobody. The only reason for priests and nuns to swear off sex was because there was something wrong with it, something bad. Perhaps Dan was misreading the Bible. Probably. No doubt.

The priest abuse and Augustine, if not Aristotle, are intimately connected, like cause and effect. This whole idea of an all-male clergy, celibate,
no sex ever in any way, is that sex is evil. The abuse was baked in right
there. It was all fucked up, and even a kid who was never touched would
be fucked up in his head for life. A vow of celibacy meant that you would
live your life without sex. You wouldn't jerk off, and you would never have
sex with anyone. Ever. For the rest of your life. Jesus. Jesus never had a
girlfriend, unless you counted Mary Magdalen.

Priests were a bunch of bullshit. Jesus wasn't a priest. There were
no priests. The Jews had priests. The pagans had priests. The Christians
didn't have priests. They were different. Peter wasn't a *bishop*. 'Apostolic
succession'. Of what? The apostles weren't priests. They wouldn't know
what you were talking about. A priest was God's man on earth. He had
the power to transform bread and wine into the body and blood of Christ.
Transubstantiation. That was absurd. In the Bible, Jesus is called Rabbi. A
rabbi is a kind of priest, right?

No. Jesus was a *teacher*. Rabbi means teacher. Disciple means learner.
They were learning from him. They were following him, *away* from the
priests. They called him Rabbi because he was their teacher, and he was
their *only* teacher. He taught them to leave the temple priests. He taught
them that they were all equal.

Be not ye called Rabbi; for one is your master, even Christ; and all ye are
brethren. And call no man your father upon this earth; for one is your Father,
which is in Heaven. – Matthew 23, 8-9

Neither the Romans nor the Jews even saw Christianity as a *religion*
– because it had no *priests*. The nuns and priests all meant well. Some of
them did. Probably. Most of them. What does that even mean, most of
them? Most people won't fuck you up for life, what good is that?

CHAPTER ELEVEN

Dog Ryan was wearing a football uniform. Where in the world could Dog Ryan get a football uniform except from a football team? Maybe Dog Ryan thought he'd catch a pick-up game of football at Fox Park. Guys showed up there with their own pads and helmets once in a while. But a good game of tackle football with a bunch of guys required planning during school to get it organized, sometimes days in advance, and Dan hadn't heard anything about a game. Dog Ryan probably stole the uni from somewhere or somebody.

"I'm playing for St. Edmund's."

"Edmund's has a football team?"

"You didn't know?"

"How'd you get on it? We go to Ascension."

"Doesn't matter. As long as you go to *church* at St. Edmund's."

A technicality.

"I get it."

"You ever go inside St. Edmund's church?"

If there was a church around, Dan would go inside it. Besides Ascension, he had been inside St. Bernadine's and St. Edmund's and the Lutheran church near South Park and the cathedral downtown, and Saint Andrew Catholic church in Deleavan, Wisconsin. When there was no Mass being served and the Ascension church was empty he would go in, dip his fingers in holy water and make the sign of the cross and bow his head and genuflect at the aisle and go into a pew and kneel down and say a quick Hail Mary and then he would wander all around the aisles by the side altars and under the Stations of the Cross and into the nave and maybe even up the stairs to the choir loft with its organ at the top, beneath the dome, which had once been shining gold and now was green, surmounted by green Jesus, arms outstretched, as if wondering why, why, why?

"Yeah, I've been in St. Edmund's.

"Good. So you can say you go there then."

At the Ridgeland-Commons field, there were a couple dozen players uniformed like Dog Ryan, only cleaner. It was Edmund's football team. Edmund's had a football team. Who knew there even was such a thing? And Dog Ryan of all people was on the team. And Doggie ran off to practice. Dan watched from a distance. The coach wore a ball cap and a Vince Lombardi aspect.

"Run back to the huddle – run!"

They had started by doing calisthenics – jumping jacks, push-ups, leg raisers, starting with bicycling, then lowering the legs and shouting *twelve inches*, then *six inches,* and emitting war cries, and then they broke into groups – running backs over here, quarterbacks and receivers over there, linemen over here. Dog Ryan fit right in. He was an average player for these guys from Edmund's, who seemed to Dan not quite on a par with the Ascension lads. Some bigger guys, but nobody as tall as Shock or anywhere near as athletic, and nobody as big as either Jimbo Kidd or Jimbo Wilkinson.

They ran a scrimmage, mostly running plays, not passing. Afterward, Dog Ryan went up to the coach and started talking to him. The coach was listening to him, and then Dog was pointing Dan out to the coach, and the coach gestured for Dan to come join them on the sideline.

"I hear you're a football player", the coach said.

"Yes, sir."

"You *go to church* at St. Edmund's, don't you?"

"Sure."

"Good enough," the coach said. "We'll see you at practice tomorrow, then. You got pads?"

"Yes, sir."

"Wear your own pads and we'll suit you up afterward."

"Yes, sir!"

It was almost dark, and there was a cool fall breeze that sent the oak leaves cascading onto the sidewalk of East Avenue as they headed back toward Clarence alley. It was Indian Summer, and Dan was going to play football tomorrow, his first step toward maybe being one of the greatest football players of all time, like Johnny Lattner or Jim Thorpe, as played by Burt Lancaster.

"You know why he wants you to wear your own pads?"

"See if I'm any good before he gives me a uni."

"You gotta earn it."

"Well, you earned it, Doggie, how hard can it be?"

Dan would be like Jim Thorpe, All-American, as played by Burt Lancaster. Dan would stay up late to watch that movie whenever it came on and be inspired to tears and spend the night dreaming of football plays, of scoring touchdowns for Fenwick's Fighting Friars, for Notre Dame, for the Chicago Bears, no, he would not play pro football, he would do something else, be a spy maybe, but why think that far ahead? For now, it would be enough to score a touchdown. He could sleep on that.

The next day at Ascension, there was a time warp, stretching out interminably while he endured the interval before football practice. Finally, it was time for football practice at Ridgeland-Commons, just off Lake Street in the middle of Oak Park, not far from St. Edmund's but more than a mile away from Ascension, and far from Clarence alley. There was a fall chill in the air, the sky was gray in the late afternoon, and people had to rake the leaves in their yards, and the smell of autumn leaves was cleansing, and the smell of the grass and earth when you rolled on it was fortifying.

The coach blew his whistle. "Listen up. We've got a game coming up with St. Eulalia, and we are going to be ready to play football, you understand me? We are going to block, and we are going to tackle because that, gentlemen, is the game of football. You understand me? In its entirety. Blocking. Tackling. You understand?"

Dan could see that it was going to be important to understand the coach, but it didn't sound like much fun. You take care of blocking and tackling, and the rest will take care of itself. What could that even mean? Football was about dodging people, getting away from them, escaping, outrunning, about throwing and catching, about tight spirals arcing through the sky. Football was a game of skill and coordination and speed and grace and athleticism. The NFL had that contest: Punt, Pass, and Kick. It was a *skills* test.

Now there they were, headed for the blocking sleds. Each was built for two players to put their shoulders to and give it a go. For the first time in his life, Dan plowed his shoulder into a blocking sled, imitating the guys who'd gone ahead of him. He was wearing cheapshit shoulder pads, and it hurt, and he was glad when they switched to something else. Then he found out it was tackling, by way of a tall canvas punching bag you could knock over. That was ok. That was fun. It wasn't that Dan was afraid to tackle, but he didn't much care for head-on collisions, and he didn't want to be steamrolled. He was a pretty good tackler when he could take an angle on the ball carrier, and especially when he ran somebody down from behind, which he discovered he could do just about every time the offense ran a sweep to the opposite side from where he was playing cornerback. One kid's name was Tomasetti, but Coach Payne always called him Tuffinetti because he liked the way he hit.

Cornerback was where the coach put him as soon as the scrimmage began. He must have wanted to find out if Dan could play or not right away. They both found out at the same time. If the play came at him, Dan could side-step the blockers and still manage to pull the ball carrier down at an angle or from behind. If they decided to throw the ball, that was even better, because Dan was a ball hawk.

On defense, things have to remain fairly simple. Since the whole idea is to stop whatever the offense initiates, it doesn't do much good to apply ironclad strategies that ignore what the offense does. Let the offense follow strategy; your job on defense is to mess that strategy up, to disrupt, and you can always just take the ball away from them if you get the chance.

Dan liked all of that, and on a team like this, you could play both ways, play on both offense and defense. So now Coach Payne would see what Dan could do with the ball in his hands.

There were *holes* between each of the offensive linemen, and the holes were numbered.

Numbers! Dan's nemesis. But how hard could it be? After all, they ran the same play over and over again. That's why they called it practice. They would run a sweep to the right, to the right, to the right, then to the left, to the left, to the left. The running back would get the ball in a direct snap from center.

The first time they ran the play with Dan as the running back it was like a dream. He followed his blockers patiently. He was so short that the defenders had a hard time spotting him back there. He hid behind his blockers, and this caused the defenders to hesitate ever so slightly, and that's when Dan got the jump on them. They were all running in one direction in pursuit and running hard, because they knew the play, when suddenly Dan veered back against the grain and cut right through them. He did it again and again.

"We got ourselves a cutback runner," the coach exulted.

Dog Ryan was on the sideline in his dingy uni in the red glow of the September sunset, his helmet off and dangling from the facemask that Doggie gripped with one paw, and he was grinning. He had recruited a cutback runner for St. Edmund's.

The coach took Dan for a look at the game unis, even though he wouldn't be getting one just yet. The jerseys were like those of the Cleveland Browns, white with brown numbers for the road, brown with white numbers for home. The pants were gold. No stripes or piping, just solid, shiny, sleek gold.

"Classy, huh?"

"Yes, sir."

And then Dan fucked it all up by telling the Ascension lads about playing for St. Edmund's and he had invited them to come out to practice at Ridgeland-Commons and join the team, and when they all turned up in their make-shift unis, Shock, Rug Olsen, Gaffney, Jimbo Wilkinson in his high-topped black spikes, Dave Doody, and all the Clarence Alley Boys, the coach took Dan out of the line-up and moved him to the bench, and it occurred to him that perhaps instead of being the greatest football player of all time like Jim Thorpe as played by Burt Lancaster, he would just be an espionage agent like Sean Connery as James Bond.

Danny made the freshman football team at Fenwick, but he only got in for a couple of plays all season, and he only got to line up with the running backs instead of the linemen because one of the assistant coaches had been Ciaran's teammate. Otherwise, he would've been doomed to life as an undersized lineman, good for nothing. Apparently, Dan hadn't done anything to stand out – because they hadn't done anything yet that he was good at – so when it came time to separate the skilled players from the unskilled, Dan ended up with the linemen, instead of with the backs and receivers.

This had all happened before. Danny was playing for the Carroll playground flag football team, and they were losing because they couldn't gain any yards running the ball, and they had no passing attack. Dan was playing center because he was the only kid on the playground who could snap the ball properly. Late in the game, trailing 6-0, Dan convinced the quarterback to try a trick play. Instead of hiking the ball to the quarterback, Dan would just touch the ball to the quarterback's hands and then snatch the ball back and take off.

It worked like a charm. Dan was into the secondary before anybody realized he had the ball.

Then they were after him. They weren't going to catch him, of course. He was as fast as the defensive backs, and he had the jump on them and zipped past them and headed for the endzone, nothing between him and the goal line but open field. There was only one problem: where was the goal line? There were no goal posts. It was just a playground field. So, Dan raced ahead of the horde of tacklers, but to what end? Where was the last yard marker, and didn't he just pass it?

If he hadn't slowed down, they never would've caught him. What Dan thought was the goal line was the ten-yard line. They caught him on the eight. And his team couldn't score from there. They ended up losing 6-0.

In the *Oak Leaves,* the story read: "Carroll Playground threatened late in the contest when Danny Finnegan broke free for an 80-yard run before being caught on the Field Playground 8 yard-line, but Field held on downs and Carroll failed to score."

At least his name was in the paper, not just that, but an 80-yard run! The greatest athletic achievement of his life. "You, sir, are the greatest athlete in the world," and he had fucked it up. It was a joke. They caught him from behind, not because he was slow, not because he was tired, but because he was stupid.

Now he was with the linemen again. He had no chance. It was awful. To play football and not touch the ball was unthinkable. He was doomed.

"Finnegan?"

"Coach?"

"Are you Ciaran's little brother?"

"Yes, Coach."

"Get on over there with the backs. Tell them I sent you."

That was how Dan ended up with the backs. Two hard-nosed runners had the starting backfield spots nailed down. Dan was not a hard-nosed runner. He was a scatback, a shifty runner, like Willie Gallimore, a cutback runner, adept at finding holes in the defense to dart through.

Dan had still been with the linemen when he got his bell rung by Bill Bonuski in the head knocker drill, designed to separate the men from the boys. Two players would line up facing each other between two tackling dummies, get in their three-point stance, and, when the coach blew his whistle, explode into each other, one player trying to block, the other trying to get by, only there was no getting by; you had to go through.

Bill Bonuski was the biggest, strongest, best player on the team. He played defensive end and tight end on offense, which was a waste because Fenwick never threw him the ball. But he was a good blocker, and he lined up opposite Dan and steamrolled him and set his head ringing like a bell clanging, exactly like the opening chords of *Ticket to Ride* over and over and over again. It wouldn't stop. He only wanted to go home and get into bed in a dark room, a black room. It was only later that it dawned on him that he'd had a concussion.

Fuck football. Fuck football? It had been his whole life. No, it wasn't. Nothing had been his whole life. Think about what you're doing. You're abandoning your quest to follow in legendary footsteps, the storied tradition of the mighty men, decades in the making, a long tradition, dating back to the school's opening in 1929, Fenwick football, Follow Fenwick's Fighting Friars, the Chicago Catholic League, the legendary Tony Lawless, Heisman trophy-winner Johnny Lattner, the immortal John Jardine.

Football was a game for somebody who didn't mind getting hit in the head, who didn't mind getting hurt, and Danny did. If he hadn't known it before, Bill Bonuski taught it to him in one smashing lesson. The football fantasy had been years in the making, dating all the way back to Knute Rockne and Jim Thorpe, All-American, as played by Burt Lancaster. It would die slowly and painfully.

Toward the end of the last game of the season, with the game out of reach, Dan Finnegan finally got on the field for a few plays. He trotted out with Ron Principia when St. Phillips punted with just a little over a minute remaining. Principia was deep to field the punt, and Dan was in front of him to block. It should not have been the other way around. Danny was a better runner than Principia, and Principia was a better blocker. Their roles should have been reversed. Instead, the punt sailed over Danny's head, and Principia fielded it cleanly, and here came a guy to tackle him, and Danny was supposed to block him, but he missed, ole, he whiffed, and all he could do was watch helplessly as the guy brought Principia down. Danny would forever be looking over his shoulder at the teammate he had betrayed. Principia was kind of a jerk, but that was beside the point. He was Danny's *teammate*.

On the next play, his first and last in the Friar backfield, Danny got the ball on an off-tackle play up the middle, against a stacked defense, just to run out the clock, yet Danny struggled to make the best of it, gave it the old college try, gave it all he had, even squirmed for an extra yard when he hit the ground. He took the ball on the handoff and dove headlong into the pile, thrashing about, looking for a hole that wasn't there, wriggling and squirming, and the ref whistled the play dead and verbally admonished Dan: "Son, when you're down, you're down." Truer words were never spoken.

CHAPTER TWELVE

F enwick High School opened its doors in September 1929. Twelve
Dominicans. The building was made of granite and limestone. "Fen-
wick, the only high school sponsored by Dominican Friars in America,
a national lighthouse for the Thomist educational philosophy." Thomas
Aquinas was born in 1225 and educated at the University of Paris by
Albert the Great, whom he then surpassed by reconciling Aristotle and
Christianity, with the resulting Catholicism.

In the hallowed halls of Fenwick, sunlight lanced through the
stained-glass windows, featuring Saint Albert the Great, and shone on the
life-size portrait of Saint Ken Sitzberger, in his USA warm-ups and wearing
his Olympic gold medal, and destined to die of cranial injuries suffered
under mysterious circumstances. Turned out he was a huge coke head, and
a drug deal must've gone bad.

The Dominican shield was painted on the locker room wall. The shield
was chiseled into the masonry on the front of the school, protecting the
stone Saint Dominic, as he protected us from sin. The school colors were
black and white. The shield, the colors, the stone, the saint, all-male, like
ancient Spartan warriors.

And maybe the Dominicans did challenge prejudice by setting up shop
in Oak Park, a hotbed of anti-Catholic sentiment. To be a WASP was to be
anti-Catholic. To be an American was to be anti-Catholic. The Chicago

Catholic League was created to promote solidarity and strength among Irish, Polish, and Italian *Catholics*, to bring them together and demonstrate their superiority. Blacks, as always, were an afterthought.

There were as many Black students attending Fenwick in all its history as there were heathens in heaven, and therefore Daniel Finnegan's education had nothing to do with race, nor did his life, because people of other races were not a part of it, except when you walked onto a basketball court or a track or the football field or got on the el or crossed Austin Boulevard. The first Black kid didn't show up at Fenwick till 1955. He didn't come from Chicago. He came from Melrose Park – Pizza Park. The wops had made their own suburban ghetto to keep their Blacks in. If you were Black and you wanted your kid to have a Catholic education, you could send your kid to St. Mel's or St. Phillip's. Not Fenwick.

"The dao is the vast treeless grassy plain of western China. Everything looks the same in every direction all the way to the horizon. Go where you want, as fast or as slow as you like."

The world of the soul. The idea at Fenwick was to always be doing something – before school, during school, after school.

High school seemed filled with enviable lives; it was just that yours was not among them. But Danny could look around and see others who might envy him, and he felt sorry for them, extending his sympathy as well to those who should have envied him, but probably did not. There was Sam Jessup, chubby, unattractive, pasty-skinned, black-haired and hairy, on his back and shoulders too, and going bald already on the top of his pate that encapsulated a highly intelligent brain, a mind at the top of his class in Latin and calculus, while the rest of him was physically weak and uncoordinated, the epitome of the non-athlete, sedentary, dandruffed, pigeon-toed, walking right into one of the Nathan DeGrorio's ad-hominem attacks.

In 1610, Father Sandoval wondered if maybe enslaving Black people might be a sin, so he sent a letter from the Americas to the Pope, and word came back that you could go ahead and buy and sell slaves "without any scruple" as long as it was for the service of the Church. So, by the time Ed Fenwick came along, slavery had the blessing of the Church and the Pope.

The Dominicans were founded by Dominic DeGuzman in 1216. He called it the Order of Preachers. He believed in an educated clergy, so he sent the friars to the great universities of medieval Europe.

What lay behind it, what lurked beneath that big F in the middle of the gym floor, behind the stone facade, the ornate austerity of Aquinas and Aristotle, the Gothic architecture, the shimmering patina of black and white? Fenwick. What was Fenwick? A tradition, an aristocracy of intellect and spirit, humanism raised to divine heights. Bullshit. Not what, but who. Who was Fenwick? Who was Bishop Edward Dominic Fenwick? The first bishop of Cincinnati, we were told, and we pictured him there in Cincy, which must be a city not unlike Chicago, and there he was with his little red cap on his head and wearing his red robes, and he was praying over the hopes of the Cincinnati Reds. You never stopped to think about *when* Ed Fenwick was Bishop of Cincinnati. And what the hell did Cincy have to do with Chi, let alone with Oak Park? The Dominicans wanted to set up shop in Oak Park, where the saloons stopped and the steeples started. It was 1929. What a time to start something, when the economy was about to crash.

What's in a name? Edward Fenwick was born in Maryland in 1768, a little late in the game to acquire sainthood, which was more easily attained by the holy ones living in the murky past when it seems existence was more frequented with miracles than in the periods of history that we actually know something about. Ed Fenwick was born eight years before the American revolution. His parents owned a plantation in the English colony of

Maryland. They were slaveowners. The Fenwicks were devout Catholics who owned slaves. This was entirely possible, plausible, and permissible in 1768, just as it had been in 1668, but it would become problematic by 1868.

At age 16, Ed Fenwick left home to become a priest. While Horace Greeley was advising "Go west, young man," Ed Fenwick did the opposite and headed the other way, to Europe. To Belgium. Ed Fenwick left the USA just as the USA was getting started, ostensibly, to seek European enlightenment.

It's easy for us to rail against slave-masters and to abhor slavery. None of us owns slaves. Most of us have *never* owned slaves. But slavery made this country what it is. Slavery and genocide.

The noble redskin gave his life. The Indians wouldn't *be* enslaved. The Africans sold other Africans into slavery. There were these Muslim traders, see. Spread the blame around, whitey. We were honkies. They were brothers. Not only did Dan not feel a sense of brotherhood with other white men; he was beginning to feel a strong sense of revulsion, aversion.

Here was a guy, Ed Fenwick, everybody's coming to the new world to make their mark, follow their dream, and he goes from America to Europe, becomes highly educated, although nothing of his writing seems to be of note, returns to America, sells the slaves he inherited, and uses the money to establish a priory in Ohio, dancing around the free territories and the slave states, and at the end of this saga of success, Ed Fenwick winds up the Bishop of Cincinnati. How's that for some shit? You can't apply contemporary morality to previous historical periods. But you can find out where the money came from.

In Europe, it would be necessary to learn Latin and Greek as well as French, Spanish, Italian, and German. That was the sort of curriculum that Fenwick, the man *and* the school, would pursue, beginning with mathematics and science. Eddie Fenwick was 16, and he wanted to be a priest. Same as Mean Gene.

Ok, Dan had wanted to be a priest too. He used to come home from Sunday Mass and make his own little altar up in his bedroom and put a cup on the altar to be the chalice, and put a nice cloth napkin over the chalice, folded just right, so the chalice would not be unveiled until that magical moment in the Mass, and Dan would deck himself out as the celebrant, in his makeshift vestments. Dan wanted to be a priest because he liked the costumes and the dramatic ritual, the Roman collar, the red and the black, the hats, mitres, and staffs. Dan wanted to be Pope! He had grown out of that by the time he got to James Bond.

Gene would actually become a priest, would go to Quigley, the seminary school, instead of Fenwick. Mean Gene. Father Mean Gene. Gene and Mary Jule had moved away from Clinton Avenue all the way to somewhere on the south side of Chicago. They were 7 years old at the time, and the south side of Chi was like another continent, deepest darkest Africa. Somehow, while Dan lost track of Gene over the years, Mean Gene had transformed himself from miscreant into man of God. What kind of man of God? Holy Orders. Mean Gene was going to take Holy Orders, when he wouldn't take orders from anybody.

Ed Fenwick was damn near a saint. But how much of a saint could he have been at 16? Maybe he just wanted to get away from home. Go to Europe. Life on the plantation was stultifying. He fancied himself a young man of culture, Aristotle, Aquinas, and higher education. Age 16 would be just about the time Ed Fenwick would be at Fenwick. Add the Aquinas touch, and Ed Fenwick became Fenwick the Friar.

Ed Fenwick sold his slaves. He didn't set them free; he sold them in 1808, when somebody who was damn near a saint should have known better. It was that money that funded Fenwick's Dominican province. By the time Ed Fenwick got to be a bishop, it was well into the 19th century.

Ed's father owned slaves, and Ed inherited some of them. Some, not all. He had to share the family slaves with his brother. Then there was a man named Waller who *sold* Ed some slaves. So, Ed owned slaves, and he bought some more, yet he was damn near a saint.

Consider the historical context of the Dominicans a hundred years or so later, when they built their all-male, all-white school in the all-white Chicago suburb of Oak Park, and they named the school after Ed Fenwick, even though Fenwick owned slaves. Eddie Fenwick owned *people*.

Slaves are people who have been turned into slaves. You don't own slaves. You own people. You treat them as slaves. He enslaved people. He was a slaver. Every slaver coined slavery.

So, when Eddie Fenwick was done inventing slavery for himself, he wanted to use the people he had bought as capital to finance a priory and a school – in service to God and humanity. Do we have a problem here?

Students take time out from their lunch period to visit Our Lord. Our needs are both spiritual and intellectual, and they must be attended to before we develop chronic deficiencies that will turn the rest of our lives into an empty charade. How do we do it? Religion, academics, and athletics, to strive for perfection as sons of God. The City bestows upon youth its greatest challenge and highest responsibility – to fulfill the City's hopes. Fenwick relates Faith to youth and its urban life.

Father Owen Farrell, the hippie priest who was new to Fenwick, took over The *Wick*, the school newspaper. The *Wick* provided an opportunity for students to explore issues and the precepts of journalism. The servers' club would allow you to express your love for God in a most personal manner. You could join the debate club and be like William F. Buckley, Jr. Debate topic: Whether the US should eliminate military assistance to foreign countries. Each side had its debaters. The skill demanded was to be able to argue on either side. The best debater won. Or did the best argument win? Could you argue for slavery and win? Offering military assistance as foreign aid is debatable. Which countries and why? To defend our national interests. Our values. That's where it gets debatable.

Dan quit the football team because he was not a brute. It may have been simply because he was not as brutish and brutal as the other brutes, not big enough, strong enough, although he would always maintain that he was fast enough. He was not a brute. If he were a brute, he would love to hit, love contact, and he didn't, not a bit.

Now, after quitting, Dan awoke every morning with the same intention: Don't do anything today that will make you hate yourself any more than you already do. He would begin with a confession, admitting to himself his hatred for himself. Then he went about separating his self from his life, as if they were separate entities. He didn't hate life, even if he hated his own life. Life was beautiful, life was worth living, if he could only somehow remove himself from the picture. He envisioned life without him, and then life had a fighting chance.

Dan thought quitting the football team was the most heinous act of cowardice imaginable – although he would top it. He thought he had humiliated himself, and he had, but it was indubitably the right choice. It was a choice between having your brain scrambled or not.

There was never any doubt that he would take up another sport – but he wasn't hungering for more humiliation. That was just extra baggage. That was just a choice he made to feel like shit.

He didn't know there was any other way to feel. He hadn't learned enough, hadn't read enough.

Nathan was telling him there was no God, and that made everything permissible, didn't it? Follow your heart. Try out for the basketball team.

It's spring, anything's possible, new life is sprouting. What about basket-ball? Yeah right. What makes you think you can make the team here when you couldn't even make the team at Ascension?

Dan tried out for the basketball team and made the taxi squad, which was separate from the team. It meant you could dress out and attend practice and stand on the sideline, but you didn't even get on the court; you were just there to watch and be ready in case someone got hurt or something.

So, Dan quit that, too. Now he was at Fenwick, and he was a non-ath-lete. Nothing to separate him from Nathan and Sam Jessup or Franklin Bill – except that they were smarter than he was. He was a better athlete than they were, but he didn't *play* anything. Except alleyball. Schoolyard. Playground. Park. Schweez taught Danny the Elgin Baylor shot in the driveway at the hoop mounted above the garage door. Schweez could actually make the shot himself. He learned it from his older brother, who showed him how Elgin Baylor would flip the ball up over his head, with his back to the basket, with Wilt Chamberlain between him and the hoop, blind, and bank it in. This was a shot that could come in handy if you were ever pinned near the hoop by Wilt the Stilt, or maybe the Shocker. It was Schweez who first invented fictional basketball leagues. He would have tournaments in his basement all by himself, being both teams on his tiny court, using a rubber ball that he could palm, and announcing the action, play by play.

The football season was over, and it had been a disaster. Dan was crushed by the reality that he would never be a star running back, he would never be Jim Thorpe All-American as played by Burt Lancaster, that he would sit the bench, suffer more injuries, maybe another concussion, and, worst of all, that it would not be fun, which seemed if not the supreme goal, at least the one you should choose over pain and suffering. Still, there he was at Fenwick, where school spirit was elevated to the spiritual.

The *Tribune* and the *Sun-Times* were lying side by side on the landing at the top of the steps, glistening with flakes of snow. Dan opened the front door and took one icy step outside to pluck them both up, and quickly stepped back inside and closed the door against the winter. When his dad picked up the *Trib*, the sports section would be missing. The *Sun-Times* at least stayed in one piece. The sports pages began at the back, so Dan read the paper in reverse and rarely went past the sports section. That was all he cared about, that and what movies were playing.

Dan started paging through *Time, Newsweek,* and *US News and World Report*, all of which came in the mail, and now Dan himself subscribed to *National Review*, and it thrilled him when it arrived, addressed to him. Nathan DeGrorio, of course, subscribed to *National Review* and *read* it. Dan read Buckley's column, so he could quote him, and he read the movie reviews and the letters to the editor and little squibs, but nothing too taxing on his brief attention span.

The crucial events in his life were things that never happened, all the things he set his heart on, imbued with his imaginative power, circled around endlessly, but when the moment of truth arrived, he turned tail and ran. He was a schlemiel. He was the superfluous man.

Dan's first communion was a debacle, a farce, bordering on sacrilegious – but only as literature, as a story, with Dan as the hero of the story, who has emerged out of history from the 19th century and Ireland and Germany, the nation states, into the middle of America in the middle of the 20th century in the middle of things, written in the middle of the night. It seems right that his faith is shaken, and he is sent spinning between belief and denial.

He is burdened with guilt. He feels responsible for his baby brother's affliction. He feels he caused it by terrifying the infant in his crib, and if that wasn't enough, perhaps he had unconsciously wished for it to happen, out of sibling rivalry. What a putz. He's a little boy, a little red-blooded American racist, homophobic, sexist boy, who wants to be an athlete, an athlete who is secretly an artist, an artist who creates no art, and yet he loves it. It. Art. Sport. Life. God. He wants to be a priest. That too? An actor, a pretender, a liar, a coward, a loser.

But quitting football is a lifesaver, and will become, over time, one of the best decisions he will ever make. It spares him a world of pain, both physical and emotional – because even if he had played on, he wasn't going to supplant the starters in the backfield. The team would have been just as sorry with him on it, the comparison with his brother, the Golden Boy, just as stark. Instead, he gained a lifelong pursuit that would keep him healthy for half a century. It shamed him then, his wise choice, as well it might have, since he didn't choose it out of wisdom. It's a lucky break – quitting football. But there's no such thing as luck. Hazard. Necessity. Contingency. Hegel, Marx. Nietzsche.

This kid Dan doesn't know shit, hasn't read Marx or Proust or Spinoza or the whole Bible. He hasn't paid much attention in school, just enough to get by. 'C' was always good enough. He's horny, he's scared, he's smart enough not to act stupid, he thinks, but that's about it.

All those years, he dreamed of being a Fenwick Friar, and before he knew it, the whole experience turned into a nightmare. There he was, at the all-boys Catholic high school; at least at Ascension, there had been girls, and he could sit in the desk behind Molly Jordan and watch her blue stockinged toes dangling her shoe, and he could see the fine arch of her foot and the round of her heel. At Fenwick, he would just sit there and think of that. He didn't realize that Ascension would fuck him up, and Fenwick would fuck him up exponentially more.

In the *Grundrisse,* Marx is talking to himself, finding a way to apprehend reality, historical reality as a necessity, not a contingency. Nietzsche, from his privileged point of view, sees just the opposite. Contingent means it all depends. It means this depends on that, which could go either way. Necessary means it could and will go only one way. One thing has to happen. Marx is writing for himself, talking to himself, but his mind never strays. He stays on point. Proust would have been reminded of something or other, been led astray, remembering, and then inventing, seeing things through Swann's eyes or Charlus'. Tolstoy can mix the two approaches. And we're always trying to reconcile the two forces, the two personalities, in an effort to see if we can get our friends to be friends. For a while, you could make an effort to like both Buckley and Gore Vidal, but it wouldn't hold up, because *you* were changing, not just shifting and changing sides, but becoming another person. Not only could you not reconcile Buckley to Vidal, get them to patch things up, get them to like one another, you couldn't even get you to like *you.*

Ian Fleming gave birth to his creature when he wrote *Casino Royale,* branding his blunt instrument of a spy with the blandest name he could come up with, cribbed from the book on ornithology he'd just read by James Bond. Dan was theoretically two years older than Bond, but two-year-old Danny Boy would not meet James Bond in the Lamar theater for another decade. Fleming would die, a dozen Bond novels later, living just long enough to go to the movies and see *Dr. No* and *From Russia with Love* and *Goldfinger* and realize he had created a monster.

And it should have ended right there. The books exist entirely separately. The experience of Ian Fleming's novels, the experience of reading them as an adolescent boy sitting amid the shady branches of the tree he had climbed in Fox Park for privacy and meeting there with international intrigue, sex and violence, to be conjured in the imagination solely by the stimulus of the text, Fleming's plotting, and style.

There was something about the books, the good ones, the works of art, classical music, the Bergman movies, naturally, that plunged you into not only thought but sadness, melancholy, and the contemplation of Death. It was fine and beautiful, this life, or that life, your own or that of someone else, someone you loved, and all of it was passing, not just flying by, but flying in all directions, dispersing into the universe, the expanding universe with no center to it.

Nathan DeGrorio was in training to be a film critic. Not a movie reviewer, mind you. He connected with Pauline Kael in the *New Yorker* first, but he was catholic in his reading if not his faith, and it wasn't long before he happened upon John Simon, and Nathan instantly took a liking to Simon's attitude. This man Simon, he *hated*. You can't love the good, he said, without hating the bad. But there's so much more bad than good that you end up hating most of the time. To consider the number of hours spent in the dark, essentially alone, despite being surrounded by an audience of which he considered himself only provisionally to be a member, enduring movie after movie that he would not deign to call film, knowing that he must then re-create the experience on paper for readers so that they would know just how awful it was, there is no escaping the conclusion that John Simon's life, insofar as he was a critic, was pretty miserable, as he became accustomed to greeting each day with the almost certain prospect of more dreck, more execrable viewing, more odious faux entertainment, more balls of shit. He becomes dispirited. The movies he sees and reviews are laughable, but he's not laughing. He doesn't laugh at what's funny; he *appreciates* it. If the work of art is meant to produce an emotional response, and you hate it, has the artist not achieved his goal?

If his goal is to be hated. Is it the purpose of the critic, then, to determine which emotional responses are appropriate? The critic criticizes not just the art and the artist, but also all those who respond to it. The critic doesn't speak for everyone. The critic speaks for God.

James Baldwin went to Sweden to talk to Ingmar Bergman about his movies, leaving behind President Kennedy and the USA, and discovering a world of black and white. "It then occurred to me," he said, "that my bitterness might be turned to good account if I should dare to envision the tragic hero for whom I was searching – as myself. All art is a kind of confession, more or less oblique. All artists, if they are to survive, are forced at last to tell the whole story, to vomit the anguish up."

Susan Sontag was brilliant, beautiful, and young. John Simon was brilliant, charming, and mature; they were both lethal, and they hated each other. Sontag wrote *Against Interpretation*. Simon put it nicely: "Against Interpretation? Might as well say Against Criticism." Dan was taking *Against Interpretation* with him to college, where it would only get him into trouble. Camp. Seeing the world as an aesthetic phenomenon. Her point was that interpretation misses reality.

In their senior year, the students at Fenwick took a retreat. They got on buses and traveled to Lisle, Illinois, and stayed in dorm rooms, one student per room, for the weekend, to enhance the solitary nature of the quest, and Dan had managed to smuggle inside his duffel bag his paperback copy of *The Magus*.

No one knew about it, except Nathan DeGrorio. The hardcover edition of *The Magus* was behind glass in Nathan's bookcase. On its cover was a painting like something out of Bosch, another bit of culture that Dan might otherwise have skipped over like a puddle, had not Nathan indirectly turned him on to it, and then, he found that you do not dip a toe into surrealism. It's all or nothing.

In the book, the narrator, Nicholas Urfe, learns through a bitter, beautiful, and mystifying experience just what Nathan had held all along: life is all that matters. Nicholas is presented with a series of inescapable choices, for which all probable outcomes are bad, so that no matter what he chooses, he loses, so that the challenge of the game is to figure out that it's rigged.

The Magus is a page-turner, and Nathan had turned Dan on to it, so he lay on his cot in the narrow dorm room, and Nicholas Urfe took over, with a name like Franklin Bill, easy to make fun of, and he was a cynic, a nihilist, but he hadn't yet discovered the repercussions of being such. First, he had to discover love. Then it had to be snatched away. And then there he was in Greece, with everywhere white stone, blue water, ancient mythology coming alive, the dream life merging with reality. A line was being drawn, a distinction was being made, that was neither clear nor permanent, between thought and action, mind and body, books and sports, Athens and Sparta. Shadow play. Black and white.

There were prayers and discussions and sitting in a circle, and Father Farrell, the hippy priest, was the moderator, and they tried to make Jesus their friend, and it was all instantly forgettable. What Dan took from the retreat was reading *The Magus*.

Dan had no more idea what *The Magus* meant than the moviemakers who turned it into such a mess that Michael Caine, who played Nicholas Urfe, called it one of the worst movies ever because no one even knew what it was about. Maybe only Nathan did, but that didn't stop it from enthralling Dan, or prevent his retreating to that Greek island and seeing the myths animated and have a weapon forced into his hands and be ordered to kill someone to save his own life, the kind of question that you might by analogy have to answer, to be forced to execute someone or die yourself, so that if you allowed that analogy to work on you, if you followed it through, the existential crisis was happening every moment, and that was why he would feel like he was getting nowhere, even if he were crashing his car at 70 mph down East Avenue into a stoplight.

Nicholas Urfe meets a girl named Allison and shacks up with her, and then a few months later, he breaks up with her and takes a teaching job in Greece. He's an antihero. Everything about him says that he is, and he knows it. All of which resonated with young Dan, even though he had never slept with a girl, let alone shacked up with one; all those fuckups lay ahead of him. A self-fulfilling prophecy. The tone is confessional. Nicholas Urfe whips his former self for the sin of pride, as well as ignorance, blindness, insensitivity, and cowardice. Dan didn't like him either, but he knew how he felt.

The lines from "Little Gidding" that intrigue the narrator echoed in Dan's head: "We shall not cease from exploration/ and the end of all our exploring/ will be to arrive where we started/and know the place for the first time."

What makes *The Magus* metafiction is that you have an authoritative character in the novel espousing the thesis that the novel is dead. And Nicholas or Nick or Nicko gets the idea that the Magus might be Death. Death, remember, who played chess with the Knight on the shore in *The Seventh Seal*.

There was the cover art on the hardcover edition of *The Magus*, a copy of which stood behind glass in Nathan's bookcase in his bedroom alongside the expressway. Dan wanted to exist among those masks in that masque, and mix with sex, and running went with that, with Greeks, and even long hair, but football did not. Football went with war.

Everything about Urfe's encounter with the Magus bespeaks the central fact of his life, which is that he has nothing better to do. *The Magus* contained a powerful anti-war message: Stay alive. It wasn't pure cowardice, because nothing was pure; it only meant live and let live. Which is fine, provided you're not in a piece of aluminum hovering fifty feet above guys with weapons trying to kill you.

Conchis escaped the battlefield by falling down and playing dead, and then he ran away and sneaked back home. He confesses this to Nicholas. He takes over the narrative with his story within a story of World War I and his girlfriend, Lily. Conchis was a deserter in World War I, and he wants us to feel sorry for him. Nicholas is prepared to do just that. He understands desertion. So did Dan. He was transforming from hero into antihero.

Captivated by Lily, Nicholas is all set to dump Allison, but he's got to know if Lily really likes him. He needs to know if a girl likes him. It's the sort of thing an eighth grader would need. Even Fowles admitted that the novel met the needs of a teenage boy's psyche. Nicko is horny, he fucks around, he smokes cigarettes, he has no family, he is completely independent, free to fall in love on an island in the blue Aegean. He's abusive and misogynistic, and although he might confess to the former, he is blissfully unaware of the latter. Nicko is a cad.

The reason *The Magus* made such an impression on Dan was not that he devoured its 600 pages in one weekend during what was supposed to be a religious retreat, but rather that the book devoured nearly a year of his life. As the mysteries deepened for Nicko, Dan grew into young manhood, a place where you find that you both belong and do not. What are you, queer?

The question of whether Dan was queer had to overcome the hurdle of why he liked girls so much. On the other hand, in order to conceive of oneself as desirable to the object of desire, one must consider as desirable a member of one's own sex, oneself, one's self.

"Member. Good one."

If *The Magus* was telling Dan his life story, holding up a mirror to his future, he'd see his own pursuit of mysteries, each ending in maddening futility. Nicholas Urfe was an unwilling actor. Nicko does some fancy footwork to tell us he's a coward. He even confesses this to the girl of his dreams, but only to get in her pants. He wants her and us to believe he must really be a hell of a guy, owning up to all his faults like this. He wants to tell us the truth and have us believe it's really a lie.

It was either a great work of art or it was silly. Sounds like the Bible. Fowles himself called *The Magus* adolescent. Exactly. That's when shit happens. You're unsure of almost everything, everything's a mess, and the few things you are certain about are completely wrong.

Franklin Bill was playing chess. He was an excellent player. It didn't matter. It wasn't just that this kid's name was Franklin Bill, two first names, that made him ripe for derision, it was being overweight and not seeming to care about that or that his hair was greasy and kept shading one eye, or that he wore black-rimmed glasses that he kept having to push back on the bridge of his nose, it was that he insisted on being called Franklin and not Frank, and so kids heralded him with *Frank-lin* as they beat the shit out of him.

Chapter Thirteen

They were putting on a play for Nicko. He had a role to play, and maybe that was all Dan was doing, playing a role. In fact, he had many roles. Everyone did. The best you could do was try to be one thing *at a time*, but even that was not always possible, so you had to hope your roles did not conflict; otherwise, you could turn into your own worst enemy, which was exactly what was happening to Dan.

At any given moment, someone acting a role is no longer acting. At any given moment, it doesn't matter whether someone is acting a role or not. There was a difference between pretending to be something and really being that thing, but if, in a moment, the line could be crossed, and they were the same, a unity of opposites, being and pretending, then what?

"What makes you think you could be an actor? "

"That's just what it's called. "

"What do you call it? "

"It's just wanting to be someone else."

The antiwar movement was fueled by a generation of pussies who didn't want to fight, who didn't have the balls, the spoiled brats, faggots. Now we're onto something. Or back where we began.

In *The Magus,* there was not just more sex than Danny-boy had ever imagined, there was all the sex he *had* imagined, which made its reading engrossing, the kind, it has been observed, that might be done with one hand. It was an occasion of sin. It was quite an occasion. On more than one occasion. More than occasionally. Perpetually and ever after.

Those lines from *Little Gidding* – what kind of faggot crap was that? T.S. Eliot. That quote. It was underlined in the book Nicko found on the beach, the book Lily left for him to find, the first scene in the elaborate masque, with its unmistakable message: This is a wild goose chase.

That's not what the quote said at all. It said we shall explore without end until we finally arrive at the place where we started, and we will know it for the first time. We will know it. We *will* know. We *will*.

Nicko inspired hatred for Oak Park and everything it stood for. So did Hemingway. "Is that how one learns?" Nicko asks. "By marrying and having a family? A steady job and a house in the suburbs? I'd rather die." He held it in contempt. But everything that Nicko recounts is meant to show us how wrong he was about everything. Wrong about Allison. Wrong about himself. He was not at all the person he had imagined himself to be, more than that, *thought* himself to be. The image he held in his mind of himself was not who he was at all. He would never have found himself in a crowd.

You will never be at peace. You will never be happy. Truly happy. What is truth? Truly sappy. Veritas. Turning everything into black and white.

The all-white boys' Catholic high school in the all-white village. There was nothing any one of them could do about it. They had no control over having been born white or being where they were. They were not free agents. If they were, Nathan would have transferred to Oak Park High, but he couldn't. Why? Why couldn't he? He was Nathan DeGrorio, wasn't he? He slammed the door in his mother's face. Why couldn't he tell her he was transferring to Oak Park High? Sounds like bullshit.

Black and white are contradictions. They contradict each other. Black and white and color are contradictions. They contradict each other.

Dan was full of contradictions. They were pulling him apart. Of course, everyone was full of contradictions, and everyone *is* full of contradictions, and that's where a mirror comes in handy because it can show you just how things are, things you could not see or know otherwise.

Remember, you're looking at a mirror-image where everything is reversed, and your eye is pulling some kind of trick too because everything is really upside down.

Theirs were all lives not of quiet desperation but muffled. That's why it's called the suburbs. The Finnegans were the first generation of suburbanites, a phenomenon of America in the mid-twentieth century. It was all brand-spanking new. The wealth of nations. Look in Dad's wallet. Look at all that change in the porcelain pup. With the money he stole, Dan would be parsimonious, he would be shrewd, he would buy two boxes of plain popcorn instead of one of buttered popcorn at the movies, which he attended by himself, after the fashion of Nathan DeGrorio. Contradiction: if you wanted to be like Nathan DeGrorio, you had to be without Nathan DeGrorio.

All the while, there was a tapestry being woven, a montage, in black and white and color, with a soundtrack and hit songs and movie stars as well as sports stars. The ambiguous ending of *The Magus*. The ambiguous ending of *Citizen Kane*. What does it all mean? What do you want it to mean? If it can mean *anything*, then what does it *matter*? Is that the same question, or another one? Was this a loss of innocence or a loss of ignorance? Either way, there was no going back. Once you've lost it, you turn into something else. Complicit. You know too much. You're becoming disillusioned. Becoming? You've been telling yourself you didn't do anything wrong, but you were doing everything wrong, and at the same time something horrible, history, was being done to you and everyone else. You didn't have a prayer of sorting it all out. No one did. Not Nicholas

Urfe on his island, nor Bergman on his, but getting high didn't seem like all that bad an idea, and the more tempting it got, the more it seemed like sin. Thank God, sin was going to go out the door with God. She came in through the bathroom window. Lady Madonna. Eleanor Rigby. Lovely Rita, Meter Maid.

"I had a wonderful novel to write about Oak Park but never would because I did not want to hurt living people." – Hemingway

There were quail and red-tailed foxes on the prairie then. You could find arrowheads and spearheads and even axe heads in mounds made by the Potawatomie along the Des Plaines River. Ernie walked all over town. He walked down Euclid Avenue all the time, so he walked by the Euclid castle, and you'd see him pass right beneath Dan's bedroom window on the second floor, Ernie and his mates trooping along beneath the cathedral arches of the oaks, heading for the woods.

There was Hemingway on the Oak Park Huskies wrestling team and the swimming team and the football team, and then he took up boxing and then fighting marlin in the Gulf. Would you get in the ring with Papa? Are you willing to fight a ghost?

Hemingway was the starting center for the Huskies junior varsity football team, and the team went 7-1 in the *Suburban League*, which is impressive. In his senior year he played for the varsity, but he wasn't a starter. In fact, the captain of the team called him Lard-Ass.

Hemingway went to Oak Park High, played a little football, and lettered on the *wrestling* team, so he was tough. Hemingway was 6-2, but he wasn't 6-2 as a freshman, not when he was just 15. Maybe he was 6 feet when he started high school. Hemingway had covered this same terrain where Dan rode his bike to Thatcher Woods, and later, in high school, when the harriers ran there, along the paths by the Des Plaines River, that was where Ernie used to forage and fish in the river. Ernie had done that right here. When Dan and the guys ran along the railroad tracks, they followed Ernie's footsteps.

Hemingway graduated from Oak Park High and left Oak Park in the summer for a job on the *Kansas City Star*, and in six months, he learned to write according to the Star's style sheet. Uncle Tyler in Kansas City got him the job. Hemingway set a pattern. Eighteen years in Oak Park, then split.

Ernie had an older sister. Oh boy, did he have an older sister. Marceline was stronger, faster, smarter. She went to college. Ernie never really considered going to college. Ernie went to Kansas City to be a reporter. He'd learn how to write journalism first, before learning how to write fiction, their main difference being staying power.

Ernie was in Kansas City when his dad, Doc Hemingway, sent his son the current issue of the *Oak Leaves* with the news from back home. Ernie wanted those *Oak Leaves*. He wanted to know what was going on back there in Oak Park, and how the football and wrestling teams were doing. But that was all.

Ernie's dad, the doctor, the head of obstetrics at Oak Park Hospital, wanted Ernie to go to Oberlin College, like his sister, or he could go to the U of I in Champaign. Or, Ernie thought, why not just get a job writing for the *Tribune*? Ring Lardner was writing for the *Tribune*, and Ernie could write like Ring Lardner, in a voice that sounded like Ring Lardner. He could write like Sherwood Anderson, too. Ernie could write so much like Sherwood Anderson that he would write *The Torrents of Spring* and make him look like a fool.

Ernie came home to Oak Park from the war, wounded, traumatized, and in love. And then she casually mentioned in a letter that, oh yes, her former fiancé had re-entered the picture. She was shacking up in Italy with a rich wop. Sucker. Three months later, Ernie gets another letter from her.

The wop dropped her. Said she was an American adventuress. But now she wants back with Ernie. She can go fuck herself.

Ernie and his buddy Bill Horner rent an apartment at 1230 N State Street, near Lincoln Park. Ernie is going to be a serious writer, not just a newspaperman. He is figuring he could substitute his war experience for a college degree. No professor could teach you the shit Ernie had learned in a week in the trenches. Ernie had a diploma in shrapnel, and he was reading hot new poetry by Pound and Eliot. And then Ernie meets another older woman to fall in love with. The first one was 7 years older, and this one was 8. Just saying. Another rich broad.

Ernie would punch your lights out if he heard you say it, but to call it like it is, Hadley was a drip, a sucker. Agnes would keep him guessing, but this broad was easy; he could play her, not the other way around, and she got him introduced to Sherwood Anderson.

Hadley might have been from St. Louis, but she was indistinguishable from an Oak Park girl, *north* Oak Park that is. Hadley would be 30 by the time she married Ernie, good and desperate. What's he, feel sorry for her?

Ernie was 21, but he was as grown up as anyone who'd been to college and graduated, due to his wartime and journalistic experience, but now he was working for this bullshit advertising firm downtown in Chicago. His new girlfriend Hadley gets the two of them invited to a party on the north side, where they meet this guy Sherwood Anderson who's just getting famous for his fiction, and he happens to write like Ernie does, so Ernie thinks, or as he's trying to, simpler, straighter, sharper. Great. But how's he going to eat? That's what Ernie wants to know: how do you support a wife? A guy's got to support his family. The thing was, he didn't want to be here anymore, not Chicago, not Oak Park certainly, not even the good old USA. He wanted to get back to Italy. Ernie was an artist, and that was what made him distrustful of both journalism and the ad agency, and Oak Park, where the saloons stop and the steeples start, Saints' Rest.

The big fight was coming up, the heavyweight championship bout between the champ, Jack Dempsey, and the Frenchman Georges Carpentier. Dempsey was a barroom brawler who had beaten the piss out of the giant Jess Willard to win the belt. Ernie bet $700 on Carpentier. What a sap!

Ernie was staging his own boxing matches on the roof of the apartment building downtown on State Street, where he was rooming with two other guys. They'd go up on the roof, and they'd box. To Gertrude Stein and the arts crowd in Paris, Ernie was a rube, not because he was from Oak Park, but because he hadn't gone to college. Yeah. Ever hear of the College of Hard Knocks?

Ernie, however, was not a rube. It wasn't just being from *north* Oak Park that made him *not* a rube; it was having been in *war*. Somebody might know a lot more about something than he did, but nobody knew more about being alive than somebody who'd been in *war*.

"I had seen nothing sacred, and the things that were glorious had no glory and the sacrifices were like the stockyards at Chicago if nothing was done with the meat except bury it."

You can hear the Chicago in his voice when he says, "*at* Chicago".

Begin again and concentrate. That was Gertrude Stein's advice to young Ernie after she'd read his stories and must've thought they were shit. Funny thing is, Ernie didn't tell her right then and there to go fuck herself. Instead, he began again and concentrated. You'd think he would've told her to go fuck herself. After a while Ernie did tell her to go fuck herself, although he apparently didn't have the balls to say it to her face.

Dan was coming of age in the Affluent Society, where it was natural to act like an arrogant asshole. That was Dan's excuse, but just one of Dan's excuses. What was he supposed to do?

Stop the spread of communism.

Exactly how do you propose to do that? By sending in troops? By force? And that's going to what? Communism must be something you could fight. We had stopped the spread of fascism in just this way. All it took was World War Two. So that was how and why his brother was going to wind up in Vietnam, flying a helicopter.

Mind and body. The aesthetes and the jocks. The draft dodgers and the baby killers. There was no in-between, no compromise. The enemy were gooks, less than human, but if that were true, why would we give a shit about saving their gook country? Someone on your team, a teammate, a comrade on the battlefield, someone who fought alongside you, who risked his life along with you, he wasn't going to betray you and trick-fuck you the way your intellectual and artistic friend would.

Guys went over, got shot at by gooks, and shot back, and started hating gooks, started killing gooks indiscriminately, soldier, civilian, man, woman, young, old, and they hated the war, and they hated anyone who wanted to stop the war. No one could think straight. This could not have been the way the world looked to Dan's mother because she was the mother of a son in combat, and on the front door of the brick castle on the corner of Euclid and Van Buren, by which all must pass on their way to church, hung the emblem and star that meant a soldier came from here.

To choose between Nixon and Humphrey, between war this way and war that way, was no choice at all. Dan wasn't old enough to vote. You had to be 21 to vote. And since he couldn't vote, what did it matter? Either way, the war was going to go on. Dan didn't protest the war. His big brother was fighting in the war. No, he wasn't fighting – he was flying. He ever fire a shot in anger? Don't know. Ever fire a shot? Doesn't talk about it. He was flying a helicopter; he wasn't shooting at anybody. One time, Ciaran said something about the war. He said that you never get over the shock that someone you don't even know is trying to kill you. Their intent. On the surface, absurd. Why are you shocked – you're invading their country? But on the sensory level, this is the way the human mechanism reacts to war, and it is not good. None of it is.

The 60s started out with Kennedy as President, but that didn't last for long. Johnson had to finish Kennedy's term. Then Johnson ran against Goldwater and clobbered him. But the next four years were enough to make Johnson puke, that is, to make him quit. He didn't seem to be able to get us out of the mess that Kennedy had gotten us into in Vietnam. Where? Why? So, Johnson quit after one term. Gene McCarthy started running in March. Then Bobby Kennedy announced he was running. Johnson dropped out, and Humphrey jumped in. All of that allowed Nixon to creep back into the picture. Where was Charley Clover picking his nose now?

Speaking of gross, Dan's pen pal was running for President, too. George Wallace. When it was Goldwater against Johnson, Nathan DeGrorio was pulling hard for Goldwater. It wasn't the same as when everybody at Ascension, besides Charley Clover, was for Kennedy, the *Catholic*.

The whole school wasn't going to get behind Johnson the way it had Kennedy, but nobody, except Nathan, was *for* Goldwater. And with all this shit going on, Johnson versus Goldwater, Vietnam, Cuba, all that, Bobby Kennedy was *fucking* Susan Sontag. Art and politics intertwined, like Michael Caine and Candace Bergen on the cover of the paperback promoting the movie of *The Magus* that even they couldn't figure out.

The Magus was exactly the wrong book to read on the senior retreat if you wanted to find God, and it was exactly the wrong book to read if you wanted to support the war in Vietnam. Dan didn't support the war. He wasn't for the war. He couldn't defend the war, and wasn't about to.

Barry Goldwater said to bomb the hell out of 'em. Buckley didn't even think Goldwater was all that smart. Good man, on the right side, but not all that smart. Buckley was willing to go to war over going to war. Goldwater lost in forty-four states. During the campaign, it was fun to be for Goldwater because nobody else was. It made you stand out. You knew what AU/H2O stood for, just like UNCLE.

What sort of role model was Nicholas Urfe, or John Fowles, for that matter? They were very different people, not to speak of the fact that one was real, and the other was not. Nicholas Urfe was the creature of John Fowles, and a mere fantasy, sort of an antihero, *sort of*, because he speaks to the reader as though he has our sympathy and understanding, but he is not likable. He's trying to tell us how he has been humbled, but he is still arrogant and conceited. Dan didn't see it that way. Instead, he read with a kind of foreboding, a vague sense that what happened to Nicko in the book was going to happen to him in real life. Metaphorically speaking.

He would, though not on a Greek isle, discover himself to be a cad, to practice to deceive, but, above all, to be deceived, to deceive himself, to be the fool. It didn't take a magus for him to be revealed. He could see himself because he was willing to look in the mirror, but he had to look closely, and that meant missing everything that was going on in the background.

Now, to bring it forward. Dan had no way of knowing it, though you could have convinced him of it in a minute, but the whole Cold War was bullshit, a monstrous waste of time, money, energy, and lives.

Look at what was happening to Cuba, and to the sprawling Soviet Union and its satellites. The Cubans had been cut off from all trade with America, left to live on leftovers, and the Soviets were plowing their economy into a military that served no purpose but to suck the life out of *itself*, while America could always sell more shit and learn to live on shit and love it. The Soviets were doomed.

Buckley started *National Review*. It blithely answered the leading question: Why the South Must Prevail? by clearly stating: "The claims of civilization supersede those of universal suffrage." Buckley thought that racism would save the world from communism because, in the end, the difference between the Soviets and Red Chinese was that the Soviets were white, and the Chinese weren't. They would not in the end abide one another. So, Buckley saw the Soviets ultimately as our allies because we're both white.

It was March and cold, and Johnson went on TV and said, "There is division in the American house right now." Then he quit. He wasn't running for re-election. He was out. McCarthy and Bobby could fight it out. Four days later, Martin Luther King was shot to death. To Black people, the message was: "You tried non-violence, and this is how it works." Riots broke out in more than a hundred cities. In Chicago, DeMare gave an order to shoot to kill. "As long as I'm mayor of this city, there's going to be law and order in this city," sez DeMare.

Gene McCarthy wanted to end the war. He was *going* to end the war and pull our troops out *now*. But he couldn't even get the nomination, much less get elected. Humphrey was going to end the war as soon as he could do so *within reason*, but he didn't win. Nixon won and took the war up a notch.

Bill Ayers at least knew that the war was bad enough that you should do something about it. Dan was oblivious. He had his mind on other things.

There were girls whose names you forgot or never knew, nameless girls, like you were some kind of Don Juan, and you weren't, you were just too shy to ask their name, or you didn't really listen when they said it and instantly forgot it, not that there were that many of them, in fact there were only two that he could think of that he could not name – and that girl who let him put his arms around her and place his hands on her belly in her sleek white translucent one-piece swimming suit while standing behind her waist deep in Ridgeland-Commons pool, yes, he remembered that in sensual detail, but not her name, and the girl who had asked him to the Trinity sophomore prom. The prom! What a cad he was. Couldn't even remember her name? Why? Because he had treated her like such shit. Blotted her name out of guilt. She had a little bit of a mustache going, but no, she had done nothing to be treated like that. Another good reason for sending Dan to Hell, if you happened to be God and looking for a reason, which is absurd because if you were God, you would be reason itself.

He never saw her again. It was a shitty thing to do. Kind of thing only an asshole would do. Sitting in the car, not talking to her – because he knew he was going to hurt her, and he was sorry. Sorry for something that hadn't even happened yet. Sorry because he knew it was going to happen, and he was covered in guilt and shame, and it was sticking to him, and he couldn't get it off, not then, not ever.

Chapter Fourteen

We don't mean to hold Dan's immaturity against him. Of course, he's immature; he's a kid. But the world he lives in is not a kid. In that world, there's a war in Vietnam, and riots in Chicago, where racism and the expressways cut through a crumbling west side by way of the Eisenhower and south along the Dan Ryan, where Mayor Daley rules, all that has no excuse for being immature.

We read the Bible, the Old Testament, and we identify with Moses and the Israelites, as we would with the protagonist of any story. But if we are not Jews, if we are not the descendants of those ancient Israelites, then are we not the descendants of the people they opposed, their enemies, and of people all the world over who were not Jews?

James Baldwin recalled how, as a youngster, he would watch Hollywood westerns, and it only gradually dawned on him that as a Black man he had more in common with the savage redskins being conquered than with John Wayne. Dan had more in common with pagans who worshipped Baal. It was very confusing. Jesus said the spirit is willing, but the flesh is weak, and the runners answered him that we will make the flesh as strong as the spirit.

The getting of treasures by a lying tongue is a vanity tossed to and fro of them that seek death. – Proverbs 21:6

A tissue of lies. Living tissue. The only way for him to be honest would be to admit that he was not honest. You can't be honest by lying. But by lying, you may become honest. If you pretend to be a good student, to act like one, your actions may be indistinguishable from those of a real good student or a thief or a lover. They are the same, identical. Then you are a good student or thief or lover. What began as a lie becomes the truth.

Sophistry? Bullshit? Was Dan two people, schizophrenic, bi-polar, multiple personalities? Or did he just want to become something other than himself? Or was he perfectly normal, whatever that meant?

He was definitely fucked up – because everyone was. Every human being that was alive in that moment in history was out of their mind if they could rationalize and reconcile themselves to the fact that Death was stalking them, while at the same time, they were hating and killing or praying. Death!

Homer enjoins us in *The Odyssey* to *live as one already dead*. What can this mean? It suggests that we view our life as an event of the past, over which we no longer have any control, and the most we can apply to it is our feelings, memories, recreate it as we will, and to reflect upon it all as something we did or something that happened to us that we regret or gave us joy or sadness, pride, embarrassment, the good, the bad, to accept, not to judge, but to confess, and then, to live as if seeing all there is from beyond the grave, all those you love, which can only make you love them more, and the more love you have, the more powerful you are, the more alive. To live as one already dead is, in a sense, to have conquered Death.

Ethics. How to live. That's probably a good thing to figure out. That's what this book is about. *In Black and White and Color*. There is no distinction between nature and the supernatural. They are the same thing. There is no supernatural in the sense that it is beyond nature. But there is a supernatural in the sense that it includes and is included within nature.

"Artists do not stem from their childhood, but from their conflict with the mature achievement of other artists; not from their own formless world, but from the struggle with the forms which others have imposed on life." – Andre Malraux, *Psychology of Art*

Daniel was an artist. He may not have been a very good one, but he was an artist nonetheless, and his world had *no* form. He was in conflict with the forms imposed on his life, the ones that kept shifting the focus, that kept the kaleidoscope flashing from black and white to color.

Malraux's theory is contra-Freud. Is not childhood the heart of art? That was where it all came from, the essence of personality, of being. Instead, all shaped by art? Isn't it pretty to think so?

He was a bad artist because he closed his eyes. He was a bad artist because he hadn't written anything, painted anything, acted any role except in deceit, deceiving himself.

Live. Breathe. Everything is moving, becoming. It was becoming when all those world events took place, and the repercussions would shape your life, and you didn't even know it was happening. Hiroshima. Before Dan's time. The bombing of Dresden. That happened- to Kurt Vonnegut, he of the craggy face and mustache, Twain-like, whose science fiction was before its time, who was against the war in Vietnam.

Wait a minute. There's a war in Vietnam? What for? Exactly. You even know where Vietnam *is*? It's in Southeast Asia. You know how we know? Because of the war there. That's how Americans learn geography.

When Ciaran got back from boot camp at Quantico, he would walk down Van Buren to Oak Park Avenue and look at the houses and say to himself, "There are normal people in there, living normal lives." That sense of strangeness came just from *starting* to become a Marine. He had yet to go to Vietnam.

The troops were being exposed to Agent Orange, which would not only give them cancer but would also cause diseases and disorders in their spouses and children. Ciaran went to war. He was a second lieutenant in the Marines, a helicopter pilot, not someone who dropped bombs on people. A helicopter dropped you off somewhere in the jungle where no plane could land, or a helicopter saved your ass when it dropped down out of the sky and got you out of a tough spot, retrieved wounded. Ciaran was no war monger, but he was a sharpshooter and had a sharpshooting medal. So did Oswald.

Ciaran would rise to the rank of Captain. If you were a Captain in the Marines, you were the true gen of Not to be Fucked with. Something Dan had known all along. "Too bad about the Lane game."

It was winter, and Danny was nine years old and in the third grade, and his big brother, a senior at Fenwick, was walking him home from school. It was a few weeks after the Friars had been crushed in the snow in Soldier Field in front of 90,000 people by Lane Tech 19-0. It was Coach John Jardine's first Prep Bowl, and the Friars ran into the Public League champions that had eliminated Vocational High and Dick Butkus.

Danny slipped on the ice and fell, and some kids on the other side of the street laughed, and Danny's books and papers were scattered in the snow, and Ciaran was helping him up. They were teenagers, high school kids, three guys from Oak Park High who thought they could say whatever they wanted because there were three of them, and, besides, they were all the way across the street, so one of them shouted, "Too bad about the Lane game."

Ciaran looked up, and then he took off, sprinting straight for the hecklers, who paused fatally before attempting to scatter. Most people when they run curl their hands into a loose fist that tightens slightly with speed and adds force to the pumping of their arms, which helps lift their feet and thereby run, but not Ciaran, who ran with his fingers extended straight out and his hands became axe blades that cleaved the air with an amazing rapidity that produced *speed*. Ciaran tackled one of the guys and rubbed his face in the snow, as the other two ran off, and then he stood back up, brushed the snow off his pants, and walked with sure steps back across the street to where Danny was watching and holding his books.

"You ok?"

"Yeah."

"Let's go home."

And so they did, or maybe it never happened. Maybe Dan just made it up, a story he could tell about Ciaran to ward off bullies. Maybe something like that incident in the snow happened, but probably nothing approaching Dan's rendition of the incident took place. He just made it all up. He just made up shit all the time.

"Why? Why do you just make up shit all the time?"

"I don't know."

And that was a lie, too. He made things up to mess with time, to alter the past and shape it into something he could use now. See, if this happened, which it didn't – but pretend it did, then. And in this way, you could proceed indefinitely in an advanced state of fantasy, adorned with specific sensory details, the snow, the night, the books and papers, even the dialogue. All of it is bullshit.

Ways to amuse yourself. It was snowing hard, and the wind was blowing, so the snow would whack you in the face. The Rope Trick! Here's what you do: it's a snowy night. Snowflakes falling in the darkness, and a car's headlights beam through the white flakes. Lovely. Meanwhile, there are a couple of kids in the street on one side and a couple on the other, and they look like, what the hell? Hey! What you do is you *pretend* you're holding a rope. And this is funny? Hell yeah, it's funny. Look how mad they are. Come on! And then you run away.

William F. Buckley's theatricality struck a nerve in Dan, just as the priests celebrating Mass did, and Kirk Douglas did, playing Spartacus, Burt Lancaster as Jim Thorpe, All-American, and, above all, in print and on-screen, James Bond. Dan didn't want to be Bond, which would have scared the shit out of him, but acting, pretending, that seemed to be right up his alley. The beauty of it was that it could happen almost entirely within your own mind, sometimes with the aid of a mirror or glass you could see yourself in, sometimes by drawing pictures or by writing a story, or inventing fictional players to play in fictional leagues with fictional standings and statistics and imaginary games, all of which he would doodle at during class instead of paying attention. Pretending, making up shit, lying, faking, deceiving, disappointing, and disappearing, that's what he was good at; he had a real gift for it. Dan could pretend to be a hero, but he would be much more believable as a schmuck. He was no Sean Connery, let alone Kirk Douglas or Burt Lancaster, while his brother Ciaran lived in reality a Hollywood action pic, and followed up his stint in Vietnam, where he flew over 700 combat missions, by joining the FBI. War hero becomes an FBI agent. Beat that.

There was no way to beat it, any more than there was of Dan sticking a harpoon in Moby Dick. It wasn't about supporting the war; it was about doing your duty. So, you put the question of supporting the war or protesting the war out of your head. Not to reason why, but to do and die. Vietnam was turning into the Charge of the Light Brigade.

Besides, no one was asking Dan to support the war *or* protest it. The whole thing couldn't touch him till he turned 18, and by then it would probably be over, and even if it wasn't, he'd be in college with a deferment till he graduated four years later, and surely the war would be over by then. If Ciaran wanted to go wading into battle, that was his business.

"Your brother's over there."

Ciaran was featured in a *Tribune* series, *Our Men in Vietnam*, recounting his combat missions, air medals, and Purple Heart, and his play as a Friar football player. He'd been shot? No one knew until he got home. Shrapnel. Where? Where do you think? He's flying a helicopter. It's like he's sitting on top of the enemy.

The Great Pretender. That was what his mother called Danny-boy. It was also the title of a movie starring Danny Kaye. Danny Finnegan was the Great Pretender Manque. But all these alternate lives he was living were horrendous at heart. It would be awful to be Jim Ryun, really – for Dan anyway. It would be hell to be James Bond. How could he sleep at night? All the great basketball players were too tall to live a normal life. Football scrambled your brain. To be Buckley, you'd have to have read all those books and still come out of it wrong on the most basic questions, like: Are Black people human beings?

The movement, the peace movement, the mass movement was to move the nation out of war, was to remove the war machine from Vietnam, but it was going to take time, a long time, when a year is a twelfth of your life or a sixteenth or a twentieth, *years* of protest would have to take place.

Downtown, it was all happening downtown. "And it's one, two, three, what're we fightin' for? Don't ask me, I don't give a damn; next stop is Vietnam!" Buckley and Vidal were losing control just watching the convention from their swivel chairs. The whole world was watching what was happening downtown and on the lakefront in Lincoln Park. A huge anti-war protest timed to blend in with the attention given to the Democratic convention had met with DeMare's ire, and there was hell to pay. Father Farrell, the hippy priest, was going down there. To Lincoln Park for the demonstration, the protest to stop the war, DeMare was gonna call the goon squad out on all those people. "For God's sake, father, don't go in there!" And Father Farrell said, "For God's sake, I am going in there."

Terry Flaherty's dad had been mugged downtown by some Black guys, and that turned the whole Flaherty family virulently racist. Their prejudice appeared and shortly thereafter Connor was downtown, heading home after work, and had just taken a seat on the el when a Black man reached through the window from the platform and tried to grab the watch from off his wrist, unsuccessfully, only nobody in the family would think of calling him a Black man, no, they said *nigger*, it was right there, anytime, anywhere, under your breath if need be, but audibly too, *aloud*, to the point where kids said it so much, even if you were racist you got sick of hearing it, and didn't want to say it anymore yourself. It was like they were obsessed with it. Couldn't they think about anything else? Who goes around thinking about Negroes all day? Because, in Danny's world, you could easily go *years* without seeing a Black person *in person*.

Emmett Till left Chicago for a short vacation to visit his cousins in Money, Mississippi, and he came back in an open casket with his face so mushed up and misshapen, his eyes were about to pop out, and young Cassius Clay looked and looked at Emmett Till lying in a box like that.

Benny Kid Parrot was killed by Emile Griffin in the ring, and it was plain to see what a pitiable thing boxing had wrought, and yet it would never die. But for Danny, there was a distinctly different tone to the boxing world after Benny Kid Parrot was killed on TV. Danny and Schweez watched it together on TV in Schweez's basement rec room, a man being killed with punches.

It took a couple of years, but the Cubs finally started to turn things around, and they finished third in the 10-team National League. First time in the first division since 1946. The Cubs' story builds to their collapse. It takes 18 years, as long as it took Sophocles to write *Oedipus Rex*, as long as it will take Dan to get out of Oak Park.

The Cubs were too good to be true. But to Dan, they looked like world beaters. He didn't know that Ernie Banks was washed up. Didn't know Leo the Lip was wearing out his starters. Didn't know that the clubhouse was a snake-pit. There was this surge of hope, of great anticipated relief, the skies about to break open and pour down the welcome rain after a long, long drought; generations had passed, and now there was thunder and lightning. But the Cubs were going to burn out like a cigarette butt tossed in the street.

Ernie Banks, Mr. Cub, said, "Let's play two." And it was ninety-six degrees in Wrigley. Durocher imploded, and so did the Cubs. Leo Durocher went off on Ernie Banks, said he couldn't run, couldn't field; toward the end, he couldn't even hit. "But I had to play him. Ernie Banks owned Chicago."

To Dan and all the rest of the Cub fans in the world, it seemed the cruelest of jokes that not only did the Cubs blow an 8-game lead in the last weeks of the season, but they lost to the *Mets*, who went on to win the World Series in only the eighth year of their *existence*. But for the Met fans who were Brooklyn Dodger fans who had cheered all their lives for a team that disappeared, and those who were not Dodger fans were Giants fans to whom the same damn thing had happened, and their team had been around since *the beginning of baseball*, it was sweet. Cub fans were sad, Met fans were happy, but everybody had a right to be.

Dan was a senior, but he hung out with the juniors on the cross-country team, Dave Thornton, Bob Mooney, and John Wilkes, whose father was a doctor. The Wilkes were rich and lived in north Oak Park and were members of the Riverside Country Club.

It was all soul music for Davo, who lived on the south side of Chicago, down Harlem Avenue past Summitt, and he carried it in his head when he ran. He had a smooth gait, and when he turned on his kick, the music in his head turned to a double-beat. He'd turn his head to Dan as they ran and say: "Double-beatin?" And Dan would nod. And off they'd go.

On the track, when they would jog the curves and sprint the straightaways, Davo would lead the jog through the curves, setting the pace at that of a double-beatin' snail that would emerge from the turn and explode. Rockne Stadium had a cinder track, and you could hear the crunch-crunch of each runner's steps. The sound your spikes made digging into the cinder track gave your cadence a delicious sense of devouring space, churning. Whose idea was it to make a track out of cinders? God bless him. Running cross-country, the sound of the wind was what you heard when you ran.

The way you felt when you ran was fine, your head cleared, your lungs filled with air and you could breathe, freely, through your nose and through your mouth, smell the fresh air, relax, your body stretching itself, unhinging, unfurling, smoothing out all the kinks, blood circulating, heart pumping a steady beat, arms swinging like pendulums doubly synchronized to move in tandem with the opposite leg, each stride falling forward of its own weight, the ball of the foot bouncing, thrusting, easily, striding. Getting in shape came in two phases. Once you had worked hard enough, it felt better to run than to walk, then, a little later, it felt better to run fast than to run slow.

The gods of running. Jim Ryun was at the top, but he was only just arriving there. In running, there was, beyond the sense of defeating everyone, there lay breaking records, setting records, there was a sense of building on the past, of standing on the shoulders of the great runners all the way back to the Greek who ran from Marathon to Athens to gasp "Victory" before he died.

The Fenwick cross-country team ran two miles from school, past Frank Lloyd Wright's house, every day to practice in River Forest at the House of Studies, which was what the Dominicans called their college of philosophy for neophytes of the Order. A road led onto a driveway in front of the Gothic castle-like structure in the form of a cross with a bell tower at its heart, like a medieval castle, which is what Ed Fenwick went to look for in Europe when the USA was just thinking about getting started. There were no other roads or pavement in the entire two-square-block property; it was all just grass in a field. Alongside the athletic fields for football and baseball, there was a grove of apple trees.

Enter the *curriculum,* which takes us back to the Romans and the Coliseum. Back to Rome. Buckley liked it there. Latin. Not Greek. The Greeks were dangerous. The Greeks were crazy. The Greeks *believed* in crazy. Back to the chariot races, round and round we go.

Chapter Fifteen

Not only were the students at Fenwick all Catholic, all white, and all male, but they had almost all spent eight or nine years in Catholic grammar schools. They were from St. Luke and Ascension and St. Bernadine and St. Vincent Ferrar and St. Catherine of Sienna and St. Peter Canisius and Our Lady of Victory and Resurrection and Immaculate Conception and St. Giles and Providence. The girls from Ascension were headed to Trinity or Nazareth. Some of the boys were headed to Fenwick. *Some* of them. You would be chosen based on your superior potential for academic success – that's what they were looking for in those pressure-packed entrance exams. You had to take the entrance exam and *pass* the entrance exam, to get into Fenwick. It was going to be hard.

There would be math. What if you failed? What if you didn't get in? You'd go to Oak Park High. You'd just go to a public school. A *public* school.

Oak Park High and Fenwick. With one glance at the two buildings, you could see the difference between the two schools. The public school was a modern institution. The Catholic school was a castle from the past. Ascension hadn't been that way. Ascension looked like a school, but it was connected to the church, all one property, all one block. Fenwick looked like a monastery out of the Middle Ages. The Renaissance. Heaven, forbid, the Enlightenment. A castle, there was even a moat around it. Not really.

There was no water in it, but there was a floor below ground level, with a flagstone wall, protective and intimidating. Were it filled with water, it would be a moat. The wall was irresistible. Kids had to climb it, walk along the top of it, jump into the pit, only to discover they couldn't climb out, and would have to beg for some priest or monk to come save them, and they never did that again. This was Buckley's conservatism standing athwart history yelling, "Stop!" Fat lot of good that was going to do. History does not stop.

What if he didn't get in? Dan couldn't even think about that, not because of his blind determination to succeed, but because of blind fear; it was too awful to contemplate. Blindness, deafness, and dumbness were the only explanations. There was no thought involved. There was only desire. He held none of it up to the light, not Fenwick, not the nuns and priests, wait, there was Nathan DeGrorio, and Nathan DeGrorio was going to Fenwick too, and he critiqued everything.

At Fenwick, life would change from color to black and white. On a cold Saturday morning, more than a thousand eighth-grade boys were sitting in classrooms in the castle fortress of Fenwick, taking the test to see who the best of them were, the aristos, because those were the only ones who were going to get in. And of those who got in, a solid third of them would never make it to graduation.

An interminable time later, a letter of acceptance or rejection would appear in the mail to determine his Fenwick fate, to discover whether or not Dan could follow his brother and father and become one of the Fighting Friars.

Every day, he would wait anxiously for the mailman, and every day, no word came, no letter of acceptance or rejection, so he filled the time preparing himself for when the news hit him, rehearsing it in his mind. If he got in, he would yell as loud as he could and run outside and jump and cheer and pump his fist and take a victory lap around the whole block. If he didn't get in, he wouldn't say anything, and he would go to his room and shut the door on his life. But he played the alternate scenes in his head so many times that when the letter finally arrived, and he had gotten in, he only smiled and thought, well, it wasn't as hard as I thought it would be. He was in. He was a student at Fenwick, he was a Fenwick Friar, and the world was turning back into black and white.

Black and white were the coolest colors a school could have, and there could never be any cooler, because they were the essences, and the others were only colors, while white and black were simultaneously all colors and none.

When the Blackfriars Guild, which is what the Fenwick drama club called itself, put on a play, girls from Trinity played the female roles. Blackfriars was appropriated for the moniker of the yearbook as well. The Blackfriars theatre was part of Shakespeare's legacy, after the Globe burned down and the troupe moved indoors, where they could perform at night.

Some of the Fenwick priests would depart each year as missionaries. One left for Kyoto, Japan, seeking to Christianize the future leaders of Japan. Then there could be Catholic Japs just like there would be Catholic Gooks, who were the good Gooks and on our side in Vietnam.

Schweez didn't get accepted. He might have killed himself then and there. Schweez failed the entrance exam. He was crushed. His life was over, and then on the third day, he rose from the grave. Well, not three days. Three months. That fall. Strings had been pulled. They let him in. How did it happen? The same way Kenny Gretz managed to graduate from Ascension despite not having completed his science notebook. It was an idle threat, and he knew it. He called their bluff. Kenny was smarter than Schweez, who should've just kept quiet, should never have told anybody he was rejected, should just have waited till his parents bribed the priests to let him in, he should've lied and said he'd been accepted. Instead, Dan knew from the start that Schweez got in without passing the test, and he probably wasn't the only one.

The legendary Tony Lawless had been Connor's coach, Fenwick's first football coach, and won the Friars' first Catholic League championship and their first Chicago City Championship. The Chicago Catholic League had been in existence for a decade, working its socioeconomic voodoo on the city at large, Chicagoland, before Fenwick even came on the scene. Why was there a Catholic League? There was no Jewish League, no Episcopalian League, no Muslim League. But there were Irish Catholics and Polish Catholics and Italian Catholics, lots and lots of them, and there were all those parishes that superseded towns or neighborhoods. The Catholic League was a way of isolating and unifying at the same time, putting a new spin on separate but equal, even as the country was giving the lie to the whole premise. The Catholic League was saying: We are separate and *unequal* – because we are *better*. The Irish and the Polish and the Italian Catholics invented the Chicago Catholic League to protect themselves and make themselves strong.

Tony Lawless was Knute Rockne redux; he even looked like him, acted like him, talked like him, but instead of dying in a plane crash in the prime of his life like Rockne, for decades and decades, Tony Lawless *ruled*. Tony Lawless coached the Fenwick football team for 27 years, winning five Catholic League championships and two Prep Bowls. The great Johnny Lattner played for Lawless at Fenwick in 1949. Then he played for *Notre Dame*. He won the *Heisman Trophy*. How do you replace Tony Lawless? With Jardine. How do you replace Jardine? You can't.

At Fenwick in PE, your name was stenciled across the back of your shorts, like it was the name of your butt. Above it, your name was stenciled on the back of your shirt. You wrote your name on the side of your shoes in black marker. You were 13 years old; how well do you think you are going to stencil? Perfectly? Gump is going to stencil perfectly. You are going to fuck it up.

This was the *first day* at Fenwick. The freshmen were within the fortress, in the gym, which would later be named the Lawless Gymnasium, under the austere gaze of no less than the legendary Tony Lawless himself. They had learned the preliminary rules of PE, how to dress out, the proper stenciling of your name on the back of your shirt and shorts, the shirt always tucked in, and trickiest of all, stenciling your name on the sides of your shoes.

"Why?"

"Go ahead and ask if you really want to know."

"That's ok."

The freshmen listened in scared silence, attending to exactly what would be expected of them each day of the week, and beginning today, each class would end with the students showering and then returning in their uniforms, with their wet hair neatly combed, tie re-tied, blazer buttoned, and then sit silently in the bleachers until the bell rang and they were dismissed.

"Now hit the showers!"

And everybody did. Everybody except Nathan DeGrorio, who simply went to his locker and changed into his street clothes, then resumed his seat in the bleachers and immersed himself in Proust.

Tony Lawless looked up from his clipboard and saw Nathan sitting there by himself in the bleachers. He was just about to light into him when the rest of the class began to stream in, and Furnace Face, as Nathan would dub him, decided to wait and make an example of Nathan. When the freshmen were all silently seated again, waiting for the bell, the great man held their anxious attention while he scanned the roster.

"Mister . . . DeGrorio?"

Nathan raised his hand.

"Did you take a shower?"

"Why? Is there one missing?"

It was so perfect, everyone had to laugh, but they didn't, not a one of them, not so much as a snicker, because they all knew their lives hung in the balance – this was the *first day*.

The bell rang. Of course, the instant the students were out of the gym, Mr. DeGrorio, having been instructed to remain, they exploded in gales of laughter, but it lasted only until the first priest appeared in the hall.

Cross-country was the opposite of football; its participants were the inhabitants of two different planets. John Wilkes snuck up behind Davo, and with one quick move draped his jockstrap over Davo's face.

"Moosefuck! "

For Dan, there would be three years of running, running on sidewalks in the shade of oak trees, running north to the House of Studies, by Hemingway's house, by Frank Lloyd Wright's house with a tree growing in the living room. Frank Lloyd Wright's prairie-style homes were ground-hugging and horizontal. When the harriers ran by the Frank Lloyd Wright house on their way to the House of Studies they could hear in their heads that song by Simon and Garfunkel "So Long, Frank Lloyd Wright" and whenever they would hear it, they would think of running by that house, and they would think about how they were running out of time too, that one of these days they were going to run by that house and it really would be *So Long, Frank Lloyd Wright* because they would never run past it again, and for the rest of their lives, whenever they would hear that song, it would take them back there, running together, laughing, joking, confessing and absolving.

"Architects may come and

Architects may go and

Never change your point of view

When I run dry, I stop a while and think of you.

So long, Frank Lloyd Wright

All of the nights we'd harmonize till dawn

I never laughed so long

So long, Frank Lloyd Wright

I can't believe your song

is gone so soon

I barely learned the tune

So soon

So soon"

Hemingway's house was at 600 N. Kenilworth, on the corner. Three stories high. The conservatory was acoustically perfect. Ernie's mother, Grace Hemingway, gave recitals and lessons there. "I'll go hunt big game in Africa," Ernie said. Really, it sounded like something only an asshole would say. Ernie had to test himself. "I'm going to go hunt a lion." Who says that? Who *thinks* that?

That crack Hemingway made to Scott Fitzgerald when Scott said, "The rich are very different from us," and Hemingway said, "Yeah, they have more money." What was he talking about? He grew up in north Oak Park in a three-story house with turrets and servants. Ernest, maybe his friends called him Ernest. Wouldn't that be just like north Oak Park? You can safely insult Hemingway now, because after July 2, 1961, there's no earthly way he could slug you.

Kids didn't read his books, but they would hear about him. He was the most famous guy who ever came from Oak Park. Came and went. He didn't want to come back here. Ernie wrote this to his pal Bill Horne: "Me

I like life very much. So much it will be a big disgust when I have to shoot myself."

Hemingway's name alone had entered Dan's consciousness; he was one of the most famous men in the world, and he was from Oak Park, but thereafter, he became a ghost, alternately friendly and horrifying, that would haunt Dan for the rest of his life.

"All true stories end in death," Hemingway said, and like a lot of things, it was true, and it wasn't true. It was true that there was nothing else a living being could ultimately do but die. But it was not true that every story ends in death, because not every story has an end.

Hemingway was the guy who wrote dirty books. *Across the River and into the Trees* had come out, and in it his alter ego, Colonel Cantwell, was half a century old and bedding down a broad in her early 20s, and the church-going cultured Oak Parkers, like Hemingway's own mother, did not approve. Ernie's mother said plainly: "I never read any of Ernie's books."

Hemingway had had to watch Winston Churchill get the Nobel Prize for *Literature* before he did for *Old Man and the Sea*, one of his more meager works, on the heels of an outright bust – *Across the River*. He was living in Cuba then, trying to walk a tightrope between Castro and Batista, but disposed favorably toward the revolutionaries, and that would come back to haunt him, spurring his paranoia. He'd been making enemies politically since the 30s and the Spanish Civil War. So, it was no surprise when Batista's soldiers showed up at the Finca in the middle of the night, wanting to search the place.

The revolution took over Cuba, and Hemingway got the hell out of there, heading for Ketchum, Idaho. He was falling apart. He never should have left Hadley, and he knew it. That was the biggest mistake of his life. His marriage with Pauline was doomed from the start, based on a fatal error, filled with regret, longing, and shame, and only getting worse, more complicated, more kids, more responsibilities, more mistakes, and add politics to the mix, boom. Sex and Violence. *Men at War*. And a Woman appears. Martha Gelhorne – "She came at me in sections" – long-legged, red-haired, tough-talking, smart and sexy Marty Gelhorne. She took him for a ride, his third wife, don't look back. How could this be a mistake when it was just an attempt to correct the original mistake, which was really two mistakes, leaving Hadley and marrying Pauline? He just wanted to get laid. Hadley's pussy had been sweet, Pauline's not so much, but she was rich, and he would never have to worry about money, and he could do whatever he wanted, buy a boat, for instance. In an effort to please him, Pauine had a salt-water pool installed in their backyard in Key West, while he was away at the Spanish Civil War, cheating on her with Marty, and Pauline was home, trying to hold on to her man, her world famous man, the manliest man in the world, any way she could think of, and when he got home, and the cement was still drying around the edges of the pool, he took a penny out and pressed it into the wet cement. "There's my last cent," he huffed, like *he* bought the thing, like some bust-out asshole, like *she* wasn't the money.

"Bullshit," Marty told him. She must have called him on his shit, so he went looking around for someone who wouldn't call him on his shit, and that was how he wound up with the diminutive Mary Welsh, the spunky correspondent Hemingway bedded in London, on the eve of World War II. Mary rarely called him on his shit, but now, with terms of comparison, Hadley's sweet pussy and Marty's long legs, Hemingway could see in Mary how far he had fallen. All of that was in his mind, while in his body, havoc reigned, and there was blood in his piss, and his head hurt from the blows it had taken and given – two plane crashes on the same day, a skylight falling on him while he sat on the crapper, headbutting the door to escape the plane. All that happened before he got the Nobel Prize, and he was too weak to attend the ceremonies. How the hell he got through the rest of the 50s was a miracle. He easily could've shot himself then. He was never going to feel any better, and he knew it.

It's pretty clear if you were born in Oak Park, Illinois, but you live in Cuba and you have pompously come to consider yourself Cuban, and you support the revolution that has declared the United States the enemy, that you are a traitor. Hemingway would have to leave Cuba. He didn't want to. He had no plan. He had no life. So why was he alive?

In the throes of depression, afraid, lonely, paranoid, sleepless, delusional, ashamed, overcome with guilt, strapped to a table, hooked up at the temples to a machine to shoot an electric current through his brain, he would have a dozen of these treatments before they would let him out. The doctors had zapped his brain with electric shock. His memory was destroyed. He had nothing to write with anymore. We write what we remember. If you can't remember shit, you can't write. You can't make shit up out of nothing. "Memory," he said, "is where I store my capital." In his mind, Hemingway was broke. And he was broken. Hemingway was close to Pop's age. On a Sunday in July 1961, Hemingway shot himself to death first thing in the morning. Danny was in fourth grade at Ascension.

Hemingway, dead from a gunshot wound. Accidental. He was cleaning his gun. Bullshit. Hemingway killed himself by sticking the end of a shotgun in his mouth and pulling the trigger with his toe, taking out his entire cranial vault. Twelve-gauge. He had used it to shoot pigeons. Suicide is not all that outlandish or uncommon. People diagnosed with something they know is going to kill them, something that *is* killing them, and they just want to beat it to the punch. How is that cowardly? How is that cruel? To the people left behind – when you've gone on ahead. When *behind* and *ahead* lose all meaning.

"Any man's life, truly told, is a novel." – Hemingway, *Death in the Afternoon*

Hemingway hated Oak Park and couldn't wait to get the hell out of it, but Frank Lloyd Wright loved it and built his own house and studio in Oak Park, the noble village on the prairie, shaped to the good earth.

The idea of Hemingway was black and white that burst into color like an impressionist painting. The Hemingways were north Oak Park cats. They had a music room in their spacious house, Dr. Hemingway and his wife and family, the three kids, Ernie, his sister Marceline, and their little brother Leicester, whom they called Baron. Come on. They were rich. They spent their summers on vacation at their lake house in Michigan. Doc Hemingway was doing well enough to buy an acre of land for a *summer house* on Walloon Lake.

Ernie was 16 years older than his little brother, Leicester, the Baron, a gap greater than that between Ciaran and Dan. Hemingway was in the rifle club at Oak Park High, but he was nearsighted, and he was a shitty shot. Nick Adams was the name Hemingway gave himself in his fiction, a character who shared his experiences. It was not himself, because he knew more than Nick did.

And there was no Rifle Club at Oak Park High. Ernie made it up. And then he got his boys together, surrounded themselves with his dad's and his uncle's guns, took photos, and wrote it up for the *Tabula*, the yearbook, and got away with it. There it is in the yearbook for 1916.

Ernie was one guy who tried to be both artist and athlete. And he wrote great books and lived a life of physicality, a life that required muscle and skill and timing and coordination, and that was how he perceived beauty, and no doubt ran headfirst into all the contradictions between body and spirit.

Ernie said he saw a lion in Africa cover 100 yards in three seconds. It took Dan 12. He thought he might be able to get a tick under 12. He dreamed it, and then, a week later, in practice at Rockne, he ran 11.9.

Ernie could find something good and clean in killing. Come again? At a good party now, in Dan's circle, there wouldn't just be booze and making out, but some people would be in a corner talking about the existence or nonexistence of God, and when it got really late and only a few people were left, they would get to talking about death and ghosts and when each of them would die, and then they'd get out the Ouija board, which was sort of on the money once. It said Schweez would die real soon. And he did, two years after high school, still trying to get as strong as his brother, bench-pressing, and the barbell fell on his throat, and there was no one spotting him.

Soldiers with machine guns were on the steps of the Capitol, prepared to quell riots. Quakers were lying naked on the floor of the DC jail because they had refused jail clothing, crazy with dehydration because they refused to drink. Did Buckley have some smartass shit to say to them? They weren't cowards afraid to fight in a war; they weren't spoiled brats blowing shit up. No, but they were Quakers. What do you expect? That's what they do.

"Hell no, we won't go." If you don't have a whole shitload of people chanting it, it's not going to work. But if you do have a whole shitload of people and they're chanting "Hell No We Won't Go", a real chorus of strong voices, it gets hard to ignore. Especially if you never much wanted to go to begin with. The peace movement, or antiwar movement, would by its nature be attractive to anyone who was just afraid to fight in a war, not to cast any aspersions. Debate topic: Resolved that all American citizens should be subject to conscription for essential services in time of war?

Spring rolled around, and the news broke about a massacre in a place called Mi Lai, and there were our boys in uniform killing around five hundred women and children and old people. Mi Lai revealed that some of the soldiers had been transformed into baby killers, and the logic of the war was laid bare in the explanation: "We had to destroy the village in order to save it." That was either a perfect statement of nihilism, or patently absurd, or both. The argument for going to war was that when you were called up, you went. "Ours is not to reason why, ours is but to do and die." If everyone sat back and decided for themselves, not if a war was just or not, but just whether they felt like going, where would we be? We'd be right here. What difference does it make? This was existentialism. This was the absurd. This was beyond him. Dan was spinning out of control into space, out into the universe. He had now smoked cigarettes and drunk every kind of alcohol he could get his hands on.

Learning nothing and getting nowhere, "And it's one, two, three, what're we fightin for? Don't ask me I don't give a damn; next stop is Vietnam." You could burn your draft card. "Hell no, we won't go." *We*?

Vietnam was such a total disaster that it killed the draft. It was too embarrassing, dispiriting, to go to war and have the soldiers refuse to participate, burn their draft cards, or run away. Bill Ayers was going to fight it *and* run away. His dad was way up there at Com Ed. Mr. Ayers, at the very top, the boss, Connor's boss.

LBJ had said we were living in a Great Society. It was great enough to reach across the world into Southeast Asia to help people out. Far, far beyond America, far, far beyond Oak Park, Saints Rest, there were gooks, who were akin to chinks and japs, to be added to the list of despised races, which amounted to all that were not white.

Dan remained steadfast in his belief that the war could not touch him, and, besides, he wouldn't even have to worry about it for at least the next

four years because he'd be a student, 2-S. He'd have a deferment. He didn't
thank God for it, providential as it may seem, he might thank his lucky
stars because there was evidence, true evidence, that his was a lucky time to
be born; it slid neatly between the Korean War and Vietnam to make his
generation free from military service.

Deprived of the chance to be a soldier. Glory. The chance to prove your
manhood, find your courage. Dan could live with that. He had not distinguished himself in his lone position of leadership, and he was a coward.
Other than that, he'd make a fine soldier, utterly expendable. Fortunately,
he was lucky. Luckily, he was fortunate.

If life was a movie, and he was the star of the movie, the protagonist,
an extra turned into an antihero, against his will, but, being a coward and
a quitter, he was incapable of fighting it off. His destiny was to be an
antihero, and you can either accept your fate or you can try to escape it,
in which case you will run right into it. Having nothing better to do, Dan
decided to do both, now one, now the other, but he would not play a
villain, nor would he attempt any more to be the hero, although out of
necessity, he would play antagonist to many. The war was out.

The Republicans convened in Miami Beach. ABC had already signed
Buckley up to comment, but he had to have an opponent, so ABC asked
him for suggestions, and then ABC asked Buckley, whom did he *not* want
to debate, and, stupidly, he replied. That he honestly replied Gore Vidal
doesn't matter. He was stupid.

Dan was trying to reconcile himself with this society and culture, using
William F. Buckley, Nathan DeGrorio, and Jim Ryun as his guides, each
of them blazing a path he could neither follow nor comprehend. Ryun was
training for the Olympics, or thought he was, but he was training for a race
he had no chance of winning.

Nixon was a Republican. President Eisenhower had been a Republican too, but he had also been a five-star general, and he had led the invasion of Normandy and had been the leader of the Allied forces against the Nazis. All was well. It would never be better than that. Those were the good old days of yore, the likes of which would ne'er be seen again, the bullshit lie of the fifties exposed in the sixties, all there in black and white.

If you were a Frenchman, you saw the USA moving into Vietnam after you had ignominiously slinked out. The French have a somewhat older culture. Ed Fenwick could have told you about that. Culture, that is. Western values. The French were old hands at imperialism, and here came the Yanks, while back in America, there was rioting in the cities, and the general population was marching on the Pentagon.

And the Church's view on things – from philanthropic heights? Catholicism was not just of Chartres or even the Pieta and the Sistine ceiling and Gregorian chant and all the monks, particularly the Irish, preserving the great texts, but Catholic culture, from burning people alive at the stake for heresy to burning them with napalm and gasoline gel. It was oppressive, the weight of all those centuries, and it was meant to be oppressive because the whole enterprise was a power play. Seeking dominion.

Father Farrell was the hippy priest. If he found out the world was going to end in 24 hours, he'd go out and plant a tree. Crazy. A balcony ran around the pool, with a railing you could climb over and jump into the pool. Nobody wore a swimsuit in the pool, except for the swimming team. Everybody else swam in it naked. Does this seem crazy? Don't think about it. Hear The Tale of Father Farrell. Here The Tails of Father Farrell. The hippy priest. He was going to go down to the inner city and fight for justice. He was going to go down all right. He was going to go down on them. And someday later, maybe he would go down in flames in Hell. Maybe. God knows. But when the boys went on retreat, Father Farrell could no longer help himself, so he helped himself. He could not resist temptation. What if you went into the priesthood because you were attracted to boys, and every day you would encounter a whole school of them, and with a wave of your hand you could bless them and have them bow down, or bend over, or be sucked, and you would have God's blessing because you had been blessed by God? Father Farrell fought for peace and racial justice, so why shouldn't he get his rocks off once in a while? A kid fell asleep, so Father Farrell took his clothes off. Wait. What? He wakes up on a couch where he must've fallen asleep, and he's got no clothes on. What? His clothes are right there... what the fuck?

Fenwick was the embodiment of racism and perversion, and that was what had made it holy. What Dan conceived as sublime in life, joining together the corporal and the spiritual, black and white, veritas, was simply a derivative of slavery, of sin. Monstrous priests existed, and in number.

Spring came, and with it Dan's slow awakening from his torpor, languishing in the cold and medieval castle on Washington Boulevard, the gothic walls now the symbol of spiritual tyranny and the image of melancholy winter.

Fenwick was a fortress that was built to crumble. It wasn't built for that purpose, only with its inevitability assured, to take nothing away from Aquinas and the Dominicans, but how were they to explain away their part in the Spanish Inquisition?

One reason pedophiles and perverts pervaded the priesthood was that Catholic school children were thoroughly and completely repressed, closed off from their yearnings, weirded out and wary of intimacy and affection, fearful of death and the fires of Hell, and driven into the arms of those who must be trusted: cops and priests. They were fucked.

Are we saying that our boy Dan here was a victim? He wasn't the victim of Father Farrell. Somebody else was, some other kid, some other *kids.* In stories, we like heroes who do something, as opposed to people that things just happen to. But all of us are victims. Shit happens to everyone, terrible awful shit. The priest-abuse at Fenwick had nothing to do with Thomas Aquinas, nor did racism and sexism. Or did it? All or nothing. Did or didn't. Can't be both.

Over the summer, Terry Flaherty got a girl pregnant and had to get married. His life was over. There was Tony Liano walking down the hall-way. He would always bump shoulders with Dan and try to intimidate him. What was he doing at Fenwick? He was a stupid asshole, and there were supposed to be no stupid assholes at Fenwick. There were assholes, but nobody was stupid, or they would flunk out, and that's what Tony Liano was doing at Fenwick, flunking out.

Dan believed in the power of dreams. If you dream that you can do something, you can do it. But you have to dream it first. A real dream that comes in your sleep, not a daydream, that you're king of the world, whatever. It's got to happen on its own. When Dan dreamed that he broke five minutes in the mile, then he knew he could do it. He had done it before in his dream. It was the dream that had this power.

Dan had a dream that Tony Liano wanted to pick a fight with him, which was real enough because Tony Liano did want to pick a fight with him. Tony Liano wanted to show everybody that he could take Dan in a fight. He wanted to punch Dan in the face and have Dan just take it, too scared to fight back, but in the dream Dan did fight back, and he bloodied Tony Liano's fat lip, and in the dream Tony Liano could taste his own blood, and the next day, the day after the dream, Dan passed by Tony Liano in the hall at school and they bumped shoulders and Tony Liano could see in Dan's eyes that he wasn't afraid of him anymore. And that was all it took, because Tony Liano wasn't stupid, or at least not that stupid, and he knew Dan was going to fight back, that you couldn't just punch Dan Finnegan in the face and walk away and tell everybody you took him. That wasn't going to happen. What was going to happen instead was a fight, and Tony Liano decided it just wasn't worth it.

Chapter Sixteen

There were enough lockers in the locker room at Fenwick for every student in the school, a thousand lockers, row upon row of lockers, a bottom locker, and a top locker. Everyone wanted a top locker. It was easier to deal with. A narrow bench was in the aisle, just wide enough to sit on while you tied your shoes. The locker-room gave onto the showers and bathroom, where Davo would deposit his 3:01 shit or otherwise be stomach-plagued throughout practice. Davo was famous for pronouncing upon his daily 3:01 as a predictor for the quality of the day's practice. There was another set of lockers beyond those for athletes of the highest rank, and within it, there was a stairway that led up to the coaches' office, the training room, and the equipment room. From there, another set of stairs led up to the gym. The basketball team would emerge from these stairs at the start of a game, but the entrance was otherwise off-limits for students. Students were banned from both sets of stairs unless they were being issued equipment or getting therapy in the training room, where there was an ice bath and training table for ankle-taping.

Dan looked up the stairs from the locker room. There was nobody around, no coaches, athletes, priests, students, janitors, nobody. It was weird. But also, reasonable – they all had cause to be somewhere else. So, he mounted the stairs and peeked around the corner into the training room. The lights were off. There was a light on in the equipment room. The top

of the door was open. It swung open to allow a student-manager of one of
the teams to stand behind the sacred threshold and hand out uniforms or
equipment. In one motion, Dan swung himself over the bottom door and
into the sanctuary. Jerseys, pads, helmets, basketball uniforms, warm-ups,
home unis, away unis, all of them black and white, the cross-country
uniforms, baseball unis, stirrup-socks, practice unis, game unis. For an
instant, he just gazed in worshipful silence, and then he pounced. If he
snatched something new, it would be missed, but something of an earlier
edition might not, and if he had to choose between the home and away
football jerseys, he'd go for the away, the black ones with the white numbers
and white stripes and trim. He snatched #30, Ciaran's number, stuffed it
under his shirt, swung over the half-door, and scrambled down the stairs
to his locker, where he deposited the stolen goods in his duffel bag. What
would he do with it? Where would he wear it? To a party, to impress a girl.

"What's her name?"

"Patty Moody."

"She nice?"

She had dark red hair, and she was just a couple inches over five feet
tall, with a body like a gymnast, compact and round-muscled, and the
dark redness of her hair distinguished her from the bright red-haired or
orange-haired redheads with pale skin and freckles. Her skin was not pale,
but that of a healthy and robust girl. Dan was smitten. Neither Betty
nor Veronica. There was a third option. How many options could there
be? Options? Types of girls. *Types*? How about the brainy type? Never
occurred to him. A girl you could talk to? Yes. That was different. A girl
who would laugh at his jokes. If a girl thought you were funny, you maybe
had a chance.

Davo had a girlfriend named Cindy Tucker, a cute blonde, and now
Dan's girlfriend was Patty Moody, a cute redhead, and John Wilkes had

a girlfriend, the busty, beautiful, dark-haired, long-legged Linda Yuloski. Their other teammate, Mooney, didn't date.

"What's up with that?"

"Who knows?"

Guys who ran cross-country didn't need to explain to each other why they liked being alone. Aside from drinking, which only Dan and Davo indulged in, and girls, which excluded Mooney, the four friends hung out together all the time.

"You wanna go to a whorehouse?"

Dan wanted to go to a whorehouse about as much as he wanted to go to Vietnam. He'd pass. It scared him. Just the sort of thing he would fuck up. He could even fuck up fucking. He didn't want to get the syph like Nicholas Urfe.

He was still a virgin, and he was going to graduate still a virgin. Damn. He reached an agreed upon limit with Patty Moody, after a month or so and a dozen dates, and she would let him touch her bare ass and her tits, and finger her pussy, but there was to be no fucking and no oral sex, although for some reason she liked sticking her tongue in his ear, which turned out to be a thrill, because he could *hear* how her tongue felt.

"I love you."

"I love *you*."

This was the full extent of their romantic dialogue, and it proved they were in love. He would say it to her between kisses, and she would breathe it to him in his ear in advance and retreat of her quick tongue. He gave her his ring, and she wore it on a chain around her neck.

It didn't take much to turn Dan against the war, and his being against the war was a good reason for not fighting in it. So, he would settle for going to school. He'd be leaving Patty Moody behind, and, even more touchingly, he'd be leaving Patty Moody's behind.

"Come on over, I'm babysitting. We can watch a movie on TV. On the couch."

"I'll be right there." Halleluiah! Patty had to babysit. Dan would hop in the Corvair and drive to Berwyn, and after Patty's little brother went to sleep, Dan and Patty would sit on the couch and make out while a black and white horror movie played on TV. Dan and Patty made out in Dan's Corvair, parked here, there, and everywhere. And there was a blanket in the trunk of the Corvair, and they made out on the blanket at Ravinia Park at the Blood, Sweat & Tears concert, and they made out on the blanket in Grant Park, and on the sands of North Avenue Beach on the shore of Lake Michigan.

Patty Moody lived in Berwyn and went to Trinity, way the hell away in River Forest. How'd her family swing that? They were working class. Her dad was a mechanic with grease around his cuticles. How'd she get there? By bus? By car? For four years? That can't have been easy. All Dan did was walk out the door and walk a few blocks to Fenwick. Davo had to get to Fenwick all the way from the south side of Chicago, on the other side of Summit.

Patty had a little brother who was a hemophiliac, so there was always something sad, tragic, and dangerous hovering about their family, a burden they had to bear, like that of Dan's little brother, the presumed epileptic. And Patty had a younger sister, Debbie, two years younger, dark-haired and lithe and slender, where Patty was rounded, and the two of them darted angry eyes at each other.

Fenwick was all boys. Trinity all girls. Let's dwell on that concept for a moment. Separate the sexes when they reach puberty, solely for educational purposes. Dan began learning to cheat.

"You're cheating on her?"

"No. I'm learning."

"You're cheating on Patty Moody."

"Don't tell her, all right?"

"Don't tell her you're cheating on her. And what are you going to say when she finds out?"

"She's not gonna find out."

"What are you going to say?"

"I'm going to lie."

"You're planning to lie?"

"I'm not planning on it. I'm just predicting. Sounds like something I'd do."

"You'll deny it?"

"I'll make some shit up."

"She'll know you're lying."

"She'll suspect I'm lying, but there will be no way to prove it."

So, it would just be one of those things that hovered over the relationship to the end, her suspicion that he had cheated on her, and his concealed guilt. Ronnie. Her name was Veronica, but she was called Ronnie, and she had short brown hair like a pixie, like Judy Carne on *Laugh In*, and she lived in Cicero, and she was sexy and had a good sense of humor and she was smart, and she liked to make out, so it was worth it to drive to Cicero to see Ronnie.

When Dan admitted to himself that what he wanted was wrong, he felt clean of it, that at least he had been honest with himself, and to be honest with himself meant he must lie to other people. A moment of clarity, it soon passed, and he became agnostic again – about himself, wondering whether he really existed or not, but, more than that, whether it mattered. That's called depression. Those are called suicidal tendencies. And Patty was in love with him? What was the matter with *her*?

If being honest with yourself meant lying to other people, then telling them the truth would mean lying to yourself, that is, pretending. You can't lie to yourself and know it's a lie. What are you – two people?

At least.

He lost his patience. He lost his temper. He lost his cool. He lost his mind. What he wanted to lose was his virginity.

You find yourself wondering whether she would do it, your working-class Catholic girlfriend, Patty Moody? No. Bill Ayers' petit-bourgeois girlfriend. Would she wrap a hand grenade in her skirt and blow up the draft board? Is she bourgeois? Very. And Bill Ayers' father is the boss of Commonwealth Edison? The kid's a class traitor.

Patty was a perfectly normal girl, an average girl for Trinity in Dan's stereotypical view of things, a good girl, good grades, didn't get into trouble, and didn't have radical ideas or particularly deep thoughts, didn't question the existence of God or think about things like that. What Dan knew about her was how to make her laugh and beyond that, not much, just the way her skin felt and little by little the curves of her breasts and bottom and what she tasted like and smelled like, the tone of her body, her freckles, her rich dark red hair, her full lips, her mouth, her tongue, but what she really thought, no, not at all, except that it was not what he thought. Patty was Dan's girlfriend, but there was never even a thought of taking her to see a Bergman movie, never a thought that she might read *The Magus*.

They went on a date to see *Elvira Madigan*. It was romantic and tragic, and Patty shrugged. She was a year younger than Dan was, a year behind him. All his friends, besides Nathan, were juniors; just as the year before, all of Dan's friends had been seniors, and he had taken part in their illustrious achievements vicariously. He was part of the City Champion cross-country team, albeit a completely inessential part, not even scoring any points.

Only the top five runners score points for a team in cross-country. Dan was a world away from that. On the City Championship team, Dan was barely in the top ten. He was awarded a minor letter. A *major* letter required a black pullover letter sweater to be emblazoned with a big white F. If you were a senior, you wore a blazing white pullover with a stark black F on your chest. A white minor letter was small enough to fit neatly on one side of a black buttoned sweater.

Dan and Davo were running east to Austin Boulevard, through Columbus Park, alongside the expressway to Central Avenue and Rockne Stadium. The wind was blowing, now hard in a gust, then steady in a gale. Davo was from the south side, and he liked soul music. He *only* liked soul music.

"Did you see her pussy?"

"Patty's?"

"You didn't, did you? "

"Why?"

"To see what you were getting into. She just let you put your hand in her pants. "

"She did."

"But she won't let you lick her pussy, and how long have you been going with her?"

"I don't know."

"What? Why don't you at least try? You should ask her. Just say, just come right out and say: Would you like me to lick your pussy?"

"Just like that?"

"That simple."

"I think you're full of shit."

"Try it. You'll like it. Where you going?"

Davo would have to catch him now, and they were really running, with *miles* to go. It felt great.

"You can't worry about hurting people's feelings."

"But I do. I worry about hurting people's feelings. Feelings are about all we've got. I don't want my feelings hurt."

"Your feelings get hurt too easily."

"My feelings are easily hurt. "

"This is what I'm saying."

"So, why don't you pity me?"

"You want my pity?"

"If you can spare some. What, are you saving it up?"

Dan Finnegan, age 17, high school senior, well on his way to realizing his dreams would never come true, while knowing it all along – because that's what makes them dreams – they're not real. They can become real. Are we talking about dreams you have in your sleep? Because sometimes those do come true, or at least they seem to have a real power. You dream something – like punching Tony Liano in the face, and then the next day at school, you pass him in the hall, and you can see in his eyes that he's afraid of you now, he senses your new power, your newly discovered power that you must have had all along. How do you think that happened? By a miracle. Really? No. It's *your* mind when you dream. It's you, in the dream, not Tony Liano. You write the play, and you play the parts. It's not Tony Liano, it's your idea of Tony Liano. You dream it, and it changes you. So, the next day, when the two of you pass in the hallway, you look at him and he looks at you. And he can see it in your eyes, the change in you, and he responds to it with avoidance. He looks away. Not those dreams. Aspirations, goals. Winning a gold medal in the Olympics.

"By losing my life I should not have lost very much; I should have lost only an empty form, the empty frame of a work of art." Proust

Somehow, Nathan DeGrorio had gotten himself into Fenwick, and now he couldn't get out. As Mark Twain said: "It's easier to stay out than to get out." If the lure had been to learn Latin like Buckley, the lure had lost its luster. Latin was a dead language. Nathan wanted to learn French so he wouldn't need to read the subtitles in the new wave cinema of Godard and Truffaut, and he wanted to be at Oak Park High, not Fenwick, because at Oak Park, there was a film study class, and there were *girls*.

Not that Nathan had any respect for women, except when he did. For the most part, he openly proclaimed that he operated under what he called the Heidegger No-Brian Theory of Women. But then Pauline Kael and Penelope Gilliat entered Nathan's life by way of the *New Yorker*, yes, the *New Yorker*, and as he devoured their prose style and assessed their analyses of film, and he granted them intelligence and merged them with images of Liv Ulman and Bibi Andersson, like that moment in *Persona* before the film burns up, to raise the idea of woman to the sublime, if not quite to where Dante put Beatrice.

"You don't understand women."

"Why should I? You understand them. And you don't like them."

"That's not true."

"Which part?"

They had a film study class at Oak Park High, so why the hell was Nathan studying Religion at Fenwick? Theology. Twelve years of Catholic education. All that Latin. "Greek to me." The priests were right about Latin, though. Our grammar plays out there, so that if you could diagram a sentence in English, you could master Latin grammar, and vice versa. Funny thing was, Nathan hadn't been able to diagram a sentence back in eighth grade at Ascension. Mother Edna. Nathan called her Craphead. He could've come up with a better name, but it wasn't worth the effort. He was a fabulous writer, with an immense vocabulary and an energetic style, but he couldn't diagram a sentence to save his life, and Craphead recognized the difference between the two friends and remarked that if they could combine their capabilities, they could "go far". How were they supposed to do that? Collaborate? Nathan was not a collaborator. You had to stretch your definition of friend to call him your friend. If somebody asked him if he had any friends, he'd say no, and he'd be telling the truth.

Nathan actually *liked* Father Kenmeister, oddly enough, the driest, dullest, most boring of all the teachers at Fenwick; he didn't even try to make it interesting or fun, which of course was exactly what Nathan liked about him. He was an aesthete. Speaking in a monotone, Father Kenmeister just laid it all out, take it or leave it, Emily Dickinson, Steven Crane. Melville. Most guys left it. Nathan took it up the ass, metaphorically speaking. Nathan was in love with Emily Dickinson. Intellectually. The way he was in love with Pauline Kael and Susan Sontag. With Sontag, it might have been more. It was certainly more with Liv Ullmann. Father Kenmeister's English class was the one refuge in the day for Nathan, so Dan tuned in then, too. Not that Dan had to ape *everything* Nathan did and liked and hated – for one thing, no one could ever keep up with all his hates. It was just that Dan followed Nathan's lead as his intellectual superior. It allowed Dan, when not with Nathan, as was usually the case, to act like he was a lot smarter than he actually was, smarter than everyone else, because he was Nathan DeGrorio's proxy.

Nathan would give you shit for any cliché, any catch phrase, you used, no matter how necessary it was to habitual human interaction.

"How's it going, Nathan?"

"It? What's *it*?"

Go ahead and try to argue with him. He'll just make you look and feel like a fool. But if you had an emotional reaction to a work of art – that was the purpose of a work of art, wasn't it, to make you feel something? "Hey

Jude" was a shit song because it had all those bullshit nanananas in there. The Beatles were ok, but their shit was shit just like anybody's shit. "You're a sap. You like sappy shit."

"Most people do."

Nathan DeGrorio declared himself a libertarian at 12, with a superior intellect, *bearing*, pedigreed, sophisticated, and then he'd casually drop into the middle of the conversation the word *faggot*.

The mail. Something would come in the mail. Nathan DeGrorio got mail. Dan would ask his mother if he could subscribe to *National Review*, and she would write a check to William F. Buckley, Jr., and *National Review* would arrive in the mail, yes, something would come for Daniel Finnegan in the mail.

Nathan DeGrorio had his own terrible inconsistencies. He was skinny, but he looked fat. His stomach wasn't large, but the way he comported himself in a perpetual slouch that advanced his belly before the rest of him, which proceeded in a duck-walk, with toes pointed out, combined with his general disdain for athletics and his pale body's lack of tone and definition, made him seem fat and pudgy, which jibed with his abnormally large head, which jibed with his abnormally large brain, even though he wasn't fat at all. Everything about Nathan told you that he succeeded by means of intelligence alone. He was a non-athlete, but he made fun of other people's lack of coordination. He was in no way good-looking, but he made fun of other people's looks. He made fun of everybody and everything. He made fun of strangers passing by on the sidewalk.

"Nice face," he'd say under his breath, but audibly. Something insulting, sarcastic, and funny as shit, and you'd have to laugh, so even if the stranger couldn't exactly hear what was said, they knew they were being laughed at, knew they'd been humiliated, some poor old woman or a mother with a baby or, most often, somebody who looked like they deserved it, so you laughed in affirmation. But don't get carried away, because Nathan could just as easily turn the sarcasm on you.

The Sharon Statement of the Young Americans for Freedom: "In this time of moral and political crisis, it is the responsibility of the youth of America to affirm certain eternal truths." Eternal truths? Responsibility of Youth? And Nathan believed in *this*? Why was Nathan going to Fenwick? To be like Buckley? Nathan could make fun of everybody because everybody was beneath him, but he didn't make fun of Buckley, and he didn't make fun of Ingmar Bergman, because they were not beneath him; hell, they might even be above him, Bergman that is, not Buckley. Nathan and he were even, with Nathan slightly ahead, since Buckley was saddled with his mannerisms and affectations. People who tried to make fun of that which was not beneath them but, rather, of that which was above them, were stupid and essentially made fun of themselves.

For Dan, the priestly phase had been followed by the Bond Phase, the Buckley phase, and the Ryun phase. The lifestyle of James Bond was antithetical to running track. Bond smoked 60 Turkish cigarettes a day and drank martinis. Dan's parents were martini masters, with transportable works, always prepared with gin, vermouth, and olives.

"You smoke? You wanna smoke a cigarette?"

"Hell no. What kind?"

"Benson and Hedges. They come in a flat box. You slide it open."

"Cool."

Yet Bond was somehow in shape, and he'd fire back at his boredom with a brace of exercises that made his stomach muscles scream! Then, of course, there was his judo training and karate, the martial arts, a technique of unarmed combat that would allow the weaker to win, if properly applied, a mindset discovered by Dan in the boxing ring where Larry Sullivan taught him that the tougher guy can always beat the shit out of you, but only if you let him. That night, Dan let him. But for the first round, he had him, sticking and moving, he was faster, smarter, quicker to the punch, and then he just started slugging it out, whaling away, and he got the worst of it. Stupid. He could've won. Dan could be one of the guys, or he could be Nathan's only friend. He could not be both. Or could he? Everything started to bleed into the real world. The real world was impinging on his fantasy. Nathan's take on *The Magus* was: "You can't treat life like a detective novel. Because every solution is an illusion."

Sam Jessup was headed for valedictorian, and he was captain of the chess team, a ham radio operator, but, like Ingmar Bergman, he was apolitical. Sam Jessup noted, in explanation of his lack of interest in the war or its protests, that he wasn't worried about getting drafted anyway, because he had an ace in the hole – an irregular heartbeat. Nathan laughed.

"That's great, Sam, you're not gonna get killed in the war. You're just gonna be walking down the street one day and – " Nathan stopped to convulse, then halfway dropped to the ground, only to straighten up and deadpan: "I'm happy for you, Sam, really."

Through it all, there was a crushing sense that life was flowing past you, and there was no way to catch hold of it. How to belittle. "Your problems don't interest me." Nathan would come right out and say that, and then, not surprisingly, he'd say: "My problems don't interest me either." That was the secret of Nathan's superiority: apathy. Very little rose to the level of his interest.

Dan followed Nathan into Krochs & Brentanos on Wabash Avenue to purchase the new Bond paperback: *You Only Live Twice.* – "Once when you are born, and once when you look death in the face." But Nathan didn't purchase books. He stole them. He put them inside his coat and walked out with them, and no one saw him do it. Dan didn't see him do it either. They were walking down Wabash Avenue, a block from Krochs, when Nathan withdrew a volume of Proust he'd been holding next to his heart, by way of a hole in his coat pocket.

Nathan's books were all hardbound, and they were behind glass. They were in perfect condition. Nathan wouldn't think of marking them up, underlining, or making notes in them. None of the albums in Nathan's record collection had scratches on them, and he kept them in their paper sleeves inside their album cover, and when he took them out to play them, he wiped them off with a cloth before he played them, and he always let the arm automatically set the needle down gently at the beginning of the album, he never set the arm down by hand to selectively play one track or another the way Dan and everybody else did. Nathan would listen to the whole album, allow the arm to lift off on its own and shut off, then he would wipe the disc again, replace it in its paper sleeve, and put the sleeve back inside the album cover, then put the album back in place in his collection and slide the glass door shut. Almost all of the books were stolen. He hadn't figured out how to steal a record album yet. Too bulky. Books he could just stash in his coat or jacket.

Nathan was a man alone, the perfect conservative. His cursive was round and compact and straight up and down, no slant to it.

"When the student is ready, the teacher will appear."

Dan was ready. And there was Nathan DeGrorio. Nathan always seemed older than the other kids. He wasn't taller than they were. He was short and pudgy, with chubby cheeks. It was his demeanor and the way he carried himself that fooled everybody into thinking he was really a middle-aged man, with the *Chicago Tribune* and *National Review* tucked under his arm, wearing rubbers over his shoes, and keeping a handkerchief in his pocket. The fact that he was 12 years old was generally overlooked. Nathan was a cynic. How absurd is a cynical 12-year-old? He didn't ride a bike. He didn't own a bike. He played no sports. He didn't go to parties or dances, which was unthinkable.

"What have you got against dancing?"

"It's stupid."

"What's stupid about it?"

"It looks stupid. It makes you look stupid."

"It makes *you* look stupid. It doesn't make Fred Astaire or Gene Kelly look stupid."

It didn't make Nathan look stupid because he never danced. If you preferred Sinatra to the Beatles, you wouldn't be going to the sock-hop. You were staying home and reading a book.

There must've been close to two hundred hardcover books behind glass in the bookcase in Nathan's bedroom. Only hardcovers, no paperbacks. Nathan was a master book thief, so good that he never got caught, and his appetite for books required constant replenishment.

All these stories of Nathan happen over time. It begins at Ascension, the incident on the corner in winter with Stan Roe, when they served as patrol boys, and then the Uncle Freddie Show, and then their days in thrall to the Man from UNCLE. Nathan's world is the opposite of the sports world and the Clarence Alley Boys. Incidentally, Susan Sontag stole books, too.

When James Baldwin wondered in his debate with Buckley what happens to the minds of white children when they are immersed in this warped vision, he was talking about Dan. The Oxford debate. Nathan thought Buckley won. The Oxford students felt decidedly otherwise.

Nathan and Buckley couldn't see or did not wish to acknowledge what was happening right before their eyes and all around them, and consequently, neither could Dan, and they weren't going to get anywhere until first admitting how wrong they were and apologizing. They had to start over. And it would never happen for Buckley or Nathan, but maybe it could happen for Dan. Maybe he could redeem himself.

CHAPTER SEVENTEEN

"**S**ince the prophets perceived the revelations of God with the aid of the imaginative faculty, they may doubtless have perceived much that is beyond the limits of the intellect. For many more ideas can be constructed from words and images than merely from the principles and axioms on which our entire natural knowledge is based." – Spinoza

And that is not only why we tell stories, but why the stories have the capacity to reveal truth and beauty, different names for the same thing.

"Now we see why the perceptions and teaching of the prophets were nearly all in the form of parables and allegories and why all spiritual matters were expressed in corporeal form, for this to be more appropriate to the imaginative faculty." – Spinoza

Picture it. The angels didn't exactly have bodies, but they came exactly to a point, and that was why scholastic theologians could argue about how many angels could fit on the head of a pin. There was no other way to explain it, finally, although Aquinas appealed to Aristotle, than as a miracle. But that would be contrary to the nature of God, who would not be God if He had to resort to miracles, in effect admitting His mistake. Aquinas and Maimonides agreed that God can do anything logically possible. So, you couldn't trip them up by asking if God could make a rock so heavy that he couldn't lift it, a logical impossibility. However, this weds God to logic, with logic, not God, calling the shots.

How can you write history like this? How can you even write a story like this? Past, present, future, all in a loop, all happening at once? If it is seen from God's perspective, does that mean looking at it as if it's all over, complete, finished, perfect? Because then it's all past – there is no present, there is no future. It is simply as if there is no time, or, rather, there is no real distinction among past, present, and future. While at the same time, there is cause and effect, which necessarily happen in that order. It *is* all past – in the sense that it is perfect, and necessary, as Aristotle defined necessity in *The Poetics*, like a mathematical equation. But notice, two plus two *equals* four – present tense. And yet two plus two equaled four on D-Day and in 1265, and two plus two will equal four long after we're all gone. Our problem is that our consciousness never apprehends anything but effects. That means we always have a pretty good idea of how we feel – but not why. Consciousness is just the awareness of our feelings. It takes more than mere consciousness to know the causes of things. It takes reason.

"A fool's voice is known by multitude of words." – Ecclesiastes

The Bible is a book written over a long period of time, starting during or just after the Babylonian captivity, roughly the same time that the *Iliad* and *Odyssey* were coming together. The rhapsodes gave that gift to Homer. No one thinks nowadays that *The Iliad* was divinely inspired, but the Greeks did. The Old Testament is roughly comparable to Homer; the rhapsodes are like the various nameless authors taking on the name of Moses to write the Pentateuch. How can it be said to be the Good Book when it's not even a good book? Consider it better a library or, at best, an epic, a huge novel, like *In Search of Lost Time* or *Finnegans Wake* or *War and Peace*, it's in search of its author to give it some coherence. It needs an auteur. Bergman, Fellini, Godard.

If you could put in place the first 18 years of your life, put it in historical context, and see how it led to where you are now, and if you had half a century of space and time to see it through, and then tried to make sense of it, in an objective way, not just the way a reporter would, but the way a novelist would, the way Tolstoy or Proust would, then at least you would know *something*. You could make a rational statement about the nature of things in your life, just yours, the hero of the novel, your doppelgänger, although the story is told in third person by an unseen narrator, who's really a *third* person, after the real you and the fictionalized you, here finally is the Godlike you.

The Godlike you has the power to forgive. We begin with God. For a reason. For reason itself. And it joins all the themes together, weaves them together, and weaves in and out of the chronology. This is the story of Fenwick, of football, the Chicago Catholic League, Catholicism, Jardine's tragedy, the House of Studies. Protestants and Catholics at war in Ireland, but in America, playing games with one another. Life. Death. Eternity. At first, you aren't. There is no you. This is nonexistence. Suddenly, you are. This is your existence. It ends, and you exist no more. It's over. Life goes on. Forever. Into eternity. For you, however, time is up. But not for everybody and everything else, at least not yet. Until existence ends, and all that's left is eternity.

He who lives in the present lives in eternity. – Wittgenstein

Things were unthinkable because they hadn't been thought of *yet*. The trick for the historian or artist is to capture an event at the moment when something else so easily could have happened but didn't. That is, at the conjunction. *However.*

Go back to a time before something happened and recount everything leading up to it, the people, the places, the weather, all the elements of drama to be considered, plot, character, thought, diction, sound, spectacle. Epic theater. This is going to take *time*. The events are so long past. *Long* being a relative term. Take your own time. The characters present themselves in an endless stream, some onstage, some off, carrying the action toward its tragic climax and the shock of recognition.

Hey, that's *me*. That's *us*. The Holocaust. Hiroshima. The whole world is watching the collective acts of our shared humanity, in wonder. How can we be so fucked up? The Bible collides with reality. Slavery. USA. Civil War. Race. God is holding it all together, although it's not being held together at all; it's just flying apart. But you can consider it all God. Then there's humanity. Where do we fit in? We don't. Our brain is too big. Too big for our own good. That's a scientific fact. We've got just enough brain power to think up more shit to fuck ourselves up with than ways to live in peace. From certainty to doubt. Is that progress? The certainty was false. From mystery to... not clarity. Deeper mystery.

And what of humankind's achievements? What about the positive things, that fine spirit of progress in history that Hegel saw and the knowledge that enriched Dan's existence from the beginning that lay beneath his love for Bible stories, the pictures he drew, the shapes he formed with his modelling clay, donning his pretend vestments to say pretend Mass, the caves full of paintings, the war between the Neanderthals and the Homo Sapiens that had to be won – there was just no reasoning with those people – the time, who knows how long, spent as nomads, always on the move, a tight band of interdependent teammates, harriers, until life turned into its opposite, by our choice, and the seeds were planted, and that way of life was forever ended, what about all that?

Dan grows up slowly, his awareness dim, his self-absorption blinding him to the people and events around him, which force their way into the foreground, and force Dan either to recede or take note of them. They scream louder and louder for his attention.

It's easy to see that not only all of Dan's concerns and worries, but those of his dad and mom and Hemingway and LBJ and Bill Ayers were misperceived, clouded with inadequate ideas, misinformation, falsification, and lies. They didn't know they were lies at the time. In fact, they were not lies at the time. They only turned out to be lies later. Dan was overwhelmed by these forces, but so was Nixon, and to far worse effect. Nixon fucked up the whole country, the whole world. Dan just fucked up himself. So he thought. In his solipsism. "I am a man more sinned against than sinning." Let's say it's about even. Once you reach the age of reason, you're the one responsible for you. Come on, a seven-year-old kid? Twelve then, or a teenager. There are rules in place to guide you. There are guidelines. Be like your brother. It's too hard. I'm not tough like him. I'm a coward. It takes a lot of courage to admit you're a coward. No, it doesn't. It's just quitting. It's the easiest thing in the world to just give up.

Jim Ryun could still win the gold medal in Mexico City. That would be something, at least, vicariously. The same way that Buckley scoring a point in a debate made Dan feel superior.

Wasn't that a zinger! Buckley told the Negro who was complaining about conditions in the ghetto, "I didn't put the rats there." Good shot, Buckley.

All visible, visibly moving things
Spin or swing, one of the two;
Move as the limbs of a runner do,
To and fro, forward and back;
Or as they swiftly carry him,
In orbit go, around an endless track.
– W.H. Auden

A man running is a story. A man running away from something is a plot. The season was over, and when Dan walked home from school at 3 o'clock, he could stop at the convenience store and get some chips, candy, and chocolate milk, and walk slow because he wasn't in a hurry. He had nothing to do. Instead of running two miles to the House of Studies and running a round of progressions, he did nothing. Then run two miles back to school, take a long, hot shower. Now Dan felt guilty. He was doing nothing.

After the season ended and he didn't have to run anymore, he didn't, and he started to put on weight. It was those stops at the convenience store, the chocolate milk, donuts, chips, soda, and candy bars. He had a spare tire, love handles. He was soft. You have to run when the season's over. No, you don't, what for? To get better. Distance running was like a bank. If you didn't put miles into training, you couldn't make a withdrawal when the time came to race.

Dan was learning to find joy in sport that would last a lifetime. The miles were changing him. He wouldn't know for sure till he broke the plateau. A runner could see it clearly enough; there was a difference between feeling good and being happy. It was easy to feel good. Happiness had to be earned in the gray click of running.

Dan would find joy in distance running, unimaginable to the football or basketball or baseball player. The loneliness of the long-distance runner was sweet. Once you were good, and conatus ruled, your breathing and cadence were in rhythm, and you reached a state of perfect relaxation, and gravity and momentum took over, you were at peace, and your body became a conveyance, a vehicle that you could accelerate, decelerate, and steer, all with your mind.

If you wanted to improve not just as a runner but as a racer, you had to keep a record of your mileage, your training, and the times at various distances. In season, Coach P. charted the progress of the team, but if you wanted to make an impact on your own personal success, you had to study the charts and keep your own running journal, where you would keep track of everything that happened in practice and all the running you did on your own. The running you did on your own was the secret to success. If you wanted to max out, you ran twice a day. But getting out of a warm bed to enter freezing darkness and run was to the pubescent mind anathema.

You can't know why Superman Zika was a superman unless you've been in Chicago in the winter. Superman Zika ran in his white gym shorts and t-shirt, and that was it. He didn't even wear a jock. He said it made him feel free. He was Superman. If it was below zero, he'd put on a wool cap. Superman had his wool cap on. Superman just smiled. He didn't talk much. Zika didn't have much speed, and although his body temperature maintenance was unmatched, he was beatable in a race.

"He's fucken crazy."

"You think maybe running in weather like this might be bad for your lungs?

"I dunno. Maybe. What is it, like four below?"

"Eight. And the wind chill."

"N'gimme wind chill. This is Chicago, there's *wind*."

"If you can fill the unforgiving minute/ with sixty seconds' worth of distance run, / Yours is the Earth and everything that's in it." – Kipling

They would combine all the worst traits of the great runners, head flopping from side to side and arms crossing the chest like the great Jim Ryun, leaning to one side and landing with a heel strike like Pre, running a suicidal pace, or hanging so far back you were in last place, like Dave Wottle, before you started your kick. Roger Bannister broke four minutes in the mile, and the figure stuck in Dan's head and became his measure for pace. He could manage, at his peak, to maintain this pace for about 600 yards – that left 1000 yards to go, and he was completely out of gas. Dan's best race was probably somewhere between the 440 and the 880. 600 was just about right.

The mile relay team debate:

"What order are we gonna run?"

"We want our fastest guy running the anchor leg."

"Who's our fastest guy?"

"Dave."

"No, he's not. Dan's got a better kick."

"Who's got the better time?"

"Dan ran a 55."

"So did Dave."

"Dan's got a better kick."

And so it went. The hand-offs were no big deal. It was a 440 you were running, not a sprint. Still, guys mess up all the time. John Wilkes, then Mooney, then Dave, then Dan. Together, they could break four minutes. Together, they could challenge Jim Ryun. On a really good day, they could beat him.

Fat chance. Ryun had a better kick than Dan or Dave. He held the world record in the mile and the 1500 meters, and he was fooling around one day and broke the world record in the 880. He blew everybody away over the last 200 yards, long strides, arms pumping in countering pendulums. The exact opposite was Pre. Bursting out of the gate, hellbent on breaking the spirit of the other runners in the race, head tilted with the curve of the track. Pre was going to burn you out, gambling that he wouldn't burn himself out first, and when that happened, he would fade. Dead-man wasn't like that. Dead-man, Michael Bachner, didn't fade. Ever. He was dead solid steady from start to finish, like that crippled kid Chester playing golf, and at the end he was maybe a little gray and glowing, like he'd been painted with gray gloss. He wasn't even breathing hard; maybe there was evidence that he'd been sweating a little bit, a half circle of wet fabric at the neck of his jersey, but he was breathing normally, although his eyes were open abnormally wide.

Time and space in running come down to cadence and stride length. The cadence is the pattern of rapidity of footsteps, how many in a minute. The stride length measures the distance from one footstep to another, how much space you have covered.

"They're raising the distance for cross-country."

"Why?"

"It's not going to be two miles anymore."

"Why not?"

"Too short."

"What do you mean, it's too short? It's *two miles*!"

"The longer the better."

"Three miles?"

"No, Two point seven."

"You're making this up. That doesn't even make sense. Point seven?"

Point seven would make a difference. Dan was maxed out at two miles, more than maxed out. It was already beyond him; adding another point seven would make it certain. The distance had been two miles, and being raised to 2.7 was devastating for runners like Dan, who ran middle distance because they were fundamentally sprinters, but without elite sprinter speed. They just hung on at middle distance, hoping to be there at the end, where a finishing kick might win the day.

It was good news for Dead-man, Michael Bachner. He could use some good news. He didn't have much else going for him. Dead-man was not a hit with the girls. Dead-man was shy. He was not the least bit cool. He wore fruity clothes, and he wore them fruitily. He was short and skinny and disproportionate, his legs taking up, it seemed, two-thirds of him. And he was slow. How had he managed to be the fifth man on the team that won the city championship then? No one noticed. He lettered. Only non-senior who did. Dead-man was the dorkiest guy at Fenwick to sport a major letter. In a hundred-yard dash, he would finish last. He didn't appear to be very strong. He wasn't much of a conversationalist, didn't care to joke around, and in the way of boys, as a consequence, he became the butt of jokes. He was passive. If it hurt his feelings, he was used to having his feelings hurt. He was used to scorn, and he seemed oblivious to it, but that was just a defense.

Dead-man. Bachner. Call him Bachner. That was his name, Michael Bachner. Give him a little respect. Just a little. He had gone to St. Edmunds, and he lived in a big but broken-down house in the middle of the block on Gunderson Avenue with a bunch of little brothers and sisters. Dan and the guys on the team all thought of Dead-man, Bachner, as this worm, but to those little brothers and sisters, he was their big brother. They loved and respected him, whereas his teammates treated him like shit.

"He knows we love him".

"He knows we don't."

"He wants our love."

"He wants our respect. "

"He wants to be one of us, and he knows he never will."

How do you do it? Take someone like Bachner. What does he think about? What is he thinking, feeling, desiring, anticipating, fearing, hoping? Where does his mind wander? What does it feel like to be Bachner? How can a writer make that leap of imagination? Won't he know that he could be wrong? Of course. But why would he be wrong? Because he's that different from Bachner that he cannot even imagine the pain of his existence? Or does he just not want to go there? Dan was voted captain of the team because Bachner was too shy and introverted to lead the team, and no one else really gave a shit.

The wind was blowing hard. They would have to run into it. The day was beautiful, the sun so bright, the sky so blue. The frost was burning off in the morning sun, and there was bright green grass underneath it. The trees were turning colors, so there was a golden frame to everything.

"The brain – is wider than the Sky" – Emily Dickinson

In a Gadda da Vida was pounding through his head. The song lasted about as long as the race. Dan would listen to *In a Gadda da Vida*, lying in bed, rocking from side to side to the rhythm of the beating drums, like the cadence of his running, running faster and faster, harder and harder, on and on and on to the frantic crescendo, leaving him bathed in sweat, having run his race, visualized it most intently, given it his all. Now he would have nothing left for the real race. He had just doomed himself.

"When'd you wake up?"

"You mean, when'd I *get* up?"

Hard to say when he *woke* up – because it seemed like he was just lying there all night with his eyes closed, waiting. If he was sleeping, he was dreaming about the race or panicking because he wasn't asleep, or dreaming he woke up and had overslept, but that was impossible, and he told himself to stop and go to sleep, and by the time he woke up, he was exhausted.

Time to run the biggest race of your life. He knew it. Somewhere inside, he knew that he was doomed, and somewhere inside he knew that he was dooming himself. Why? All you've got to do is try. Then no one catches you from behind on the 8-yard line. If you could hang with Bachner, you could outkick him on the final straightaway. But how could you hang with him? He'd be applying pressure from the opening gun, his heart beating at 40 beats a minute, yours going twice that fast. In distance running, the general rule is whoever puts in the most work wins. It had ever been thus. But what it took to put in the most miles was a perfectly relaxed running form, the most efficient energy-conserving gait, cadence, and carriage. Michael Bachner's low heart rate was a huge advantage, as were his light frame and long legs.

You could get your second wind, find your rhythm, a breathing pattern. The worst thing you could do was panic. It was like drowning. He was drowning. If he had just waited. Distance running is all about patience, and Dan had none.

"Holding forth the word of life; that I may rejoice in the day of Christ, that I have not run in vain." – Philippians 2.16

Dan had run the course countless times before. They *practiced* there, Miller Meadow. In the dream, the sleeping and waking dream, *In a Gadda da Vida* was playing, and that long, long drum solo was turning Dan's dream race into his kick, into an all-out sprint. This was the way he envisioned it, the rhythm building and building to a climax, a crescendo, as he turned on his famous finishing kick, arms and legs pumping high and in perfect syncopation, flowing effortlessly, gliding ahead of the competition, those faceless runners he would give a sidelong glance in passing, as he went on to place somewhere in the top twenty, scoring precious points for the team, as well as winning a medal for himself. Perfect. That was the goal. It was within his grasp. He carefully examined every scintilla of speculation he might apply: the results of every dual meet and time trial at every course against every team in the North Section.

Was he going to quit that race? No. There would be no need to quit the race, no reason to quit it. He knew how to run a race. You start out slow and easy. You build your way up to top speed, which you do not want to reach until the end of the race. He knew how to run a race, so what was he thinking? What was he thinking all day long, calculating, figuring out split times, envisioning the whole race from every other runner's point of view? This was how Dan and his team were going to win the North Section championship. He had it all figured out. He was forecasting who the first 20 runners would be. Batromera from Gordon Tech would win it easily; no one had beaten him all year or was even close. Bachner would be decent, finish in the top five maybe, certainly top ten, Mooney and Davo top twenty, then Dan, he figured himself in there, scoring points.

He had run the race in his head a thousand times before the gun went off, and as soon as it went off, his energy vanished. They were all thundering across the field, the great mass without a leader yet, sprinting for position before they hit the first turn, three hundred yards ahead, where the path began and they would string out, the path wide enough for just three or four runners abreast and you would need to sprint to pass anyone, expend energy early in the race that you would need later. But Dan never got that far. He sprinted near the head of the crowd, glanced around at the contenders and pretenders, instantly realized which one he was, and dropped out of the race.

He would tell everyone he had a pulled muscle. He would limp. He would act. He would pretend. He was a pretender. He had pretended to be the captain of the team, but when the team needed him most, he disappeared. He flat out quit. Why? Because it was too hard. He was already out of breath. They were better runners than he was, that's all, and he couldn't admit it. He had to lie to cover himself. No one said anything to him about it. They all seemingly accepted his explanation without question. But anyone could see that it was bullshit. Pulled muscle. Come *on*. He wasn't hurt. He was afraid. He was just afraid.

They all ran their own race. When the lead pack came around the last turn, there were two runners about 20 yards ahead of the rest. It was hard to make out just who they were at first, and although they were moving fast, they didn't appear to be sprinting; they were just flowing and at an ever-increasing rate of speed, still maybe a quarter of a mile away. It was Bachner, the little twerp, the Dead-man.

"He that is dead is free from sin." Romans 6-7

Bartomera must have wanted to kick past Bachner, but he just couldn't do it. Whatever was left of his once mighty kick dribbled out over the open field, and he was fading all the way to the end, losing ground to Dead-man, steady as a metronome. His resting pulse was 42 beats a minute. He was maybe up in the 50s or 60s now. His teammates called him Dead-man. They made fun of him mercilessly, and then he beat them all and everybody else. He was the North Section champ!

You can pity him. You can mock him, deride him, make fun of him, scorn him, rebuke him, laugh at him, but you end by being embarrassed by him. The humiliation is all yours. You are the coward, the lustful, intemperate, impetuous youth, the fool in his folly, following the fallen angels, hunting down all the wrong paths, futilely seeking something that doesn't exist – happiness.

Coach P. looked at Dan.

"What happened? "

"I think I pulled a muscle. "

Coach P got down on his knees and prodded at Dan's calf. Dan had big calf muscles, and if he overtrained, they would tighten up and cramp.

"Did you stretch? Yes? Enough? Did you stretch enough? It's ok. I'm just telling you, you need to stretch, Dan. Don't try to do it now. Yes. It's tight. I'm sorry. We've got a week till City, stay off it till Monday, and we'll see where we're at."

He instantly regretted it, and it was instantly irrevocable. He was going to have to live with it forever. He had quit. He was a quitter. He was a coward. He had been exposed. He could have run a bad race. He could have just run a bad race, and that would have been better. He would have regretted a bad race too, but not like this. This was the worst thing anyone could do. It was inexcusable, unforgivable. You're not hurt, you're just afraid. Afraid of what? Failing. By quitting, you fail.

CHAPTER EIGHTEEN

James Baldwin handed Buckley his ass at Cambridge. Resolved: The American dream is at the expense of the American Negro. No shit. "Your people, sir, are not ready to rule themselves." Those were Buckley's words. He had the gall to say that. Baldwin wondered, "What happens to the poor white man's, the poor white woman's mind? Their moral lives have been destroyed by the plague called color." Master and slave – neither one is free.

Tom Ayers was the boss of Commonwealth Edison. His son Bill was a class traitor and proud of it. Bill Ayers and Ciaran were just a year apart. Ciaran was headed into the Marines and Vietnam. Bill Ayers was headed for the Weathermen. Ciaran had come out of Ascension and Fenwick and Oak Park. Ayers came out of Glen Ellyn and Forest Glen School.

There was a Black lady named Celeste who cleaned the Ayers' house, just like Ruth cleaned the Finnegan house. Bill Ayers went to Lake Forest Academy. He was the starting guard on the football team, weighing 145 pounds, while Fenwick was winning the Prep Bowl 40-0. Ayers spent four years at Lake Forest and hated every minute of it. Then he went to Michigan. The Wolverines. And he tried out for the football team. He tried to walk on. At Michigan, the Wolverines, he must've been delusional. He quit school after a year, ending up in Detroit, still living on Big Daddy's dime, powered by Commonwealth Edison. He decides to become a freedom rider.

"You don't need a weatherman to know which way the wind blows." So, they took Dylan's lyric as their anthem and called themselves the Weathermen, when the song plainly said you don't need a weatherman. "I am the catcher in the rye." "Bring the war home." But if the troops, the soldiers, were warmongers and baby killers, why would you want to bring them home? So they could become cops?

There was the war, and there was the war against the war. The Weathermen were studying *The Blaster's Handbook*, learning to make bombs, to go along with the weapons of the street, brass knuckles, saps, and garrotes. Working class, my ass, that's Mr. Ayers' kid. Do you have any idea how horrible this is? War. Riots. Hate. Hypocrisy. Ignorance. Fear. Cowardice. What's not to love about it? Have a love-in. A happening. And the terrible, ghastly shit the Cong did to the Americans they captured? What about that? Bill Ayers, whose father was the boss of Commonwealth Edison, had joined up with the Weathermen, and the plan was to provoke a response from the pigs, and it would play on TV.

About a million Vietnamese people were going to be murdered, but no one was going anywhere. It wasn't like we were out to conquer Vietnam, drive the enemy out, and take over. The enemy was not going anywhere. The enemy was just waiting for us to leave. A little Vietnamese girl was running naked down a country road, screaming and crying because she'd been coated with a gasoline-gel that was incinerating her, and she had her picture taken, and that was what the enemy looked like. Bomb them into the Stone Age. Gooks. It didn't take long. One day, nobody even knows what Vietnam is, let alone where it is, the next day we're fighting a war there and calling the people who live there gooks.

A flower child was putting a flower in the gun barrel of a helmeted soldier. A hundred thousand French soldiers died in Vietnam before the French got the hell out, before the French learned that imperialism was over. Still, the spread of Communism had to be stopped. Why? Dan wanted to declare a separate peace. A separate peace was the notion that one could tell the rest of the world to fuck off. Unfortunately, no one in the world was in a position to do that successfully. Go to Canada. Draft-dodger. Warmonger. Traitor. Baby-killer.

The smell of pot was in the air, strong and sweet enough to be inviting. There was weed and free love and anarchy, or there was a crew cut and see how many of you could fit into a phone booth with Dobie Gillis and Maynard G. Krebs and Jed Clampett, and Dan wanted to squeeze in next to Judy Carne in her miniskirt. In the summer, Charlie Manson sent his followers out on their killing spree. In Chicago, there had already been the black and white version, Richard Speck's Night of the Nurses. Roman Polanski's *Repulsion* in black and white was playing at the Clark Theater.

In the minds of the Weathermen, blowing shit up would make the government stop the war. They didn't want the war to come to an end; they wanted it to just stop, freeze, and then disappear. The war *was* going to end, but it wasn't going to stop in the middle. It wouldn't stop until the end.

Dan was the middle child of a middle-class family in the middle of America in the middle of the century in the middle of the cold war in the middle of the war in Vietnam, in the middle, being as close to the getting in as the getting out. Another thirty-thousand troops would have to die first, after another mind-blowing psychedelic orgy of death and rancor and mind-body split, insanity, car crashes, cigarettes, booze, broads, Beatles, breakdowns, beatings and a whole lot of laughs, sick laughs, desperate laughing, exhaustive laughing and braying, until it would finally peter out and the last helicopter would take off from the roof of the embassy in Saigon, and Ho Chi Minh would win, Vietnam would win, what was left of it, but that wouldn't come until the end, and this was just the middle. Not knowing that it was the middle only made it worse. Poor schmucks. Think they're going to stop the war. Poor schmucks. Think they're going to win the war. They were both dead wrong. *Of course,* life is tragic – we *die*.

"What are you going to do if you get drafted?"

"First of all, I'm not going to get drafted."

"But what would you do if you did?"

"Go in, I guess. I don't have the balls not to."

"You're saying it takes more balls to, what, run away? Go to Canada?"

"Amsterdam."

"But you don't have the balls to."

The combination of abortion rights, birth control pills, and gay liberation was signaling strongly to Dan that sex was for fun, that having sex could and did feel insanely good, and now Dan was getting the unmistakable message that that was good enough. Guys would wear a rubber so as not to knock a broad up. Broads would wear a diaphragm, or they'd take the pill, which is a mortal sin. Mortal sin? You want a broad knocked up? You want to have to marry her? Like a good Catholic! A good Catholic wouldn't have sex before marriage. Get real. Terry Flaherty got a girl pregnant, and his life was over.

If you preferred peace to war, you wore your hair long. At Fenwick, long hair was not allowed.

At home, long hair was also not allowed, and Dan didn't want long hair anyway. The great runners didn't have long hair. When Jim Ryun was a sophomore in high school, he had a *crewcut*.

Could you protest the war if your brother was fighting in it? *Should* you protest the war while your brother was fighting in it? Anybody can protest the war. Everybody is going to protest the war. Nobody wants this war.

"Really? Stop the spread of Communism."

"Warmonger."

Warmonger was one of the worst things you could call a warmonger because they didn't like to admit they were repressed and love-starved and pitiful; they would prefer to be called warriors, but you could only be called a warrior when your foe was another warrior, not women and children and old men that you sprayed with bullets or gas. Buckley supported the war, and Nathan DeGrorio did not. Buckley didn't have to fight in it, but Nathan DeGrorio might.

Eighteen years, from birth and infancy to being a young boy to the cusp of manhood, all while the world was spinning madly, more and more out of control, which means only that the *more* and *more* indicated that the out of control nature of things had been preexistent, pre-mid-century, in a world where a serious attempt could be made to eliminate an entire race of human beings, only to be stopped short of its goal by the allied forces of nations themselves built on slavery and genocide. These were no good old days. There were no good old days.

English lit was Wordsworth, Keats, Shelley, Byron. Dan loved Dickens and Melville and Robert Louis Stevenson. Then the world opened further and let Dostoyevsky in. Dan was Nicholas Urfe. Urfe's got the whole weekend before him, good food, swimming, booze, beautiful scenery, smoking cigarettes, learning a bunch of arcane shit, add a little mystery, and some perfume to indicate the presence of a woman. Nicko is to be some sort of judge. Suddenly, there's a man with the head of a stag. The Bosch-like

figures from the book's cover art come alive. The bridge from Fenwick to
The Magus was ritual.

The evidence presented at the trial shows Nicko for what he is, a loser
in every way, worse, a villain, who preys upon women and is doomed to
a psychological hell, a life of guilt-ridden, lonely misery. His unconscious
directs him to situations that are sure to piss him off, ignite his hostility.
Nicko was a hell of a lot more like Dan than he was like Nathan. Nathan
could read the book and be done with it. Nathan could appreciate it for its
literary qualities and philosophical content, and move on, but Dan would
be stuck there.

Dan lived with polarities, one brother older and heroic, one brother
younger and feeble-minded. Was he his brother's keeper? His younger
brother did not follow the family footsteps and matriculate with the nuns
at Ascension and the priests at Fenwick. The nuns and priests could not
care for him, so he went the secular route. The irony was not lost on Dan,
who listened to Nathan when he extolled the virtues of Oak Park High,
where he might be taking courses in film studies in a classroom he would
share with pretty girls, not that Dan had ever seen Nathan so much as
talk to a girl ever. Nathan made it seem as though he'd be sitting in the
darkened classroom studying the jump-cuts of Jean Luc-Godard with a
bevy of Playboy bunnies.

No, Dan was not his younger brother's keeper. He looked to the state
for that. It was equipped with special ed teachers. What if all the education
that Dan had received had been positively harmful to him? All of it, the
entire plot, was capturing the right side of Dan's brain, quitting the football team, quitting the race, the 80-yard run to futility, the errant throw to
first, the desperation, humiliation, anger, and isolation. Disintoxication.
That's what he needed, and he was going to get it. Reading *The Magus*
on a Catholic retreat was like the nuns taking the boys and girls on a field

trip in eighth grade to see *Lawrence of Arabia* at the Michael Todd Theater downtown in *Cinerama*. What were they thinking?

Nicko regrets not being *more* violent with Lily when he had the chance. He hates her now, and he wants to get revenge. He's ruled by emotion, hostility, hatred, anger, rage – because he's been humiliated. That was different than humiliating yourself, but not much. It felt just about the same. The only difference was who you wanted to get back at, yourself or somebody else. Your punishment: to live a life of humiliation and shame and constant embarrassment. Not constant. And everybody was capable of being humiliated. If you were Black or poor or disabled, you could be humiliated daily, in a near constant barrage, differing from day to day only in intensity, all through no fault of your own, issuing in fact from your perfect innocence. Whereas the Fenwick boys might experience the depths of humiliation when Father Farrell, the hippy priest, plumbed the depths not of their souls, but of their nether parts. How did that feel? It hurt. It scarred them for life. It, meaning Father Farrell. *Veritas.*

While he might have been discovering himself or the world around him, Dan was preoccupied with finding the right sport or art that he might practice with natural affinity such that he might distinguish himself, and instead he found nothing but his natural inclinations, his esteem for the body, his own and others', with the Greek ideal of perfection, so that you would measure yourself against the best, where you would never measure up. Same thing went for the mind. He was lost.

So, he's dealing with these polarities, these extremes, every day and night without escape. When he's scared, he might turn to his mother, maybe to his father, but probably not to either of them, because they wouldn't understand, and, besides, everybody was on one side or the other, with God and the angels or down with the devil, who, frankly, seemed to have the better argument. It's the devil who argues against God, finds holes in God's argument, holes that Aquinas tried to patch with a coat of Aristotle.

Chapter Nineteen

Sgt. Pepper changed everything. What a change had come over the Beatles. They, too, had gone from black and white to color. John said the Beatles were more popular than Jesus. Well, there were four of them. Orpheus lost his head. Or, maybe, Orpheus *was* his head. His songs were in his head, and even after he was dead and his head was chopped off, well, he was dead because his head was chopped off, but that didn't stop him, or it, whatever, from singing. His song lived on. It was nighttime in the summer at Fox Park, and the girls were out looking for fun with the boys.

Elvira Madigan was a movie at the Lamar that you went to see in the spring to be in love, just like *Dr. Zhivago* had been to cozy up in Siberian winter, with a subtle difference, the difference between Patti and Patty, the difference between being a freshman and being a senior. Or you could go downtown to the Loop to the movies all by yourself, sit by yourself, in the dark, anonymous, with anonymous strangers, all of you in the dark, and you could be *alone*.

We live in doubt and fear, but we're cocksure of ourselves and we like shit that scares the shit out of us – for *fun*. We like Halloween, we like horror movies, we like suspense, we like violence, or at least the threat of it, we take delight in revenge, we get our rocks off seeing someone get the shit kicked out of him, or her. Yes! Maybe that's going too far, but you get the idea. A little violence goes a long way, and a lot of violence goes even longer, becomes history, attractive not just for an audience, but for the public at large, the populous, for all the civilization that Eddie Fenwick went searching for back in time, sailing against the tide back to Europe, and then blasting forward to everything that history has spewed forth since. It's all of a piece, it's all true, and it's all happening at once, past, present, future – just three different ways of saying *now*. That's what *rosebud* means: it's burning up.

In black and white: *Citizen Kane,* all of Bergman, *La Dolce Vita*, *The Bells of Saint Mary's*, the Three Stooges, *Flash Gordon*, *The Maltese Falcon*, *77 Sunset Strip*. While Bergman imagines and realizes *Persona* in 1966. . . It starts with a boy born in 1951, Jorgen Lindstrom. That weird, sickly, fragile kid reaching out toward his mother's face on a giant screen in *Persona*, a kid just Dan's age, his contemporary, who would also accompany the two women in *The Silence* – Michael Bachner was a dead-ringer for that kid. Dan saw Bergman movies as a teenager. *The Seventh Seal* came out in 1957, but Dan wouldn't see it till at least 10 years later, perfectly timed to listen to God's silence. And then *Hour of the Wolf*. Black and white was one world, and color was another. They were not the same, could not be, would never be the same.

One thing that had to be said about John Fowles and Ingmar Bergman and just about every other cultural icon close to Dan's heart, with the exception of Hemingway, was that they were *not* American, and even Buckley affected an accent that was *not* American. Buckley would argue, eloquently no doubt, that it was *not* an affectation, but it was undeniable that no one else in the world talked that way. It was a foreign tongue, and in fact, there was nothing particularly American about conservatism. The roots were in Scotland with Adam Smith and in England with Thomas Burke.

The Vietnam War came on television – in *color*. Beethoven's Ninth Symphony came booming at him out of the tube carrying David Brinkley and the Nightly News. The music was so much better than the news. Better in terms of aesthetics. Music. We are particularly susceptible to music, particularly music without words, symphonies, because we see things in it, colors, landscapes, places, memories, sensations, emotions, we feel things in music we can't feel without it. We just feel things in music – we can't help it. And here comes the news. Jarring. In his head, the Ninth continued, a soundtrack now to the Vietnam War.

The many plot points emerge in the sequence that chronologically depicts Dan's growth and experience as a faux athlete and aesthete. It has a circular pattern – it begins and ends in running. In the middle of the 20th century. A stream of consciousness centered on Oak Park and the first 18 years of Daniel Finnegan's life. Snapshots. Scenes. Glimpses, all fractured, disconnected, no sense of beginning, middle, and end, but trying to get a sense of fullness, magnitude, then sort it into themes, and then join them all together chronologically, have them all happen in time in a sequence or simultaneously, the world, historic events, and Dan's life, concurrent, unfolding, happening to him then and there, the world of the 50s and 60s as it is produced and discovered. When Connor Finnegan was born, Proust was composing *In Search of Lost Time*, and he would keep at it until he died, as young Connor reached the age of reason. Finding Proust in Saints Rest.

"There is no man, however wise, who has not at some period of his youth said things or lived a life, the memory of which is so unpleasant to him that he would gladly expunge it. And yet he ought not entirely to regret it, because he cannot be certain that he has indeed become a wise man – so far as it is possible for any of us to be wise – unless he has passed through all the fatuous or unwholesome incarnations by which the ultimate sage must be preceded. We do not receive wisdom; we must discover it for ourselves." – Proust

Nothing wrong with making mistakes. That's how we learn. There is certainly something wrong with mistakes – that's what makes them mistakes. But there's nothing wrong with *making* the mistake, because without making the mistake, we would never learn what is to be discovered only by mistake. But what if there was no need to go there in the first place? You should have known better. And now you do. Wiser for all that. A wise man is not wise in comparison with other men; he is wise compared to stupid. Then, of course, there's always the fatal mistake.

The Democratic Convention was going to be held in McCormick Place, but then McCormick Place burned down. DaMare wasn't going to let that stop Chicago from hosting the Democratic convention. It would just have to be held in the ancient Chicago Amphitheater instead, where just four months before, the Fenwick Friars had whupped Crane Tech, in a game of white versus Black, to win the city basketball title.

The only problem with the antiwar protest downtown during the convention was that there was no objective to it beyond just trying to fuck things up, and things were already fucked up. Kennedy and Johnson were half-ass liberals who seemed to have backed into a war that was stupid, evil, and unwinnable, and now they didn't know how to get out. At the Democratic Convention in the Amphitheater, Bill Ayers was caught up in the public consciousness with Lenin and the Russian Revolution and Che Guevarra and Castro and the Cuban revolutionaries, so even if the domino theory, which pictured America as the last nation to fall to Communism like all the rest, was fundamentally silly, the fiery rhetoric of the Weathermen could nonetheless give plenty of credence to middle class fears. Dan was oblivious.

"You think the world revolves around you?"

"You mean, do I see things from my own point of view? I'd kind of have to, wouldn't I?"

Dan did think the world revolved around him. But that wasn't the problem. The problem was that the world revolved around him at about a million miles a second. He was living in the eye of a cosmic hurricane, a tiny spec at the center of his own consciousness, while Bill Ayers was getting ready to kill someone. Bill Ayers didn't want to fight in the war either, but there was a difference; Bill Ayers didn't want the war being fought. He was going to do something about it. Dan didn't do anything, and Bill Ayers wound up getting someone killed in his misguided attempt to stop the war. By mistake, a bomb of his blew up a janitor instead of a warmonger. Now Bill Ayers and his band of desperados were up to dirty tricks. They weren't just there to protest the war; they were there to fuck things up.

"They're comin' here from other places," sez DeMare.

If you were from Chicago, there was nothing lower you could say of someone. DeMare would grant no permits for camping overnight in Lincoln Park, like the Boy Scouts used to do, so the 11 PM curfew was going to be *enforced*. There were 25,000 Chicago cops, plus the National Guard, and their orders, apparently, were to beat the living shit out of everybody. They weren't about to let the would-be rioters beat them to the punch. The police rioted first.

Dan watched the riots on TV, just like people in France and Miami and Timbuktu watched it, in wonderment. But for Dan, there was a personal attachment. Wow, that's happening right downtown. Yet none of it touched him. Heads were being busted in Lincoln Park and along Michigan Avenue, but Dan was safe, with his short hair and his Fenwick blazer, white-collared shirt, tie, dark trousers, with a belt, and cuffs, 21 minutes away from the Loop by el, in Oak Park, beyond the cul-de-sacs along Austin Boulevard, where only criminals and fools would venture,

with the exception of the noble, like Father Farrell, the hippy priest, who
was going down there, down into the inner-city to save souls, like that
priest in that old movie where the ship was sinking or the building was on
fire and people were trapped and doomed and there was no getting them
out or rescuing them, and somebody tried to stop the priest from rushing
headlong right the hell in there, because he wasn't going to save anybody's
life, they were all going to die, but he was going the hell in there anyway
because he was going to baptize people before they died so their souls could
go to heaven.

"Don't go in there, father! For the Love of God!"

"For the Love of God, I am going in there."

Now there was one selfless act. Selfless and saintly and stupid.

Once the gas spread over the park, the Weathermen grabbed at anything they could get their hands on to throw at the cops: stones, bottles,
concrete from the potholes in the street, and fanned out in all directions,
spreading the cops' forces thinner. In the Amphitheater, Senator Abraham
Ribicoff of Connecticut was saying: "The turmoil and violence is compet-
ing with this great convention for the attention of the American people."
And then he said something about the cops using Gestapo tactics, and
DeMare's face turned purple, and he blew up. "Fuck you, you Jew son
of a bitch, you lousy motherfucker, go home!" The *lousy* was particularly
Chicago. The riot started in Grant Park. The only way out was onto Michigan Avenue. Everybody there knew it and started chanting it: "The whole
world is watching."

Gore Vidal called Buckley a Nazi. Buckley called Vidal a queer, as
if they were equivalent pejoratives, and balled his fist and threatened to
punch him, thereby completely losing the argument and worse, losing his
famous cool, his signature sangfroid. Buckley had lost another fight. He
could recover from the loss to James Baldwin because Baldwin was Black.

But he would never be the same after humiliating himself by *physically* threatening Vidal. He would never again be the imperturbable Buckley after that.

Chapter Twenty

I n the photo, Dan is wearing his letter sweater, standing in the doorway that opened onto Van Buren Street, and the sun is streaming in. Mary Finnegan took the picture with her new Instamatic camera. Dan was on his way to school, and it was spring, and he was a senior. The sweater was a snow white V-neck, with a big black F on the chest. On the right sleeve would be a stripe for every year you had earned a major letter. Some seniors had two or three black stripes on their sleeves, but no one had four. It was virtually impossible for someone to earn a major letter as a freshman at Fenwick of the Chicago Catholic League, pipeline to Notre Dame, because to earn a major letter, you had to be a starter or significant player for a varsity team, not the frosh-soph or jayvee team. A major letter meant playing, not sitting on the bench, and not being the tenth man on a cross-country team when only the top five runners score points. Dan had only one stripe on his arm, and it was not black; it was gold. The only major letter he had earned had come in his senior year. The stripe was gold because Dan was the captain of the team. And in his senior year, he had been fourth or fifth man in most of the races, except for when it counted most.

As for the pursuit of knowledge, carnal knowledge was precisely the right term for what Dan was after. He wanted to know her, whoever she was, Patty or Patti or Ronnie or Brenda Sloan or that girl in the Ridgeland-Commons pool whose name he couldn't remember – inside and out, up and down, carnally, smelling, tasting, touching, all in pursuit of knowledge, to know her, all about her, carnally, the way Adam knew Eve.

Of course, real people in the real world didn't give a shit what the Pope said about birth control.

Abortion would be another matter. As soon as a fetus came into play, all manner of God-fearing Christians could get on board with defending the unborn. Then it was beyond the pale. No one had the right to eliminate a fetus once it had come into existence inside the host's body. What about the host? Fuck her. But what about a pill that would prevent the existence of the fetus? That was ok, wasn't it? Everybody knew it was ok and acted as if it was ok. Guys had always used rubbers, and that was ok, wasn't it? No. The Pope says No. And don't touch yourself. Jesus. Jesus never touched himself. What? He was pure. Sex and sin were one, and that was why it was fun. It felt good because it was bad. Why was it so tempting, and at what cost could it be overcome? Put an end to desire.

Veronica Wipes the Face of Jesus. Daniel knelt before each of the Stations of the Cross and tried to contrive a personal meaning for each one, and here Veronica was clearly offering solace, so, in Daniel's version, Ronnie was absolving him of all guilt for cheating on Patty. That's a stretch. "We're not married. And we're not going to get married. And if she never finds out about it, what's the difference?" You could, for a time, follow a false god. Or gods. Was there no inkling of it at the time? No, none. Yes. There was. And it grew. That's called guilt. What should he do, see a shrink? You think you can get rid of it? You can't. Accept it. Live with it. Face up to it. Don't forgive yourself. You don't need to be forgiven. And you don't need to be punished. Guilt is both crime and punishment. Self-denying fanaticism. To be religious is to be sick. The moment you question the meaning of life, your mind is sick, because there is none.

Tweak your pleasure principle sufficiently to keep it in line with the reality principle, a transubstantiation of pleasure into something else. There is a way around the reality principle – a place called Fantasy. Sweet dreams.

Nothing is more frightening than a labyrinth with no center to it. We lie all the time with words, but it's a lot harder with actions. Not false moves. Those are just mistakes. We're talking about actions meant to deceive. Make it look like something else happened. The only way to cope with it is to keep repeating the mantra don't think – don't think – don't think – aloud, it has to be aloud, you have to say the two words out loud, put your tongue through the motions and make it tap against the back of your teeth and the roof of your mouth like a snare drum and make it roll, and for those seconds that you do that, and for just then, you will be all right. But it will only last an instant. You can't control your mind. It will race right past you and strike your heart. How beautiful life is, how much you love your own tears, your own heartache. The ancients had a wisdom – prisca sapientia. It has been lost. Daniel was about to undergo a paradigm shift. What was being taught under the guise of faith, hope, and love was how to hate. Do you want to be excommunicated? Hell no. Turn the candles upside down and snuff out your flame? Climb the Tower of Oblivion. Any regrets? Everything. All of it. He would go back and un-quit everything he quit, score that touchdown by running hard all the way through the endzone, he would gobble up that grounder and make the easy throw to first. Right the wrongs. It certainly wasn't a question of God anymore. Do you have to take sides? You are forced to take a side. You have no choice. That's just the way it is. Not taking a side is taking a side. Which one? The wrong one. You can't know that. You've taken a side.

Pride is the beginning of all sin. – Aquinas

Regret. A lifetime of regret lay before him. He was seventeen. It had taken just seventeen years for the world to turn into a piece of shit. No redeemer. No redemption. Are you the Holy Fool?

You wouldn't know, would you?

"My days are swifter than a weaver's shuttle and are spent without hope. O remember that my life is wind; mine eye shall no more see good. Why hast thou set me as a mark against thee, so that I am a burden to myself?" Job 7:6

His head filled with such nonsense, his heart pounding, his energy draining, its reservoir punctured, the vital force flooding out of him, and the gun went off. What Dan could not know in all his misery and angst and self-loathing was that by failing, and particularly by quitting, he was setting himself up for perpetual persistence. He would never give up now. Once it no longer mattered, he would run and play and live like an athlete until he died, and the harder he tried, the longer and the better he would live. It was a good thing. He didn't have to search for happiness.

He was happy. He was just too stupid to know it.

Maybe that was why he quit, because he saw the end coming, and he didn't want it to end; he wanted to freeze it right there. How awful that would have been, what a nightmare, to be trapped in 1968. That would be Hell. Guys got blown up. Life ended at age 18 or 20. Why not kill yourself? Why? Life is too awful. But what's different about it? It was awful yesterday, and you didn't kill yourself. You wanted to. Wanted to, and then you didn't. You didn't do it. And then you didn't get what you wanted, so that was frustrating. It made things worse. You made things worse. Things get worse on their own. There is no worse for things.

Dan was from the suburbs. He and his ilk aspired to be bourgeoisie. Connor was on the cusp, high enough in the Com Ed hierarchy to earn a high salary, but more than that, he was an inventor, and with some skillful planning, an early retirement, presto, a new career; he turned himself into an entrepreneur, more than a private contractor, he was president of his own company. He was a member of the Riverside Country Club now. Connor Finnegan was a member of the bourgeoisie. He made it. He lived the American Dream, Pop's dream when he bolted from Ireland.

Your best bet would be to join up before you got drafted, or you could go to officer training school and join as an officer. You didn't want to go in as a buck private, and you didn't want to serve in the infantry because those guys got shot, and you didn't want to drive a tank because somebody could drop a grenade in there and blow you up, so stay home. You could burn your draft card and go to prison in noble protest or worm your way out of it in a half-ass protest like Arlo Guthrie because you can get anything you want at Alice's Restaurant.

When Dan turned 18, he'd be eligible for the draft, but he'd be in college and he'd have a student deferment, and what were the chances the war would last for four more years? It had been going on since he was in grade school. All he was really worried about was holding onto the first steady piece of ass he'd ever gotten. He was loath to give it up just to go to college. She let him touch her bare ass in the back seat of his Corvair at the drive-in. They had been making out for weeks, and when they decided to go to the drive-in, they both knew it meant only one thing, and it wasn't seeing the movie. Climbing into the back seat increased the possibilities horizontally, and she was lying on top of him, and he reached behind her and ever so slowly, so that she could stop him whenever she liked, so that if she allowed him to keep going it must be because she liked it, because he liked her and it was genuine, and he didn't want to hurt her feelings, he didn't want to make her cry, and he would gladly settle for whatever he could get away with, along with the promise that there would be more where that came from, if he were polite and waited, and now suddenly the waiting was over and he was touching her actual ass, her bare bottom beneath his very fingers, so smooth and firm and his finger traced down to the crack, and she whispered, "That tickles" and she stuck her tongue in his ear.

Get some Mad Dog. Whiskey. Get some whiskey. Scotch. Bourbon. Irish Cream. That sounds good. Southern Comfort. Jack Daniels. Just gimme a beer. Hamms, the beer refreshing. Get drunk, so you can drive your car real fast and crash and kill yourself, which is a sin, and you will go to Hell. You can escape both death and Hell for a while by living.

Ciaran is a war hero, Dan is a schmuck. He's failing algebra, he's jerking off, and he's a basketball fan because he's not good enough to make the team. Nathan DeGrorio is leading him in a different direction – the opposite way, toward the arts. Dan is an inept follower of both paths. Nathan's path forks as well. Simon versus Sontag. Buckley versus Vidal. Buckley versus Baldwin. Buckley versus Mailer. Nathan versus his mom. Bergman. Welles. Fowles. Urfe. Books. Films. Trash, Art, and the Movies.

Dan will be a senior, leading the troops. He's the captain of the cross-country team. The team isn't all that good. Dan isn't all that good. He tries, but it's really not his thing, distance running.

And on the weekends, he likes to drink. The senior class in general sucks. But are they not followers of Christ? All the while, the Church has been instructing the student body in the Summa Theologica. The doctrine of the Trinity has been blowing their minds because birth control is legal, the Pope was a Nazi, and Father Farrell is a pervert.

One girlfriend after another. Playing the field, but don't let one know about the other. Can you get some booze? One thing about being a kid, it was somewhere back there before you started drinking, because things would never be the same after you'd had your first drink. You didn't have to grow up to be a drunk or an alcoholic, but still, your first encounter with alcohol is a life-changing event. The whole world changes from black and white to color when alcohol enters the picture. From that point on, there will be the people who drink and the people who don't. Danny felt destined to drink; the fact that he was Irish, just one generation removed from the old sod, simply sealed the deal.

Booze, broads, and cigarettes. In the 1950s, there were athletes in uniform hawking cigarettes on TV, but by the 60s, it was generally understood that smoking was harmful, so you did it because you were bad, because of that rush you got from a drag on a cigarette that was like a little taste of death, that was why it took your breath away. Cancer sticks. You want to die? Yes. No. Yes. No. Smoking and drinking go together like love and marriage. Have a drink, smoke a cigarette. Nice glass of Scotch and a cigarette. Cold beer and a cigarette. It's nice to eat a really good meal and afterward smoke a cigarette. It's nice to make love and then smoke a cigarette. All of this lies before you once you start in on booze, broads, and cigarettes.

Davo was Dan's best friend now. They had run miles and miles together, gotten drunk, double-dated, and hung out. Mean Gene had been Dan's best friend when they were in pre-school and at the playground. Schweez was his best sporting bud. Oddly, yes, Nathan DeGrorio was Dan's friend, even Nathan would now half-ass concede that, but he would not venture best. Somehow, the fact that Nathan didn't need any friends was attractive to Dan and made him want to establish a friendship with Nathan, another instance of a lark taken seriously, then taken too far, only to prove in the end, yes, that was a mistake. Just wanted to be sure.

Davo was his only drinking buddy, and they got drunk together in the basement of the Castle. He wanted to impress Davo, so they hopped in Connor's Chrysler Imperial instead of his drive-in make-out Corvair, and he drove Davo back to the south side. Then Dan drove home. He drove very, very fast, but he didn't get there right away. First, he had a crash.

There he was, drunk, without a scratch on him, but the Chrysler totaled, the stoplight down. The other car, the one that swiped its tail as the Imperial almost flashed through the intersection, was nearly unscathed. Running the red light, speeding, reckless driving, all of that and more, his father's insurance rate would zoom to the heavens. It was Connor's car, and that made it Connor's fault, and all of it would combine to make Connor Finnegan, son of James Finnegan of Derry, Ireland, feel like shit, dishearten him.

If Dan had been killed in that crash, it would've been sad as shit, but it would have been well deserved. He was a little asshole who had it coming. It was just lucky he hadn't killed anybody in the other car. They weren't hurt. Their car wasn't even too badly damaged. It merely grazed the rear end of the gold Chrysler as it flashed past them, a blur, and sent it spinning into the traffic light, which toppled and crashed in a rain of sparks streaming straight along the rainbow streak that trailed from the gas tank, and BOOM!

How demoralizing was it for Connor to know that his most talented and promising offspring was really a wastrel, a lazy, impetuous, irresponsible profligate prodigal son, whom he still loved, which only made it hurt all the more. And why? Because Dan's mind was incapable of doing anything but wish. A wish and a prayer.

Connor would often tell the tale of the father who sets his young son, just a few years old, on the mantel, and tells him to "jump – dad will catch you," and when the kid jumps, dad steps back, and the kid falls flat on his face, and dad says: "That's your first lesson in business: Never trust anyone." What's more fucked up here? That this could be considered funny or that it could be considered good advice? Answer: Both. That was why Connor told the story, instead of setting little Danny-boy on the mantel.

If Dan had burned to death, trapped in the car, there being no Hell, that would've been Hell, and justice would've been served, punishment meted out, for cheating on Patty, quitting the North Section Meet, getting caught from behind on the eight yard-line, losing to Larry Sullivan when he could've out-boxed him, throwing the ball into the dugout to blow the game they had won, for writing the names of his grandparents in the memoriam section of the missal that he got for his first communion, when they weren't even dead yet, and then losing the missal after stupidly bringing it with him while adventuring in the construction site of the Congress Expressway, for stealing all that change from his father's glass pooch, and last, but certainly not least, for whacking off. Whacked for whacking off. By fate. By pure hazard. By dumb luck. For all the bad shit he did, for all the stupid-ass mistakes he'd made, he was undoubtedly one lucky motherfucker.

What did he care if the Cubs fell apart? That was on them. It always was. Or if Floyd Patterson was destroyed by Sonny Liston or if Sonny Liston was murdered? What did he care if Nixon was President, or if Jack and Bobby Kennedy and Martin Luther King and Malcom X got shot to death, or Fred Hampton, or those eight nurses Richard Peck stabbed and killed, or a million people in Vietnam? If it wasn't hazard, it may perhaps have been an instance of God's grace. When the Chrysler slammed into the stoplight, reality exploded into Dan's life. He had been flying, a flight of fancy, trying to escape himself, just as he had run away from football, and now he was running away from running, driving away, flying away, and it played itself out finally with the crash, in case anyone had any doubts as to how it might end. You can step off the track, but the world doesn't stop spinning, at an incredible speed, with the winds of change swirling, men, women, and children dying in an undeclared war a world away, where his brother hovered above the battlefield that could barely be seen since it was submerged in jungle. Do you want to understand it, or do you want to run away from it? Both. You can't run away from it. You can try. All you're doing is running. You carry it with you wherever you go, not just Oak Park and Chicago and the nuns and priests, but the 50s and 60s, in black and white and color. It bursts into flame, but it isn't consumed. So, you got drunk and crashed the car. You could've been killed, you know. Flying through a red light at Roosevelt Road and East Avenue. You must've been going pretty fast. Yeah, around seventy or eighty. The speed limit is 35 there. Roosevelt Road is a major road leading in and out of Chicago. You'd have to be some kind of idiot to run a stoplight crossing Roosevelt Road at any hour, and think no one was coming through, let alone early evening, just after dark. And still, he almost made it through. Another car was travelling west on Roosevelt Road and passed through the intersection, with the green light, travelling at the speed limit, 35 miles an hour, when a blur that was his father's lime green Chrysler Imperial, shot through in front of them and the driver could not even begin to brake before he swiped the rear end of the blur, crumpling the west-bound car's front bumper, and sending the blur spinning across the intersection and into the offending stoplight, knocking it over and into Roosevelt Road, crashing, sparking. The collision had impacted the gas tank of the Chrysler, and the gasoline met the spark, and it was love at first sight, and the trail of fire blazed straight to the Chrysler, and the fire department was going to have to put it out.

Dan's door wouldn't open. He looked in his rear-view mirror at the fire in Roosevelt Road. There was the stoplight he had knocked over. He kept tugging on the door handle, trying to get the door to open, but it wouldn't give. Napoleon Solo. He calmly slid across the seat and escaped out the passenger door. He was drunk. He called on his gift of straightness to save him, the ability to act not drunk when you were drunk. There was no such thing. You'd have to be an idiot to think there was. The collision had popped the trunk open, and inside was a bucket of golf balls that his father was planning to take to the driving range. Golf balls rolled in the flaming gasoline and ignited, and became balls of fire. Golf balls of fire!

Had he been drinking? He said no. And the cops bought it. But, hell yeah. He and Davo had hammered down some Hamms in the basement, and they both were lit. He was going to drive Davo home. He did so, and he was driving back home, and the buzz was just starting to wear off, and he was somewhere in Berwyn when he started to steadily apply more and more pressure to the accelerator, and the speedometer started climbing, 40, 50, 60, and the buildings started to whip past in his peripheral vision. He was flying. Why? He didn't know. He felt like it.

The cop was asking him questions, and he was answering. He had the gift of straightness. It was Sunday evening. Oak Park was the place where the saloons stop and the steeples start, and the people from the other car weren't hurt or angry. They were just amazed. Their car had hardly been damaged. "Somebody's gonna have to pay for that stoplight. My clubs, Goddamnit, my clubs are in there. One Chrysler Imperial and one set of golf clubs. Jesus Christ!" He hadn't noticed that the light had changed. I heard the news today, oh boy.

"Were you drunk?"

"No."

Had he been drinking? Of course. Why not? What else is there to do?

"Where are you going to college?"

"I dunno."

"Seriously."

"Seriously, I don't know."

"You've thought about it."

"Not really."

"Don't be a wiseacre."

"I'm not. That's the point."

"Have you applied anywhere?"

"No".

"Running out of time."

"I've ruled out all the Ivy League schools and West Point."

"You'd never get in."

"That's why I ruled them out."

"Notre Dame?"

"Never get in."

But it's ok. Everything's ok. You can just let things happen. They're going to happen anyway. Who knows what's going to happen? No one knows what's going to happen. Sure, they do. They know the sun's going to come up and go down. A hard rain's a-gonna fall. We know that. Dan wasn't just walking chaos, he was chaos running in all directions at once, exploding with conflicting desires, just like Chicagoland, just like the USA, like the war! Benjamin Braddock was morose. What was bothering him? He was being drowned. Not just drowning – being drowned. In plastics. What the hell was Dan so morose about? Ben was graduating from college, as Dan was graduating from Fenwick. Ben was a runner too, a track star. Mrs. Robinson walked into his bedroom, by mistake, so she claimed, during Ben's college graduation party. She fired up a cigarette and offered one to Ben. Mrs. Robinson: "Oh, I forgot, the track star doesn't smoke."

God: From outside time, entering perhaps in the caves where art is found. The stories of the bible enchant our hero. He is baptized in Ascension Church and becomes a Catholic, an altar boy who pretends to be a priest saying Mass. But he's a shitty altar boy who mumbles the Latin. He chokes on the host at his first communion. He starts coming late to Mass, leaving early, then skipping Mass altogether. He's on his way to becoming a lapsed Catholic. Dan liked to sit by himself in the single seat at the back of the last car on the el, the seat that faced backward, and he could watch the city or the suburbs in retreat, rushing away from him, the land where he had just been, the life he had been living. Goodbye Fenwick, goodbye Tony Lawless, goodbye Friars, Dilullo, Saint Ken Sitzberger, Father Farrell, hippy priest. What are we celebrating? What are we so happy about? It's over.

Over? That was the start. The start is over. You'll spend the rest of your life figuring out what just happened, and if you ever do finally figure it out, you'll be right back at the start. That was the funny thing about the past, about ghosts, time didn't seem to have any effect on them, and that made it as if time no longer existed for them, which was why it boggled the mind, because the ghosts were all wrong, they were dead and gone, yet they persisted in acting as though they weren't. DeMare was still purple in the face, screaming something hateful and perversely righteous, Dead-man was still winning the biggest race of all, while he was belittled by all of his own teammates, the President was smiling an instant before his brains were blown out, his brother Bobby was lying on his back with a pool of blood gathering around his head on the floor of a kitchen in a hotel and Mother Lois was yanking Danny by the earlobe down the hall to her office to administer a paddling and then he was going to Hell.

In the life of his mind, Dan was spinning like a roulette ball, and when he dropped, it was into that cycle of critique to find out it was all bullshit. Was he or was he not going to take William F. Buckley and Susan Sontag to college? He had no idea how to get good grades because he'd never really tried; a 'C' was good enough. However, he was ill-equipped for failure. He had too many resources.

Flash Forward. In the basement of the rundown Lamar Theater, where they didn't even show first-run features anymore, Dan was an usher for the summer. The high school girl who sold popcorn was a big, luscious blond who chewed gum, smoked cigarettes on her breaks, and wanted to get it on, and her name was Candy, how sweet was that? Candy sold candy at the Lamar.

"You want to smoke a cig? "

"Sure. "

"Come on". She was chewing gum. She kept chewing it while she smoked. "You like this movie?"

"Yeah."

"Easy Rider – I don't get it. What's easy about it? I like the songs, though. You want to get high?"

She was tough and she was tubby, and she was pretty and had curves and wore tight jeans, and later that night, when they were making out, she was still chewing gum. Dan didn't love Candy, nor did Candy love Dan, but she did love when he kissed her throat. A week or so later, she quit her job at the Lamar, and a couple of weeks after that, Dan left for college, and he never saw her again. It didn't matter.

Jesus was looking east atop Ascension, when Daniel Aloysius Finnegan snuck out of town behind His back, via the expressway, all the way to the cornfields, where the dormitories of the University stuck up like match-boxes against the sunset, and the secular world took over, consumed him, and he disappeared, vanished into the crowd, and again the world burst into color.

www.ingramcontent.com/pod-product-compliance
Lightning Source LLC
Chambersburg PA
CBHW050035120726
47903CB00006B/2044